D0881158

The Center for South and Southeast Asia Studies of the University of California is the unifying organization for faculty members and students interested in South and Southeast Asia Studies, bringing together scholars from numerous disciplines. The Center's major aims are the development and support of research and language study. As part of this program the Center sponsors a publication series of books concerned with South and Southeast Asia. Manuscripts are considered from all campuses of the University of California as well as from any other individuals and institutions doing research in these areas.

*Recent Publications of the Center for*
*South and Southeast Asia Studies:*

Prakash Tandon
*Beyond Punjab: A Sequel to* PUNJABI CENTURY (1971)

Surinder Mohan Bhardwaj
*Hindu Places of Pilgrimage in India:*
*A Study in Cultural Geography* (1972)

Robert Lingat
*The Classical Law of India.* Translated by J. Duncan M. Derrett (1972)

David N. Lorenzen
*The Kāpālikas and Kālāmukhas: Two Lost Śaivite Sects* (1972)

# A Death in Delhi

This volume is sponsored by the
Center for South and Southeast Asia Studies,
University of California, Berkeley

# A Death in Delhi
## Modern Hindi Short Stories

### Translated and Edited by
# Gordon C. Roadarmel

UNIVERSITY OF CALIFORNIA PRESS
BERKELEY, LOS ANGELES, LONDON

218157

UNESCO COLLECTION OF REPRESENTATIVE WORKS

INDIAN SERIES

This book
has been accepted
in the Indian Series
of the Translations Collection
of the United Nations
Educational, Scientific and Cultural Organization
(UNESCO)

University of California Press
Berkeley and Los Angeles, California
University of California Press, Ltd.
London, England
Copyright © 1972, by
The Regents of the University of California
ISBN: 0–520–02220–3
Library of Congress Catalog Card Number: 74–187871
Printed in the United States of America

To the writers of India

# Contents

# Sources

"Assassins" by Amarkant: "Hatyāre," *Desh ke Log*, Allahabad: Adhunik Katha Prakashan, 1964.

"A Death in Delhi" by Kamleshwar: "Dillī Meṅ Ek Maut," *Khoyī Huī Dishāeṅ*, Kashi: Bharatiya Jnanpith, 1963.

"A Difference" by Nirmal Verma: "Antar," *Jaltī Jhāṛī*, Delhi: Rajkamal Prakashan, 1964.

"The Third Vow" by Phanishwarnath "Renu": "Tīsrī Kasam," *Phanīshwarnāth Reṇu: Shreshth Kahāniyāṅ*, Delhi: Rajpal and Sons.

"My Enemy" by Krishna Baldev Vaid: "Merā Dushman," *Merā Dushman*, Delhi: Rajkamal Prakashan, 1966.

"A Reminder" by Rajendra Yadav: "Rimāiṇḍar," *Apne Pār*, Delhi, National Publishing House, 1968.

"Sailor" by Ramkumar: "Selar," *Ek Duniyā: Samānāntar*, ed. Rājendra Yādav, Delhi: Akshar Prakashan, 1966.

"Big Brother" by Shekhar Joshi: "Dājyū," *Kosī kā Ghaṭwār*, Allahabad: Naya Sahitya Prakashan, 1958.

"Miss Pall" by Mohan Rakesh: "Mis Pāl," *Mohan Rākesh: Shreshth Kahāniyāṅ*, Delhi: Rajpal and Sons.

"His Cross" by Shrikant Varma: "Us kā Krās," *Jhāṛī*, Varanasi: Bharatiya Jnanpith, 1964.

"Our Side of the Fence and Theirs" by Gyanranjan: "Fens ke Idhar aur Udhar," *Fens ke Idhar aur Udhar*, Delhi: Akshar Prakashan, 1968.

"Intimate" by Awadh Narain Singh: "Ātmīyā," *Rūpāmbara* (December 1968).

"Retaliation" by Dudhnath Singh: "Pratishodh," *Sapāṭ Chehre Wālā Ādmī*, Delhi: Akshar Prakashan, 1967.

"Empty" by Ramesh Bakshi: "Khālī," *Sārikā* (October 1966).

"Relationship" by Giriraj Kishore: "Rishtā," *Rishtā aur Anya Kahāniyāṅ*, Delhi: Rajkamal Prakashan, 1969.

# Introduction

THIS collection of stories translated from Hindi may come as a surprise to Western readers who think of the texture and quality of Indian life as very different from that in the West. Alienation and inner torment are certainly no Western monopoly, however, and these stories should help to demonstrate that the modern Indian writer is living very much in the twentieth century, dealing with a relatively universal range of problems, though these problems are of course seen primarily in the distinctive context of life in his own country.

The writers represented in this volume came into prominence in the nineteen-fifties and sixties, and their work helped bring the story genre into the spotlight of literary attention in Hindi, a development since Independence in most of the other Indian languages also. Tales, fables, and stories have been a continuous part of the Indian literary and cultural tradition, but poetry for many centuries dominated the literary scene. Modern fiction in Indian languages goes back only about a century, and the modern short story in Hindi is largely a twentieth-century development, distinguished especially by the work of Premchand in the first three decades and by a proliferation of good writers in recent years.

As suggested by these stories, the modern Hindi writer deals frequently with the mental states of individuals in an urban middle-class setting, the world most familiar to the writers themselves. Major religious, social, and political problems are not of primary concern. Instead, these writers tend to turn inward, portraying loneliness and estrangement, social disruption, urban anonymity, bureaucratic indifference, and a general loss or absence of individual identity.

The more a reader understands Indian tradition, the more likely he is to appreciate the extent to which these stories depict divergence from tradition. "A Death in Delhi," for example, has greatest impact if the reader can appreciate the strength of the social and moral obligations which the narrator tends to ignore—in this case the duty to attend a funeral. Within the context of tradition, the matter-of-factness of the mourners becomes a symbol for the urban setting's dislocation of human values. Similar divergence from tradition is seen elsewhere in casual attitudes toward sexual relationships outside of marriage and in the very existence of friendships between unmarried boys and girls, in the desire of a single woman to live alone in "Miss Pall," in the indifference toward neighbors in "Our Side of the Fence and Theirs." For many Indian readers the moral sense of the college boys in "Assassins" would be in question almost from the beginning of the story.

Many of the characters in these stories are cut off in some way from traditional securities of family and community, and are left drifting, groping, aware of an emptiness but unable to identify the sources of misery or to act effectively to relieve their inner suffering. A mood of helplessness is pervasive, an awareness of feelings and emotions but with little expectation that anything can be changed. Pursuit is a common theme, and the victim a frequent character. The impotence of the individual against the forces of society is perhaps a universal theme of fiction today, but these stories provide unusual insights into both the common and the unique elements of the modern Indian experience.

Hopes, longings, and dreams are repeatedly shattered or stifled. Outer pressures are magnified frequently by a sort of split view of one's self, a tension expressed most dramatically in "My Enemy" but also dominant in such stories as "Assassins," "A Difference," and "A Reminder." Frequently the author's style reflects the mental state of the characters. Details of actions and reactions are recorded, but the meaning of those details is often unclear. Connecting links are sometimes weak. And conversation frequently shows an absence of communication. The authors often note the times when people look directly at each other when speaking, but the avoiding of another's eye or the moment of silence frequently carries greater significance. The reader is left to give meaning to the meaningless, to analyze what the character in the story has not conceptualized.

Many stories are told in the first person, or refer to the protagonist only as "he," or in some other way avoid giving a named identity to the characters. To give a full name in an Indian story would usually mean identifying a person's religion and often his caste, and could produce automatic associations or stereotypes in the mind of the reader. Many of these authors seem deliberately to be trying to reduce the distance between reader and character, through the imprecise point of view, the use of the present tense or direct thought, and the presentation of scattered visual impressions, trivial actions, or ambiguous reactions.

That the writers of these stories have a rather limited circle of appreciative readers in Hindi outside of literary circles suggests their divergence from literary and cultural tradition in a society still very attached to tradition, idealism, and morality. Many Indian readers feel more comfortable with Premchand's stories, written in the first three decades of the century, which expose weaknesses in the cultural, economic, religious, and social system, but which retain a strong faith in many traditional virtues and patterns of life. The best collection in English of these stories is *The World of Premchand*, translated by David Rubin.

From Premchand's death in 1936 until the emergence of a large number of new story writers in the fifties, the story was dominated by Yashpal, Jainendra Kumar, and "Agyeya," along with other authors such as Upendranath Ashk and Bhagwati

Charan Varma, most of them still writing currently. Some impact of Marxist and Freudian thought can be seen in these writers, as can the impact of the struggle for Indian independence.
Some European and American influences were also apparent in
these years when fiction from Western countries besides England
was being widely read in India. English literature had been an
important part of Indian education since the early nineteenth
century.

Yashpal continued the tradition of Premchand in his direct
approach to social problems and in the traditional plot-dominated
and chronological structure of his stories. Although identified
with Marxism and with revolution, Yashpal in his stories exposed
not only the problems of imperialism and of capitalism but also
tried to expose phoniness in all aspects of human relations. Some
of this concern was also found in the stories of Jainendra Kumar
and of "Agyeya," though they tended to portray the tensions of
man's inner world more than the conflicts in his outer world. The
approach of Jainendra and of "Agyeya" was to some extent psy-
chological, to a greater extent philosophical, and generally gave
more importance to character and atmosphere and mental states
than to plot or incident.

Where Premchand frequently portrayed the virtues of kind-
ness, honesty, justice, nobility, and good will, Yashpal and Jainendra and "Agyeya" frequently questioned these virtues, not only
as to whether they exist in any pure form within particular individuals, but also as to the purpose they serve in human and social
relationships. They hesitated to reach conclusions as definite as
those of Premchand, their viewpoint being somewhat broader
and their sympathies less clear-cut.

The nineteen-fifties brought an unusual number of new
writers concentrating on the story in Hindi, and they tended to
be more experimental, more questioning, more skeptical than the
previous generation. By the latter part of the decade, critics and
writers were heatedly debating whether Hindi literature was
witnessing a "nayī kahānī," a "new story" as revolutionary as the
"new poetry" of the previous decade. The post-Independence

writers tended to feel that the older writers had been too romantic, too idealistic, and too philosophical, and though these elements were often present to some extent in the "new stories," the direction for the story became increasingly defined as one which should reflect the reality, especially the grim and hopeless reality, of the modern world.

The heightened questioning of values, the disillusion, the alienation, the introduction of previously taboo subjects and of experimental narrative patterns was continued and expanded by new writers in the sixties. Many of the youngest writers have tried to describe their work as that of a "new generation," as distinct from that of the fifties as those writers had felt themselves to be distinct from the writers of the forties. The decade of a writer's first literary recognition frequently seems more important than his age, perhaps suggesting that the recognized writer tends to be seen as part of the Establishment by the less-applauded new writer. In any case, the more recent writers have sometimes charged the earlier group of *nayī kahanī* authors with reflecting an inappropriate nostalgia for meaningfulness, continuing a quest for values that are no longer a part of the "modern consciousness."

Each generation seems to be moving farther into taboo themes and points of view, and to be reflecting greater disillusion with political, social, and individual relationships. A concern for meaning gave way to some extent to a fear of meaninglessness and is now appearing as an acceptance of meaninglessness. The story "Intimate" is a good example of the attempt to write a story of total meaninglessness, with no reflection of morality or values by the author. Although the protagonist is disturbed by the absence of communication in his conversation with a stranger, he nevertheless becomes trapped in the exchange of jargon and finally of blows. The pointless encounter contrasts with the title "Intimate," as though suggesting that meaningless words and physical violence are the only intimacy available in the city today.

Plot and incident continue to be deemphasized. Interest in what happens to individuals changed to interest in what an individual feels, and now that appears to be giving way to a focus on nonfeeling, as in the story "Empty."

The dominant mood in the contemporary Hindi short story obviously reflects only a part of the mood of contemporary life in the Hindi-speaking world and in India. A similar mood is strikingly pervasive, however, in the modern stories in other Indian languages. These writers have sometimes been accused of taking up themes or postures borrowed from the West and foreign to India. Such accusations are highly debatable, and will perhaps be best answered if readers find in this collection a distinctive Indianness. True, some of the authors may have read Kafka, Camus, Sartre, and even Kerouac; but they write from their own context of awareness, often with the painful recognition that many of their readers and critics would prefer greater idealism and inspiration.

Shrikant Varma, a noted contemporary Hindi author represented in this collection by "His Cross," calls the modern Indian writer "a stranger in his own land," one whose vision of "the unhappy, miserable, and frightening human situation" has little root in Indian tradition. The reader of the stories in this volume can perhaps sense, however, that the modern Indian writer is no stranger to the modern world. He may not speak for all of India, but he speaks both for India and for mankind in a language more universal than he may imagine.

A collection of fifteen modern Hindi stories obviously can only suggest the tone and quality of Indian writing today. The choice of stories has been difficult and will probably satisfy few Hindi critics. I make no claim that these are the "best stories" in modern Hindi, nor that I have included all the best writers. For a variety of reasons, though, these have struck me as good and important stories which deserve a wider readership. The first nine or ten stories are by writers generally associated with the short fiction of the nineteen-fifties, and the latter five or six stories are by writers associated with the "new generation" of the sixties.

It has been difficult to omit some of the writers who estab-

lished their literary reputations before Independence and who
continue to distinguish themselves in fiction. It has also been
painful to omit many of the good writers and stories from the
last two decades. To be more representative one should add
women writers, Muslim writers, and writers who have appeared
in the last three or four years. Some excellent stories had to be
omitted simply because of their length, and others because they
had been well translated elsewhere. I can only apologize to the
many fine writers whose work has not been included here, hoping
that they will find increased recognition as both Western and
Indian readers begin to appreciate more fully the accomplish-
ments of contemporary Hindi literature.

The difficulties of translation from Indian languages have
been explored enough elsewhere, so that elaboration here seems
unnecessary. Generally I have tried to render equivalents for the
Hindi originals as faithfully as seemed possible within the limits
of modern idiomatic English and within the conceptual frame-
work of the English reader. Each unit of translation raises new
questions, and generally there is less difficulty in understanding
the Hindi original than in deciding which of many English al-
ternatives would be most suitable.

Although trying to avoid heavy Americanisms, my use of
language is perhaps closer to American English than to British
English or to Indian English. At times, however, the Hindi expression, especially in a conversation, translates into an English
construction which is distinctively Indian in wording or syntax.
At times I have left these constructions, which for the reader
familiar with India might have an authentic sound within the
particular social context of the story. Some readers may object;
others may find more inappropriate the translation into colloquial
American or British English of certain characteristically Indian
patterns.

The glossary provides definitions for most of the distinctively
Indian words. In the stories, spellings generally follow standard
usage rather than proper pronunciation ("bazaar" rather than
"baazaar") but "paan" has been given rather than "pan" because

of the confusion with the English word. Authors' names are spelled as they usually write them in English.

I have tried to review the full text of the translations with native speakers of Hindi, but some errors no doubt remain. I hope that these will not interfere with the major purpose of the book— to introduce a rich, important, exciting, and little-known litera- ture to those unable to read the Hindi originals. For those who might wish a more extensive discussion of the modern Hindi story, I apologize for the brevity of the introduction. This volume is intended to let the stories speak largely for themselves. A study of the theme of alienation in the modern Hindi story, including a more extensive history of the development of Hindi fiction, will hopefully be published in the next year or two.

Special thanks are due to the many writers who provided sug- gestions, encouragement, and permission for the translation and publication of their works. "Miss Pall," "Retaliation," and "A Death in Delhi" were first published in *The Illustrated Weekly of India.* "Intimate" and "The Third Vow" have been published in *Thought.*

Financial assistance was provided by the Center for South and Southeast Asia Studies, the Committee on Research, and a Summer Faculty Fellowship—at the University of California, Berkeley.

Arvind Shrivastava, Omi Marwah, Manjari Ohala, and Usha Jain were particularly helpful in going over my translations and assisting with difficult passages. Edith Irwin gave many useful suggestions on the English style and some helpful insights on the quality and interpretation of the stories.

Particular debts should be acknowledged to my parents who introduced me to India, to Dorothy Mateer and Josephine Miles who were most influential in helping me to explore Western literature, to Bonnie Crown and Milton Rosenthal who encour- aged my Hindi translations, to David Rubin and Edward Dimock and A. K. Ramanujan for their suggestions and insights, and to other friends who know and love India.

G. C. R.

AMARKANT

# Assassins

O<small>N</small> an October evening two young men met at a paan shop. The clear sky was blue and lovely, and the stirring breeze was a gentle reminder of the approaching winter. One young man was fair, tall, brawny, and very handsome, though his eyes were unusually small. He was wearing a white shirt, and a pair of pants so fashionably tight that his buttocks seemed to be trying to break through. There were shoes on his feet but no socks, and his hair was combed back. The other young man was dark, short, and robust. He was clean-shaven like his companion and was similarly dressed except that he wore a Kashmiri cap on his head, his pants were grey rather than chocolate color, and his undershirt was clearly visible because of the two buttons open on his shirt.

"Hello, brother."

"Hello, son." The fair one walked up alongside.

"Why so late, my boy?"

"Brother, it was a bore."

"Anything special?"

"Just that Nehru! There was another letter from him today."

"I see." The curves of a smile appeared and then vanished in the corners of the dark one's eyes and mouth.

"Yes, that man's giving me a lot of trouble. I've told him time and again, 'Look brother—give the prime ministership to someone else. I have bigger things to do.' But he just won't listen."

"What does he say?"

"The same old tune. This time he's written saying he's grown tired, that he wants to set the burden of the country entrusted to him by Gandhiji onto my strong shoulders. He says that I'm the only one worthy and wise enough to handle the job in this miserable country these days."

They burst out laughing but a moment later became solemn, like two tops spinning swiftly and then suddenly toppling over.

"Aren't there other leaders?" the dark one asked.

"Nehru thinks the other leaders in the country are all lazy and talk too much. You know, don't you, that the last time I was in Delhi, Nehru came to see me at the Ashoka Hotel?"

"No! Son of a gun, you never tell me anything." The dark one's eyes gleamed like buttons.

"Nehru took my hand and burst into tears, saying, 'The country's passing through a great crisis. All our leaders and politicians are corrupt and narrowminded. Those who are honest have no brains. My leadership's weak too. My officials deceive me. I've started five-year plans for the welfare of the people, but the officials are just lining their own pockets. I know that people all over the country are out for loot and plunder, but I can't take any action against them.' "

"Good god!"

"Don't tell anyone, you scoundrel. So at the end he said, 'The only hope for the country today is you. You can wipe out the conspiracies of the capitalists, the ministers, and the officials, and establish socialism!' "

"What do you think about it?"

"That sort of piddling work is not for me."

"You really ought to stoop a little, friend, for the sake of the country."

"Come now! I'm a man of principles. I just called Nehru long distance. That's why I'm late."

"Really?"

"Yes. I told him straight out, 'Brother, I'm not willing to be prime minister of the country. I have bigger things to do. First of all I have to establish world peace.' "

They both laughed.

"In a way your reasoning is quite right. Oh, I just remembered a little incident too. Yesterday I got a cable from President Kennedy in America."

"What did he say?" The fair one's eyes narrowed.

"He's asking me to come there. He writes that there's no one in the world these days as courageous as I. With me there, America will definitely defeat Russia."

"Did you send a reply?"

"I cabled back that I'm a patriotic young man and that during this time of severe crisis I could under no circumstances leave my own country and go elsewhere."

"You did the right thing! He's a good man, though. Holds me in great respect. I was the one who recommended you to him."

At that they both lowered their heads and began smiling, as though pleased at the sight of their own broad chests. Hearing the laughter of a gentleman alongside, however, they immediately became solemn again. Their eyes narrowed, their lips tightened, and their necks grew rigid. Then the fair one stepped forward with great ostentation and bought a pack of Capstans from the paan vendor. Both lit cigarettes and then, puffing smoke as casually as shunting railway engines, set off down the road.

Handsome stores lined both sides of the broad clean street. On the sidewalks, a busy crowd of all ages, occupations, and appearances was flowing in opposite directions. The two young men moved down the left-hand pavement, their hips twisting vigorously and their hands swinging out as though they were swimming. Frequently they glared angrily at the people alongside them. When a group of girl students decked out in glittering costumes passed by in a wave of perfume, the boys pursed their lips and let out kissing sounds. Reaching the far end of the market, they stopped at a sardarji's stall and had an almond drink, then went to the Banaras paan shop and ate four rolls each of Magahi paan, and finally started back on the other side of the street.

"Do you recognize that broad?"

"No." The dark one turned to look at a slim girl walking along.

"You numbskull! When I'm Prime Minister, I'll make you the Secretariat sweeper. That, my boy, is Chandra Sinha. She got the highest marks in M.A. English and is now working on a Ph.D. She's picked me as a husband."

"Or as a son?"

"It's no joke. Many a time she's fallen weeping at my feet. But as you know, I've taken a vow of celibacy."

"Your father was a celibate too!"

They both grinned from ear to ear.

"My friend, you turn everything into a joke. For the good of all classes of people in our country, I appeal to you to become serious and keep yourself under control."

"All right, speak up, O Emperor, Bastard of the Nation!"

"Then listen, O Arjuna! One day Professor Dixit came pleading to me."

"The head of the English Department?"

"Naturally—what other Professor Dixit is there in the world?"

"My mistake, Your Honor!"

"Approaching me with folded hands he said, 'You're the only person in the world who can help me. I can't live for a moment without Chandra Sinha. She was just an average student, but I got the top grades for her. I've told her several times that I'll get her a doctorate in just two years. I'm ready to sacrifice at Chandra's feet all the thousands I've earned writing textbooks and cramsheets. But she won't even look at me. She just repeats your name like a rosary. If you intervene, she'll take your advice.' "

"You must be scared, man. After all, you have a class with him for a period every day."

"Poof! Would one who's worshipped by the nation be afraid of that insect? I scolded him and said, 'Look, you make a big show of your textbooks, but can you deny that all of them were written by your students?' "

"What did he say to that?"

"What could he say? He started shaking and then fell at my feet and began pleading with me not to mention this to anyone. I thundered back—'I know you butter up the officials and the ministers. And you've ruined the lives of countless girls this way. Chandra's a virtuous woman. If you so much as look at her cross-eyed in the mirror, I'll be forced to make a basic change in the educational system of the country!' "

Suddenly their attention was drawn to a bookstall in front of which stood a young lady, fair and beautiful. Her braids were fastened in back like the coils of a snake, and a reddish-brown sari was draped with deliberate casualness over her shapely figure, making her look like some Buddhist mendicant. She was intently going through the pages of *Eve's Weekly*, the expression on her face reflecting a hope that people would think her very modern and intelligent. The young men moved in close, whistling softly, and began turning the pages of some magazines. One by one they flipped through such journals as *Rekha*, *Gori*, *Reader's Digest*, *The Illustrated Weekly*, *Life*, *Manohar Kahaniyan*, and *Jasus Mahal*. In between, they kept staring at the lady and making comments over which they laughed loudly.

"That Laski was a strange person too, pal," said the fair one.

"Why?"

"You know of course that he came to see me before writing *The Grammar of Politics*."

"I vaguely remember now." The dark one looked at the woman out of the corner of his eye and chuckled.

"One night he quietly showed up at my house and began

pleading that his book wouldn't get written without my help. I felt sorry for the man—he was a decent fellow and I thought I should do something for him. So I said, 'Brother, I don't have time to write the whole book for you, but all right, every evening for two hours I'll dictate and you take notes.' "

"Did it get done?"

"Oh, he was very pleased. In just ten days I dictated the whole book. He said that since I was actually the author of the whole book, my name alone should go on it. But I answered that I belong to a country of truth and nonviolence, and that my services were never intended for self-glorification."

The woman turned her head with dignity and gave him a piercing look. Then she paid for the *Eve's Weekly* and left with an air of indifference. The two young men guffawed. Then the dark one turned serious and began humming—"Let me live in the shadow of your eyes. . . . "

They made two more rounds of the bazaar. By then it was dark, but the shops were sparkling with bright colored lights, as though in some mysterious dream-world. They came back and stood at the same paan stall. This time the dark one bought the cigarettes.

"My friend, we've traveled abroad enough," the fair one said with a yawn. "It's time we gave some attention to our own beloved country."

"Right. My pure soul is eager for some action here at home, too."

"Let's go," came the response in English.

A little down the road, they went into The Prince. A middle-aged man with a huge mustache and an air of detachment and humility was seated at the counter. He leaned forward and greeted them with a salaam. To the right were four private booths. In the first, four people were talking and laughing loudly, at which the two young men became very sober, an expression of superiority and indifference on their faces. They entered the last booth and sat down.

"What will you have?" the fair one asked.

"The social and moral level of the country needs to be raised. Make it brandy!"

"A half-pint, and some hard-boiled eggs," the fair one ordered.

When the bearer brought the things, the fair one poured the liquor equally into two glasses. The dark one quietly poured some of his into the other glass and then laughed in embarrassment.

"Wretch! You're a coward!" the fair one snorted. "I was thinking that when I became Prime Minister, I'd make you the President of the Society for the Prevention of Corruption and the Society for the Abolition of Casteism. But if you can't drink even this much, then how are you going to take bribes from the officials? How will you make forgeries? How will you tell lies? How then are you going to serve the country, scum?"

They burst into laughter. Then they lit up cigarettes. After a sip of the liquor, they ate the eggs, stared straight ahead meaningfully, and then, drawing heavily on the cigarettes, blew out the smoke.

Their faces were flushed as they stepped outside. The crowds on the sidewalk had thinned out. The fair one raised his hands and stretched. "Your leadership has been no fun. Today there should be some creative action."

"Then prepare yourself! The assistance of young men like you is needed in the step I'm about to take for the all round progress of the country and for the establishment of world peace. If you'll take on the task with courage, it will please My Eminence to appoint you Home Minister."

"Whatever you command, Your Honor."

"Then come on, get in this rickshaw."

Some time later the rickshaw came to a halt in a small settlement of some fifteen or twenty small shacks inhabited by such people as rickshaw-pullers and pot-scrubbers. The place was located about a mile from the university, at an edge of the city a long way from any other habitation. On the corner was a shop selling paan and some other small items. Dim lights were visible from some of the shacks. The night was dark but the weather was

beautiful, and the cool, fresh breeze blowing gently was stimulat-
ing to mind and body.

They went up to the nearest shack. Leaning against the wall
on the left side of the small porch was an old bamboo cot, sunken
like a boat. In a corner to the right, a woman was sitting in front
of a clay firepit preparing dinner. She stood up, startled, but then,
recognizing the fair one, began to smile politely. Dimples appeared in her cheeks. Her age must have been about twenty-four
or five. Her coloring was almost black, but her body was firm and
she was not unattractive. She was wearing a dirty sari, the top
part so dishevelled that one could see her firm, bulging breasts.
She seemed an honest and simple sort of woman.

"You're putting in an appearance after a long time. Please
have a seat."

"What's the good of sitting outside?" the fair one laughed.

"Then come inside." She began laughing too.

"Today I've brought one of the great leaders of the world to
be of service to you."

"I don't understand. Who is he?" She looked respectfully
toward the dark one.

"He's the president of the Universal Loafers Association.
You must do everything to make him happy."

"To me everyone is equal. There'll be no cause for complaint." She laughed again.

"Where's that two-legged animal of yours?"

"He must be out grazing somewhere," she chuckled.

"Then what's the delay?"

"Nothing. The food can go on simmering. Suddenly busying herself, she squatted in front of the fire. Her lips were spread
in a light, refined smile. She removed a piece of wood to reduce
the flame, stirred the pot of dal with a ladle and finally stood up.

The fair one remained outside, lounging on the cot. After
some time the woman came back out, took the pot off the fire,
and returned inside. Now it was the dark one's turn to sit outside.
Meanwhile the clay lamp in a niche on the porch flickered like
an invalid's weak smile.

"Two rupees each, right?" the fair one said with a smile as he emerged.

"Today I'll take four each. You people really gave me a bad time." Her eyes were twinkling.

"You're a regular capitalist. You have everything in the world. All right, eight annas more apiece. But all I have is a ten-rupee note."

"I don't have any change."

"I'll break it at the paan shop."

"Give it to me," she said. I'll get it."

"Hey—you're an important worker for the nation. Why should you have to go to all that trouble? I'll be right back."

Leaving the shack, they headed for the paan stall. The woman stood on the porch watching.

"O.K. friend—take off your shoes and hold them in your hand," the fair one whispered.

"Why?" the dark one asked in surprise.

"Do what I say, and quietly. The time has come for our young men to act with wisdom, originality, courage, and devotion! I want to direct them in a fully nonviolent way."

At once they both removed their shoes and held them in their hands.

"The moment of economic and social revolution is at hand. Run, brother!"

They took off at a gallop, snickering as they ran. The woman rushed out of her shack, beating her chest, and wailing. "Help! I've been robbed by those sons of bitches. May lightning strike them!"

Some men dashed from their huts and took off after the young men. The paved streets were deserted. The two young men were running like Arabian horses. Sometimes they turned to the left, sometimes to the right. Among the pursuers, one swift runner was gaining on them like an arrow. He had come close. Before long he could have sprung forward and caught the dark one who had fallen behind. But suddenly the fair one stopped and stepped to one side. Out of his pocket he took a knife and opened it, gleaming, in his hand. Lunging forward, he plunged the knife into the man's stomach.

"Aay, they've killed me." He staggered and fell.

After that they both dashed away at full speed. Passing under a lamp-post, their strong bodies drenched with perspiration looked handsome in the light. Then they became lost somewhere in the darkness.

KAMLESHWAR

# A Death in Delhi

A SHROUD of fog covers everything. It is past nine in the morning, but all of Delhi is enmeshed in the haze. The streets are damp. The trees are wet. Nothing is clearly visible. The bustle of life reveals itself in sounds, sounds which fill the ears. Sounds are coming from every part of the house. As on other days, Vaswani's servant has lit the stove, and it can be heard sizzling beyond the wall. In the adjoining room, Atul Mavani is polishing his shoes. Upstairs the Sardarji is putting Fixo on his moustache. Behind the curtain on his window a bulb gleams like an immense pearl. All the doors are closed and all the windows are draped, but throughout the building there is the clamor of life. On the third floor, Vaswani has closed the bathroom door and turned on the tap.

Buses are rushing through the fog, the whine of their heavy tires approaching and then fading into the distance. Motor rickshaws are dashing along recklessly. Someone has just flipped down a taxi meter. The phone is ringing at the doctor's place next door, and some girls heading for work are passing through the rear alley.

The cold is intense. On the shivering streets, cars and buses, their horns blaring, slash through the clouds of fog. The sidewalks are crowded but each person, wrapped in fog, seems like a drifting wisp of cotton.

Those wisps of cotton advance silently into the sea of haze. The buses are crowded. People huddle on the cold seats amidst figures hanging like Jesus from the cross—arms outstretched, with not nails in their hands but the icy shining rods of the bus.

In the distance a funeral procession is coming down the street.

This must be the funeral I just read about in the newspaper: "The death occurred this evening at Irwin Hospital of Seth Diwanchand, the renowned and beloved Karolbagh business magnate. His body has been taken to his home. Tomorrow morning at nine o'clock the funeral will proceed by way of Arya Samaj Road to the Panchkuin cremation ground for the last rites."

This must be his bier coming up the street now. Walking silently and slowly behind it are some people wrapped in mufflers and wearing hats. Nothing can be seen very clearly.

There is a knock at my door. I put the paper aside and open the door. Atul Mavani is standing there.

"I have a problem, friend. No one showed up today to do the ironing. Could I use your iron?" Atul's words are a relief. I was afraid he might raise the question of joining the funeral procession. I immediately give him the iron, satisfied that he plans to iron his pants and then set off on a round of the embassies.

Ever since reading about Seth Diwanchand's death in the paper, I've been apprehensive that someone would show up and suggest joining the funeral despite the cold. Everyone in this building was acquainted with him, and they're all genteel, sophisticated people.

The Sardarji's servant comes down the stairs noisily, opens the door and starts to go out. "Dharma! Where are you going?" I call out, hoping for reassurance.

When he answers, "To buy butter for the Sardarji," I quickly hold out the money for him to get me some cigarettes at the same time.

The Sardarji is sending out for butter for his breakfast, which means that he's not planning to join the funeral procession either. I'm further relieved. Since Atul Mavani and the Sardarji are not planning to go, it's out of the question for me. Those two and the Vaswani family visited Seth Diwanchand's place more than I did. I only met the man four or five times. If they aren't planning to attend, then there's surely no question of my having to go.

Mrs. Vaswani has appeared on the front balcony. There's a strange pallor on her attractive face, and a touch of redness from the lipstick she wore last evening. She's wearing just a robe and is fastening up her hair. "Darling," her voice rings out. "Bring me some toothpaste, please."

I'm further reassured. The Vaswanis must not be attending the rites either.

Far down on Arya Samaj Road, the funeral procession is slowly approaching. . . .

Atul Mavani comes to return the iron. After taking it, I want to close the door, but he comes in and says, "Did you hear that Seth Diwanchand died yesterday?"

"I just read about it in the paper," I answer blandly, to avoid further discussion of the matter. Atul's face is shining. He must have just shaved.

"He was really a fine man, that Diwanchand."

If the comments go any further there'll be a moral obligation for me to join the funeral procession. So I ask, "What happened about that business of yours?"

"The machine's about to arrive. As soon as it does, I'll get my commission. This commission work is really senseless, but what's to be done? If I can just place eight or ten machines, I'll start my own business." Atul continues—"Brother, Diwanchandji

helped me a lot when I first came here. It's because of him that
I got any work at all. People really respected him."

My ears prick up at the name Diwanchand. Then the
Sardarji puts his head out the window. "Mr. Mavani! What time
should we go?"

"Well, the time was given as nine o'clock, but it'll probably
be late because of the cold and fog." This must be a reference to
the funeral.

The Sardarji's servant Dharma has brought me the cigarettes
and is setting out tea on the table upstairs. Then Mrs. Vaswani
speaks up—"I think Premila's bound to be there. Don't you agree,
darling?"

"Well, she ought to be," Mr. Vaswani replies, crossing the
balcony. "Hurry up and get ready."

"Will you be coming to the coffee house this evening?" Atul
asks me.

"Probably." I wrap the blanket around me and he goes back
to his room.

A moment later he calls out, "Is the electricity on, brother?"

"Yes, it's on." He must be using an electric immersion rod
to heat water.

"Polish!" the shoeshine boy announces politely in his daily
fashion, and the Sardarji calls him upstairs. The boy sits outside
polishing, while the Sardarji instructs his servant to bring lunch
promptly at one o'clock. "Fry some papars, and make a salad
as well."

I know the man's servant is a scoundrel. He never serves a
meal on time, nor does he cook what the Sardarji wants.

Thick fog still covers the street outside, with no sign of sunshine. The man selling wheatcakes and gram has come and set
up his cart as usual. He's polishing the plates, which are rattling.

The number seven bus is leaving with its crucified Christs
hanging inside, while a conductor distributes advance tickets to
people standing in line. Coins jingle each time he returns change.

Among the cotton balls wrapped in haze, the dark-uniformed conductor looks like Satan himself.

And the funeral procession has come a little closer.

"Shall I wear a blue sari?" asks Mrs. Vaswani.

Vaswani's muffled reply suggests that he is adjusting the knot on his tie.

The servant has brushed the Sardarji's suit and draped it on a hanger. The Sardarji stands in front of the mirror tying his turban.

Atul Mavani reappears, portfolio in hand, wearing the suit made for him last month. His face looks fresh and his shoes are shining. "Aren't you going?" he asks. Before I can ask "Going where?" he calls, "Come on, Sardarji! It's getting late—it's past ten o'clock."

Two minutes later, the Sardarji starts down the stairs. Meanwhile Vaswani spots Mavani from upstairs and asks, "Where did you get that suit tailored?"

"Over in Khan Market."

"It's very nicely done. I'l like to get the tailor's address from you." Then he calls to his wife, "Come on, dear! I'll be waiting for you downstairs." Joining Mavani and the Sardarji, he feels the suit material. "The lining is Indian?"

"English!"

"It fits beautifully," he says, jotting down the tailor's address. Mrs. Vaswani appears on the balcony, looking immaculate in the damp, cold morning. The Sardarji winks at Mavani and starts whistling.

The bier is now directly below my room. A few people are walking with it, engrossed in conversation, and a couple of cars are creeping along.

Mrs. Vaswani comes downstairs, a flower in her hair, and the Sardarji adjusts the hankie in his coat pocket. Before they go out the door, Vaswani asks me, "Aren't you coming?"

"You go ahead. I'll be right there," I respond, though unsure where I'm to go.

The funeral has moved down the road. A car comes from behind and slows down near the procession. The driver exchanges a few words with someone walking in the procession, and then the car surges ahead. The two cars following the procession also slip ahead.

I stand watching as Mrs. Vaswani and the other three head for the taxi-stand. Mrs. Vaswani has put on her fur wrap, and the Sardarji is either offering her his fur gloves or just displaying them. The taxi-driver steps up and opens the door, and the four of them get in. Now the taxi is heading this way and I can hear laughter inside. Vaswani points toward the procession and tells the driver something.

I stand quietly, observing everything, and somehow I feel now as though the least I could have done was to join Diwanchand's funeral procession. I know his son well, and at times like this one should offer sympathy even to enemies. The cold almost destroys my resolve—but the question of joining the funeral keeps needling me.

The taxi slows down near the bier. Mavani sticks his head out and says something. Then the taxi goes around to the right and moves ahead.

Feeling beaten, I put on my overcoat, slip on some sandals, and go down the stairs. My feet propel me automatically toward the procession and I fall in quietly behind the bier. Four men are carrying it on their shoulders, with seven others walking alongside—the seventh being myself. I ponder the difference as soon as a man dies. Just last year when Diwanchand's daughter was married, there were thousands of guests, and cars were lined up in front of his house. . . .

We have reached Link Road. Around the next turn is the Panchkuin cremation ground.

As the procession turns the corner, I see a crowd of people and a row of cars. There are some scooters also. A chatter of voices comes from a group of women standing at one side. Each has a different hair style, and they stand around with the same sensuality one sees in Connaught Place. Cigarette smoke is rising from the crowd of men and blending into the fog. The red lips and white teeth of the women shine as they talk, and there's arrogance in their eyes . . .

The bier has been set down outside on a platform. Now there is silence. The scattered crowd has gathered round the body, and chauffeurs holding bouquets and garlands of flowers wait for a look from their mistresses.

My eyes fall on Vaswani. He's trying to signal his wife to go over by the corpse, but she keeps standing there talking to another woman. Nearby are the Sardarji and Atul Mavani.

The face of the corpse has been uncovered, and now the women are placing flowers and garlands around it. The chauffeurs, their duty done, stand near their cars, smoking.

One lady, after depositing a garland, takes a hankie from her pocket, puts it to her eyes, sniffles a little, and then steps back.

Now all the women have taken out hankies and there is a sound of noses blowing.

Some of the men have lit incense and set it at the head of the corpse. They stand motionless.

From the sound, increased sadness has apparently reached the hearts of the women.

Atul Mavani takes a paper from his portfolio and is showing it to Vaswani. I think it's a passport application.

Now the bier is being taken inside the cremation ground. The crowd stands outside the gate, watching. The chauffeurs have either finished their cigarettes or put them out, and stand guard by their cars.

The bier has gone inside now.

The people who came to offer condolences are beginning to leave.

One can hear car doors opening and closing. The scooters start up and some people are heading toward the bus-stop on Reading Road.

The fog is still thick. Buses are passing by and Mrs. Vaswani says, "Premila has invited us over this evening. You'll come along, won't you dear? There'll be a car for us. That's all right, isn't it?"

Vaswani nods his head in agreement.

The women leaving by car are smiling and saying goodbye to each other. The cars start off . . .

Atul Mavani and the Sardarji are walking toward the bus-stop. If I were properly dressed, I could go straight to work from here. But it's already eleven-thirty.

The pyre has been lit and four or five men are seated on a bench underneath a tree. Like me, they just happened to come along inside. They must be taking the day off. Otherwise they'd have come ready to go on to work.

I can't decide whether to return home, clean up and then go to the office, or whether to use the excuse of a death to take the day off. After all, there was a death and I did join the funeral procession.

# NIRMAL VERMA

# A Difference

H<small>E</small> got off the bus and stood on the street corner. Facing him was the Town Hall, long and intimidating. On the first floor was a row of large dirty window panes in which the reflected evening sun looked even grimier. Just beyond were some business establishments—a pub, a barber-shop, and two general stores. A little farther, there was a small square.

"When does the last bus leave?" he asked the conductor of the bus on which he had arrived.

"Ten o'clock." The conductor glanced over at him and then pulled a bottle of beer from his overcoat pocket.

He started off toward the shops. This was his first visit here, but nothing seemed particularly unusual. Whenever he went outside Prague to any of the small towns, they all tended to look alike to him—a town hall, a church, a central square, and a sort of deserted somnolence.

The wind was cold although it was late May. He took a muffler from his duffel bag. The gloves were in his coat pocket, but he didn't want to put them on yet. He was carrying a sleeping bag. If he missed the last bus, he would sleep outside. He always preferred that to a hotel, provided it was not too cold.

Last summer when she went with him to Moravia, they slept outside in a single sleeping bag. They had toured all through Moravia that way. For the first time, along with her, he had developed the habit of sleeping in the open. What they saved on hotels, they would spend on beer.

For some time he kept thinking about the previous summer. Then he wrapped the muffler carefully around his throat and ears. It was quite cold, he thought, but not intolerable.

Perhaps nothing was intolerable . . . not even for her. At first she had been very afraid. Now she'd be all right. Now there was nothing to fear. Now there was absolutely nothing to fear, he repeated to himself.

For some time he stood in front of a food store, gazing intently at the show window. Then, thinking of something, he went inside.

He took a shopping basket from under the counter. Long rows of tins and packages of assorted sizes lined both sides. At that time of year there was no fresh fruit available. He placed two tins of peaches and of pineapple in the basket. He also had the clerk wrap half a kilo of salami and some chunks of French cheese. She had always been very fond of French cheese. Whenever she slept overnight in his room, she nibbled constantly like a mouse.

Coming out of the store, he remembered something and returned to buy a packet of Lipa. She probably had no cigarettes at the hospital.

He put all the purchases in his duffel bag. On leaving the store, he felt rather thirsty. There was enough time, he concluded—not a lot, but enough for a small beer. Crossing the square, he went into the pub.

Not taking a seat, he remained standing in front of the bar. "A small beer," he ordered.

Without looking up, the bartender placed a mug under the beer tap. When the foam began running over the brim, he turned the handle and shut the tap. Wiping the mug with a dirty towel, the man set it in front of him.

He put the mug to his lips. The beer was somewhat bitter and warm, but he didn't mind. Meanwhile the bartender took a sausage from his pocket and was eating it. He was a middle-aged man, with watery blue eyes.

"Perhaps you can tell me the way to the hospital?" he asked.

The bartender looked him over carefully. Then his eyes rested on the sleeping bag. "Have you come from Prague?"

He nodded.

The barman kept gazing at him with some suspicion. "On the right side of the Town Hall—a little beyond the cemetery," he said.

"Is it very far?"

The man raised his half-chewed sausage in an obscene way. "One kilometer," he replied, chuckling.

Thanking him, he placed a blue three-crown note on the counter and walked out without waiting for change.

Outside there was the brilliance of spring—not that oppressiveness found in summer—a light kind of cleansed radiance which comes after a long winter.

It was a ten-minute walk and he moved quickly. Now he was not overly worried, not as worried as he'd felt on the bus. He was feeling somewhat lighter after the beer. Leaving the square, he had emerged on an open road. The wind had died down, and from the distant fields whirring tractors could occasionally be heard, sounding like the buzzing of flies.

Nearing the cemetery, he lit a cigarette. Then he shifted his duffel bag from one shoulder to the other. On the trees around the cemetery, tender new leaves were glittering in the fading sunshine. In places along the dirt road, mud puddles had been formed by the melting snow, and in them he could see the tracks of cars and trucks. He rolled up his trousers, happy that no one was around to see him.

But she would certainly be surprised to see him. Perhaps she'd be pleased, too, though he wasn't sure of that. When leaving Prague, she had told him not to come. She didn't want to arouse anyone's suspicion. They had decided that she would spend two days here in the hospital. When she returned later to Prague, no one would know anything about it.

He stopped at the gate of the hospital. Perched on a knoll, the building looked like some college dormitory—intimate and impeccable, with none of the chilly nakedness so often found in hospital buildings.

Rolling down his trouser cuffs, he opened the gate and went inside. Ahead was a long corridor. At intervals there were pots of flowers. The sunlight had drawn slanting shadows of the corridor pillars on the immaculate floors.

Over near the stairs he noticed a large desk above which was a signboard saying "Reception." Behind it sat a woman in a nurse's uniform. She was reading a newspaper, so her face was hidden.

He approached the desk somewhat hesitantly. The nurse raised her head from the newspaper and looked at him.

"Whom do you wish to see?"

He told her the name. He realized that she was not just a nurse; she was also a woman, wearing a nurse's uniform. The thought was somewhat reassuring.

She took a list from the desk drawer. "In the maternity ward?" she asked.

For a moment he stood there hesitating and then wiped the perspiration from his forehead.

"I don't know about that. This is my first visit here. Can you tell from the list?" he asked, though there was no need to ask this since she was already looking over the list.

"Your wife's name is not listed in the maternity ward." The nurse gave him a questioning look.

"She's not my wife," he said. "I mean we're not married yet. . . . " Desperate, he tried to smile, but then it struck him that any clarification was not only unnecessary but foolish.

The nurse eyed him with a strange coolness and then slowly pulled back her hair. "You should have told me that before," she said, her tone not one of annoyance but only of cool detachment. She took a second list from the desk and once more asked for the name.

He stood in silence, waiting.

"First floor—to the right, the surgical ward." After a casual glance at him, she returned to the newspaper.

He reached the end of the hallway and started up the stairs.

There were open doors on both sides. Women in long gowns were seated on their beds. Outside the doors, nylon stockings, brassieres, and underwear were hanging on lines to dry. There was a sour, dank odor in the air, the kind of smell that often comes from the bodies or clothes of working women. Red and blue buckets filled with sand hung from the iron railings—probably for putting out fires, he thought.

As he turned toward the surgical ward, he felt as though someone had caught his hand from behind. Startled, he turned around to find a tall husky man facing him. He was wearing the long white coat and trousers which was the uniform of doctors here.

"Whom do you want to see?"

He gave the name again.

"All right, but you'll have to leave that here." He pointed his thumb at the sleeping bag.

He took the sleeping bag off his back and set it in a corner.

"What's in there?" the doctor asked, looking at the duffel bag.

Lifting the bag silently from his shoulder, he set it in front of the doctor. The doctor casually examined the containers in the bag and then smiled slightly. "So you're the man," he remarked, switching to English.

"Meaning what?"

"Oh, nothing," the doctor replied, using his own language again. "Bed number seventeen—but only half an hour. She's still very weak." His voice had assumed a clipped, professional tone. "You may go in."

But he couldn't bring himself to go straight in. He stood

there for some time, clutching his duffel bag in both hands like
a child.

Next to the door was an empty wheelchair. Ahead was a
long hall lined on both sides with small cubicles separated by
long pink curtains. A dim light glimmered in each cubicle. There
was a stretcher in one corner of the hall, on it some dirty bandages. Some nurse in a hurry must have forgotten to remove
them.

He walked inside. His back had felt very light ever since
removing the sleeping bag. He stopped in front of number seventeen. There was no sound from within. Maybe she was sleeping.

At first he couldn't see her. In front was a large bed, completely smooth and white. On it were two long sheets, also completely white. It was even hard to tell which end was the head,
since nowhere in the bed was there a hump or a dip. For a moment he thought it was empty.

It was not empty. Her head emerged from the sheets, then
her eyes. She was looking at him, and then a faint smile appeared
on her lips. She had recognized him.

With her eyes, she signaled toward the stool. On it was a
cup of milk.

"You didn't drink it?" he asked, leaning over.

"Later. Set it down below."

He pulled the stool over near the bed.

"When did you get here?"

"Just a little while ago."

Her lips had a purple tinge. The lipstick line was broken in
places.

"When did it happen?" he asked.

"This morning. Take off your coat."

He removed the coat and the duffel bag and placed them
behind the stool. The window was closed. Under it lay the suitcase she had brought with her from Prague.

"It didn't take very long, did it?" he asked.

"No. They gave me chloroform. I didn't feel anything."

"I said you wouldn't feel anything, but you wouldn't believe me." He attempted to smile.

She kept gazing at him silently. "I told you not to come."

"I know . . . but now I'm here." He leaned over the bed and kissed her brown hair, then her lips. Despite the warmth of the room, her face was absolutely cold. He went on kissing her. She just lay there, her head straight on the pillow.

"Are you happy now?" Her voice was very soft.

"We were happy even before" he said.

"Yes . . . but are you happy now?

"You know . . . this was best for both of us. . . . I told you that even before."

The sheet slipped below her breasts. She was wearing a green nightgown, with black flowers on it. In his own room, the sight of those black flowers used to arouse a pleasant tension in his body. Now they were piercing his eyes.

"What's that?" She looked toward the duffel bag.

"Nothing. I just brought a few things here for you." One by one he took each thing from the bag and set it on the bed—tins of peaches and pineapple, salami, French cheese, the packet of Lipa cigarettes. "Would you like a piece of cheese now?"

"No . . . later." She kept staring at the things scattered on the bed.

"You mustn't be careless about your diet during this time," he said.

"Did anyone there ask about me?"

"No. No one knows you're here," he replied.

She lay there for a while with her eyes closed. Her hair had been short even before. Now, from being pressed against the pillow, it looked even shorter. Last summer she had dyed it black, just to please him. But he had not particularly liked it. Since then it had been turning brown again, although some traces of black were still visible.

"Are you feeling tired?" He took her hand in his.

"No." She looked at him. Then she pulled his hand beneath

the sheet and slowly moved it down to her stomach. "Do you notice a difference?" she asked.

His hand rested there on her naked, warm belly. "You're not having any discomfort, are you?"

"No." She laughed slightly. "I'm feeling very light now. Now there's nothing at all here." She looked up at him, the dry lipstick on her lips shining in the light. He slowly withdrew his hand.

"You ought not to do much talking," he said.

"I'm feeling very light," she said.

"Did the doctor say anything to you?"

"No . . . but if I'd come a month earlier, I wouldn't be so weak now."

"Are you feeling very weak?" he asked.

"No, I'm feeling very light."

"I told you from the beginning to come here right away, but you kept delaying."

"What you say is always right."

He said nothing and looked away.

"Did that offend you?" She raised herself on her elbows and looked at him.

"No, but you shouldn't be talking so much," he replied, stroking her hair.

"Look, there's nothing now to worry about," she said. "I'm all right now."

"But you still think about it," he said.

"I don't think about anything." Then she opened the buttons on his coat. "You didn't put on a sweater?" she asked.

"It wasn't very cold today."

For some time they remained silent. Meanwhile a nurse came in. She was blonde and seemed cheerful. Glancing at the two of them, she walked over to the bed.

"You shouldn't be sitting up like this yet." The nurse placed her head back on the pillow. Then she looked over at him. "It wouldn't be good to put too much strain on her."

"I'll be leaving soon," he replied.

The nurse looked at the objects scattered on the bed. She turned to him and smiled. "You should be more careful from now on." There was a hint of humor in her tone.

He said nothing and looked the other way. On her way out, the nurse paused. "You have enough cotton?"

"Yes thank you, sister," she replied. The nurse left.

"Would you mind turning the other way for a moment?" she said softly, removing something from under the pillow.

"I'll go outside."

"No, there's no need for that. Just turn your head away."

He started looking toward the back wall, remembering nights long ago when she would get up from the bed in his room and put on her clothes, while he turned and faced the wall, hearing the rustle of her skirt.

"All right. It's fine now," she said.

He turned the stool and pulled it near the head of her bed. There was a faint odor in the air, differing from the odor of chloroform. His eyes fell on the pan beneath the bed. It was filled with blood-stained bandages. He found it hard to believe that the blood could be hers.

"Are you still . . . ?" He broke off in mid-sentence.

"No . . . it's much less now." She leaned over, pushed the pan farther under the bed, and then lay back down again. "Do you have a cigarette?" she asked.

He took two cigarettes from the Lipa packet and put them in his mouth. After lighting both with a match, he handed one to her. "Are you allowed to smoke here?"

"No, but no one sees." She took a long, deep puff on the cigarette. When she blew out the smoke, her nostrils were quivering slightly. Then she threw the cigarette in the waste-pan.

"I can't smoke." A thin, weak smile touched her lips.

He took the cigarette from the pan and extinguished it. One end of the cigarette bore the mark of her lipstick.

"Will you have a piece of cheese now?"

"No. You ought to be going."

"I'll be leaving. There's still time."

She had closed her eyes. The long brown eyelashes against her pale face looked like the lashes of a wax doll.

"Are you feeling sleepy?" he inquired softly.

"No." She opened her eyes, took his hand in hers, and started to rub it gently. "I thought you would come," she said.

He went on looking at her silently.

"Listen . . . now we can live like we did before." There was a trace of amazement in her voice.

"Remember?" he said, squeezing her hand. "We wanted to go to Italy last summer. Now we can go there."

"Now we can go anywhere at all." She looked up at him. "Now there's no obstacle."

Her voice again struck him as somewhat strange, but she was smiling, which reassured him.

The creaking of a wheelchair was heard from the corridor. In the next cubicle someone was screaming in a shrill voice. A woman raised the curtain and peered inside, but seeing him sitting there, she turned in confusion and left.

He looked at his watch and then began putting on his overcoat.

"You must eat these things," he said in English.

She nodded.

"Did you understand what I said?"

"You said, 'You must eat these things.'" She repeated his English sentence. They both smiled.

He fastened the muffler around his neck. Hanging the empty duffel bag over his shoulder, he rose from the stool.

"You're going now?"

"Yes, but I'll be back tomorrow at the same time."

She kept staring at him. "Come here."

He leaned over the head of the bed. She pulled the sheet down off her body and pressed his head to her breast.

"Someone may come in," he murmured.

"Let them," she said.

Some time later, when he stepped outside the hospital, the spring night had fallen. In the air there was a faint fragrance of fresh earth. Relaxing, he inhaled the cold fresh breeze. The openness outside felt refreshing after that cramped, overheated cubicle in the hospital. He looked at his watch. There was still ten minutes. He felt pleased that there was time for a beer before leaving for Prague.

For some time she lay on the bed, her eyes closed. When she was sure that he must be some distance from the hospital, she slowly got up. She opened the window. The lights of the small city were twinkling in the darkness outside. She was reminded of her dormitory room in Prague. Only two days ago she had left it and come here, but a great span of time seemed to have passed since then. For some time she stood there without moving. The cry of a baby came from the maternity ward, followed by total silence.

She walked slowly toward the bed and took an old towel out of her suitcase. Then she neatly wrapped all the things he had left for her. Going to the window, she threw them out into the darkness.

By the time she got back to the bed, she was feeling dizzy. The packet of cigarettes still lay on the stool. She lit a cigarette, but it still tasted strange. After crushing it out on the floor, she lay down in the bed. A tear trickled from the corner of her eye and disappeared into her hair, but she was unaware of it. She was sleeping comfortably.

# PHANISHWARNATH "RENU"

# The Third Vow

A TINGLE ran up the spine of Hiraman the cartman.

For the last twenty years this Hiraman had been driving a cart, a bullock cart. He used to haul grain and timber from Morang Raj, on the other side of the border in Nepal. And during the time of government controls, he had delivered black market goods from this side of the border to that side. But never had he felt such a tingling in his spine.

The time of controls! How could Hiraman ever forget those days? After making four consecutive trips across the border from Jogbani to Biratnagar with cartloads of cement and cloth bales, he had become fearless. Every black marketeer in Farbisganj had hailed him as a master cartman, and the big merchant there, the Sethji himself, had praised his bullocks.

It was on the fifth trip that the cart was seized, in the Terai Valley on this side of the border.

The merchant's clerk had been hidden between the bales in the cart, crouching quietly. Hiraman knew how bright the glare was from the two-foot flashlight of the police inspector. Just one shine in the eyes and a man is left blind for an hour. Along with

the light, a voice had cracked out—"Hey. Stop that cart, bastard,
or I'll shoot!"

All twenty carts clattered to a halt. "We're sunk," Hiraman
had muttered. The inspector sahab shone his light on the clerk
crouching in Hiraman's cart and let out a great bellow of laughter—"Ha ha ha! Munimji the clerk! Ho ho ho! . . . Hey, you no-
good cartman, what are you staring at? Take the blanket off the
top of this sack." Then he jabbed the clerk in the belly with his
club and said, "Off *this* sack! Bastard!"

There must have been a long-standing feud between the inspector sahab and the clerk. Otherwise the police inspector would
surely have settled for the sum of money being offered. The clerk
was prepared to hand over four thousand rupees right on the spot.
The inspector jabbed again with his stick. All right, five thousand! And he jabbed—"First climb down from there."

Having forced the clerk down from the cart, the inspector
shone the light in his eyes. Accompanied by two policemen, he
led the man to a bush some twenty yards off the road. Five policemen with guns stood guard on each side of the carts and drivers.
Hiraman realized that there was no escape this time. Jail! Not
that he was afraid of jail—but there were his bullocks. No telling
how long they'd be locked up without food or water, hungry and
thirsty in the government stockade. And then they'd be auc-
tioned. Never again could he show his face to his brother and
sister-in-law. The sound of the auction rang in his ears—"Going,
going, gone!" The talk between the inspector and the clerk was
probably getting nowhere.

The guard posted near Hiraman's cart called in a low voice
to another policeman—"What's happening? Is nothing going to
come of this?" Then, on the excuse of offering the other policeman some tobacco, he walked over to him.

Going, going, gone! Three or four carts screened Hiraman
from the guard. He reached a decision. Stealthily he untied the
ropes from his bullocks' necks. Sitting on the cart, he then fastened the two animals together. The bullocks knew what had to
be done. Hiraman got down and propped up the front of the cart

with a bamboo pole to free the bullocks from the yoke. Tickling
them behind the ears, he muttered, "Go, brothers! If we get out
of this alive, we can easily get another cart like this. On your
marks, get set, go!"

Beyond the row of carts, thick bushes lined the edge of the
road for a long way. Holding their breaths, the three creatures
crossed through the bushes—without a crackle, without a foot-
step. Then a one—and a two—and they were off at a trot! Puffing
out their chests, the two bullocks plunged into the dense Terai
jungle. Sniffing their way, they ran, crossing streams and gullies
with tails held high. Right behind was Hiraman. All night they
kept running, those three souls. . . .

Reaching home, Hiraman collapsed in a swoon for two days.
Recovering consciousness, he immediately grabbed his ears and
made a vow—"Never again will I carry that kind of load. Black
market goods? Never, I swear!" No telling what had happened
to the clerk, and God knows what had become of his cart. A
genuine steel axle it had; and maybe not both, but one wheel was
brand new. And those colorful string tassels had been braided
together with such great effort . . .

He had made two vows. First, he would carry no black
market goods, and second, no bamboo. "You're sure it's not con-
traband—or bamboo?" he would immediately question each contractor. Even if someone offered fifty rupees for hauling bamboo,
Hiraman's cart was not available. "Try someone else. . . ."

A bamboo-loaded cart! The bamboo sticks out four feet in
front and four feet in back! Completely unmanageable the cart
becomes. That unwieldly load and that incident in the town of
Kharaihiya! The contractor's super-idiotic servant, who was walking in front guiding the protruding bamboo, began staring at the
girls' school. That was all it took—at the corner they collided
with a tonga. By the time Hiraman had reined in the bullocks,
the bamboo in front had poked right through the canopy of the
horse carriage. The driver immediately lashed out with his whip
and began yelling abuses.

Hiraman swore off not only loads of bamboo but also all

loads from the town of Kharaihiya. But then when he started hauling goods from Farbisganj to Morang, even the cart was wiped out! For several years after that, Hiraman had worked in a partnership, half the income going to the owner of the cart and half to himself as owner of the bullocks. Oof! It was like working for nothing. The earnings under that system didn't fill the stomachs of even the bullocks. Just last year he had finally been able to have a cart made for himself.

The blessings of the Mother Goddess on that circus company tiger! Last year during this fair, both the horses which pulled the tiger cart had died. At the time for the fair to move from Champanagar to Farbisganj, the circus company manager announced to the row of cart drivers—"You can make a hundred rupees." One or two of the drivers were willing, but as soon as their bullocks came within five yards of the tiger cart, they began bellowing with fear—"Baan-aan!" They broke their ropes and ran off.

Hiraman caressed the backs of his bullocks and said, "Look, brothers, there won't be a chance like this again. Now's the time to get a cart of our own. Otherwise it'll be half-and-half again. Arre! What's there to be afraid of with a caged tiger? You've already seen the wild tigers in the Morang Valley. Besides, I'm right here behind you."

Suddenly applause broke out from the band of cart drivers. Hiraman's bullocks had salvaged the honor of them all. They advanced courageously and were yoked one by one to the tiger cart, the only thing unusual being that the right-hand one urinated profusely after being hitched up. And for two days Hiraman kept a cloth wrapped over his nose. No one could stand the stench of the tigress without holding his nose.

Hiraman had been the driver for the tiger cart, but never had he felt such a tingling in his spine. Today the fragrance of champa flowers periodically suffused his cart. Whenever his spine began to tingle, he slapped his shoulder-cloth across his back.

It seemed to Hiraman that for two years the patron goddess

of the Champanagar had been pleased with him. Last year the
tiger cart had turned up. In addition to the hundred rupees and
a cash tip, there had been tea and biscuits, and the chance along
the way to watch the fun of performing monkeys and bears and
clowns—all for free.

And now this feminine passenger! Was it really a woman or
was it a champa flower? Fragrance had filled the back of the cart
ever since she stepped inside.

The right wheel accidentally jolted on a small rut in the
rough dirt road. A light squeal came from inside the cart. Hiraman cracked the whip on the right-hand bullock and called out,
"Bastard! You think we're carrying gunny sacks or something?"

"Oh, don't beat them!" The voice of the unseen woman
took Hiraman by surprise—a bubbling voice, sweet as the voice of
a child.

How could anyone not have heard the name of Heerabai,
the woman who played Laila in the Mathura Mohan Nautanki
Dance Company? Hiraman's case was a rare one, though. For
seven years he had regularly hauled loads for fairs, but he had
never seen either a nautanki or a movie show. Nor had he ever
heard the name of Laila or of Heerabai—not to mention seeing
them! So when, late one night about two weeks before the fair
was breaking up, he had seen this woman approaching wrapped
in a black shawl, he certainly had felt apprehensive. When the
servant carrying the trunk tried to bargain over the rate, the
veiled woman stopped him with a shake of her head. Hitching
up the cart, Hiraman asked the servant, "Look here, my friend,
are you sure there are no stolen goods or anything like that?"

Again Hiraman was taken aback. The man carrying the
trunk signaled the cart forward with a wave of the hand and then
vanished into the darkness. Then Hiraman remembered the
black sari of the old woman selling tobacco at the fair. . . .

Who could drive a cart under such circumstances? In the
first place, his spine was tingling. In the second place, a champa
flower kept blooming in his cart. And when he rebuked his bul-

locks, there were tsk-tsks of reproach from his passenger. His passenger! A lone woman, and not the tobacco-selling old lady! After hearing her voice, he repeatedly turned and tried to glance into the covered section of the cart. Then he would slap the shoulder-cloth across his back. God only knew what was written in his fate this time. When the cart turned eastward, a ray of moonlight filtered into the vehicle. A firefly seemed to be sparkling on the nose of the passenger. To Hiraman everything began to seem mysterious, miraculous. Ahead was spread the plain between Champanagar and the village of Sindhiya. Could it be a robber woman? Or a demoness?

Hiraman's passenger shifted position. The moonlight illumined her whole face and Hiraman gasped. "Good heavens! It's an angel!"

The angel's eyes opened. Hiraman turned his face back toward the road and began coaxing the bullocks. A clicking sound issued from his mouth, where the tongue seemed to have dried up like a piece of wood.

"What's your name, brother?"

That same bubbling voice! The hair tingled on Hiraman's body. He was speechless. Even the bullocks' ears pricked up, listening to that voice.

"My name? My name is Hiraman."

His passenger smiled, and there was fragrance in the smile. "Then I'll call you friend, not brother. My name is Heera too."

"Iss!" Hiraman responded skeptically. "There's a difference between men's names and women's."

"Yes, but my name is Heerabai too."

On the one hand Hiraman, on the other Heerabai. There was plenty of difference.

Hiraman scolded the bullocks—"Do you expect to cover the sixty miles listening to our chatter?" He flicked the whip lightly at one of the bullocks. "This one on the left is full of the devil."

"Don't hit them. Let them go slowly. What's the hurry?"

Hiraman was wondering how he should address Heerabai. Should he use a familiar or a formal term? In his dialect, formal terms were used in addressing elders or superiors. He could handle simple questions and answers in the city dialect, but only in the village dialect could he converse freely.

Hiraman had always disliked the fog which settled over everything in the early October mornings, and many times he'd become confused and drifted off the road. But even the dense fog delighted him on this particular morning. The breeze brought a smell of rice plants growing in the fields along the riverbank. During the festival season, a similar aroma used to fill his village. The champa flower had bloomed again in his cart, and in that flower sat an angel. Hail to the Goddess!

Hiraman stole another look. The eyes of his passenger, his friend, Heerabai, were roving around scrutinizing him. A melody sprang up in his heart, and his body was quivering. "It bothers you very much when I hit the bullocks?"

Heerabai had appraised him: Hiraman was a genuine heera, a diamond.

This forty-year-old, sturdy, dark-complexioned, rustic young man took no special interest in anything except his cart and his bullocks. His elder brother, a man with a wife and children, lived in the family home and did the farming. Hiraman respected his sister-in-law even more than his brother did, and he feared her, too. Hiraman had been married also—in his boyhood. But before the girl was old enough to move to her husband's home, she had died. Hiraman could no longer remember what his bride had looked like. A second marriage? There were many reasons for not remarrying. His sister-in-law insisted that the only marriage she would arrange for Hiraman would be with a young virgin. By that was meant a six- or seven-year-old girl. No one pays any attention to the marriage-age laws. No parent, though, would give his daughter to a once-married man unless it was a case of dire necessity. His sister-in-law had taken a firm stand and would not budge. Even his brother's opinion counted for nothing against hers. So Hiraman had resolved not to remarry. Why court misery? And could a man take up the cart business again after getting married?

Whatever else he might surrender, Hiraman could not give up the cart business.

Heerabai had seldom encountered a man as honest and open as Hiraman. "In what district is your home?" Hiraman asked. The laugh that burst from him on hearing the name "Kanpur" startled the bullocks. But he lowered his head respectfully while laughing. Finally he stopped laughing and said, "Good heavens, Kanpur! That means Ear Town! Then there must be a Nakpur, a Nose Town!" When she told him that there is indeed a Nakpur, he burst out laughing again.

"What a world! Such names there are—Ear Town! Nose Town!" Hiraman stared at Heerabai's flower earrings. Then he noticed the blood-red jewel in her nosepin and quivered with delight.

Hiraman had never heard the name of Heerabai. He didn't consider nautanki dancers to be prostitutes. He had watched women who worked in these companies. The woman owner of the circus used to come with her two young daughters to the tiger cart, feed and water the tiger, and even stroke it fondly; and the elder girl had fed biscuits and bread to his bullocks.

As soon as the fog lifted, Hiraman astutely hung his shawl as a curtain over the opening of the cart behind him. "Only for two hours! Driving later than that would be difficult. You couldn't stand the heat of this October sun. We'll halt the cart near Tegachiya, on the bank of the Kajri River, and spend the noon hours there."

Seeing a cart approaching in the distance, he became alert, concentrating on the furrows in the road and on the bullocks. "Is the fair breaking up, brother?" asked the other driver as he passed by.

Hiraman replied that he knew nothing about the fair. He was carrying a married woman to her family home. Hiraman gave the name of a village.

"Where is this Chattapur Pachira?"

"What difference does it make to you?" Hiraman chuckled at his own cleverness.

He looked through a hole in the curtain. Heerabai was examining her teeth in a mirror the size of a matchbox. Hiraman was reminded of a garland of tiny cowrie shells he'd once bought for his bullocks at the fair in Madanpur. A row of tiny little cowrie shells.

The three trees marking Tegachiya appeared in the distance. Nudging the curtain aside, Hiraman said, "Look, there's Tegachiya. Two of the trees are banyans and one—one has a flower—I don't remember the name—like the one printed on your blouse. It's very fragrant—the smell carries three or four miles. People mix the flower with a special kind of tobacco and smoke it."

"And those buildings there behind the mango grove—is that a village or a temple?"

"May I smoke?" Hiraman inquired before lighting a biri. "The smell won't bother you? . . . That's the Namalgar estate. It belongs to the son-in-law of the raja who sponsored the fair we're coming from. Those were the days!"

Hiraman had now added some spice to the conversation and Heerabai tugged back the curtain. Ah, that row of teeth!

"What days were those?" she asked eagerly, chin in hand.

"The days of the Namalgar estate. What a time it was, and the things that happened!"

"You saw those times?" asked Heerabai.

"I didn't see them, I heard about them. The story of the decline of that rule is a sad one. They say a god was born in the house. A god is a god after all, right? If he leaves heaven and takes birth in the mortal world, he still keeps his brilliance. It shone from his forehead like a sunflower. But no one there realized what had happened. Once the Viceroy came by plane along with his wife. He didn't recognize the child, but his wife did. As soon as the Viceroy's wife saw the brightness of the sunface, she said—'Listen, Raja! This is no human baby. It's a god!'"

Hiraman minicked the harsh mispronunciations in the vicereine's speech. Heerabai laughed heartily, her whole body responding. "And then? What happened after that, my friend?"

"Iss! Do you really enjoy hearing stories? Well—a black

man's just a black man, even if he becomes a raja or a maharaja.
Where would he get the intelligence of a sahab? Everyone
laughed the matter off. Then the god gave a dream to the rani.
'If you can't serve me, then never mind, I won't stay at your
place.' After that the sport of the god began. First both tucked
elephants died, then a horse, and then slam bang . . . "

"Slam bang what?"

Hiraman was being transformed moment by moment, and
he felt a warm glow rising inside. A woman from the celestial
realms was riding in his cart. After all, a god was a god!

"Slam bang! Money and wealth, goods and cattle—all were
wiped out! The god went back to heaven."

Heerabai looked at the disappearing temple spire and sighed.

"But as he was leaving, the god said, 'There'll never be more
than one son in this ruling family. I'm taking all the wealth with
me, leaving only wisdom.' All the gods and goddesses left with
him except Saraswati. The goddess of wisdom remained behind.
That is her temple."

Seeing some merchants approaching with country horses
loaded with jute, Hiraman lowered the curtain behind him. He
urged on his bullocks and then began singing a hymn of praise—
"O Mother Saraswati, I'm making a petition. Come to our aid."

"What price do you pay for the jute?" Hiraman called out
cheerfully.

A merchant with a lame horse tossed back an answer—
"Twenty-seven or eight at bottom, thirty at top. The price de-
pends on the goods."

"How's the fair going, brother?" asked a young merchant.
"Which dance troupe is playing, the Rauta Company or the
Mathura Mohan one?"

"Only the fair people know how the fair is going!" Then
Hiraman again mentioned the name Chattapur Pachira.

The sun had climbed high. Hiraman began addressing the
bullocks—"Two miles more! Just be brave and keep going. It's
time for some water, right? I remember the time near Tegachiya
when a fight broke out between the circus company clown and

the monkey trainer. The clown began grinding his teeth and
screeching just like a monkey. God knows where these people
come from."

Hiraman peered again through the hole in the curtain.
Heerabai was sitting and staring at a piece of paper. Hiraman
was in a lighthearted mood today and kept recalling all kinds of
songs. Twenty years ago people used to sing such beautiful songs
—gazals and so forth. What sort of songs are these that people
nowadays blare through the loudspeakers? How times had
changed! Hiraman recalled one of the old songs of a dance
troupe—

> My love became my enemy! My love . . .
> Oh if it were a letter, everyone could read it—
> > if it were a letter . . .
> Alas my fate, oh my fate . . .
> No one can read my fate, my love. . . . Oh fate!

As he sang, Hiraman beat the rhythm with his fingers on
the shaft of the cart. The face of the dancer in that show had
been just like Heerabai's. Where had those days vanished? Every
month dancers used to come to the village. On performance
days he'd be scolded endlessly by his sister-in-law, and his brother
would order him out of the house.

Today it seemed to Hiraman that Mother Saraswati was
assisting him. "Bravo!" Heerabai applauded. "How well you
sing!"

Hiraman blushed. Head lowered, he began to laugh.

Today the god Hanuman living in Tegachiya must also have
been aiding him. There was not a single cart below Tegachiya,
where usually the place was crowded with carts and drivers. Only
one cyclist was sitting there resting. Invoking the name of Hanuman, Hiraman halted the cart and Heerabai started to pull back
the curtain. For the first time Hiraman used his eyes to com-
municate with her, indicating that the cyclist was staring their
way.

Before unhitching the bullocks, he propped up the front of the cart with a bamboo pole. Then he eyed the cyclist and finally inquired—"Where are you going? To the fair? From where are you coming? From Bishanpur? Is that all? Only this far and you're already tired out? A fine young man you are!"

The skinny young cyclist mumbled something, lit a biri, and stood up to leave.

Hiraman wanted to hide Heerabai from the glances of the world. His eyes darted around to make sure no cart or horse was in sight.

The narrow waters of the Kajri River made a turn to the east near Tegachiya. Heerabai watched the buffaloes lolling in the water and the birds on their backs.

"Go ahead," Hiraman said. "Wash up at the riverbank."

Heerabai climbed down from the cart. Hiraman's heart was pounding. The soles of her feet were as red as though she'd never walked barefoot.

Heerabai headed toward the river, walking slowly and with her head drooping modestly, like a young village woman. No one would ever think her a woman from a dancing company! Not a woman, a girl . . . and probably unmarried, a virgin.

Hiraman sat on the propped-up front end of the cart and looked inside the canopy. He glanced around and then placed his hand on Heerabai's pillow. Resting his elbow on the pillow, he leaned over, and then leaned over farther. Fragrance filled his body. He touched his fingers to the flowers embroidered on the pillow cover and then smelled it. What an aroma! Hiraman felt as intoxicated as though he had just smoked five pipefuls of ganja. He looked at his face in Heerabai's tiny mirror. Why were his eyes so red?

When Heerabai returned, he smiled and said, "Now you watch the cart. I'll be right back."

Hiraman removed an undershirt from his knapsack. Unfolding a towel cloth, he threw it over his shoulder and went off, a bucket in hand. The bullocks, one after the other, called out to him—"Hoonk! Hoonk!" Turning as he walked, Hiraman responded, "Yes, yes, we're all thirsty. When I get back I'll give you some grass. Now don't misbehave."

The bullocks twitched their ears.

Heerabai was unaware of Hiraman's return. She had been watching the flow of the stream when sleep, interrupted the night before, caught up with her. Hiraman went and bought some curds, sugar, and parched rice from the nearby village.

"Get up! Wake up! Have something to eat."

Heerabai opened her eyes with a start. In one hand Hiraman was holding a banana leaf plate and a clay pot filled with curds. In the other hand was a bucket of water. His eyes were filled with friendly entreaty.

"Where did you get all this?"

"The curds of this village are famous. But we'll have to wait until Farbisganj for tea."

"You fill a leaf plate too," Heerabai told him. "What's that? Well if you're not going to eat, then wrap it all up and put it in your sack. I won't eat either."

"Iss!" exclaimed Hiraman in embarrassment. "Very well. You go first."

"What's this first and last business? You sit down too."

Hiraman now felt at ease. Heerabai herself spread out a leaf plate for him, sprinkled water over it, and then served up some parched rice. Iss! I'm blessed, I'm blessed! Hiraman watched the goddess accepting the offering . . . cow's milk touching the red lips. He was reminded of the red beak of a hill parrot eating milk and rice.

The shadows were lengthening.

Heerabai, asleep under the canopy on the cart, and Hiraman, asleep on a mat on the ground, awoke simultaneously. Carts heading for the fair had stopped at Tegachiya and children were romping around.

Hiraman scrambled to his feet. Peering in the cart, he indicated that it was almost sundown. While hitching up the bullocks, he gave no response to the questions of the other cartmen. Then, starting up the cart, he said, "It's the lady doctor from the hospital at Sirpur Bazaar. She's going to see a patient in a village nearby, Kurmagam."

Heerabai had trouble remembering the name Chattapur Pachira. When their cart had gone ahead some distance, she laughed. "What about Pattapur Chapira?"

Hiraman laughed until his sides ached. "Pattapur Chapira! Ho ho! Those people were cartmen from Chattapur Pachira, so how could I mention that place to them? Hee hee!"

Heerabai smiled and looked toward the village. The road passed through the middle of Tegachiya. The village children, spying the veiled cart, began clapping, reciting some lines they had memorized—

> In a bright red marriage cart
> Sits a blushing bride
> Eating betel leaves . . .

Hiraman smiled. A bride . . . a bright red marriage cart. The bride chews betel and wipes her mouth on the bridegroom's turban. O bride, don't forget the children of Tegachiya. When you return through here, bring fruit and sweets. May your bridegroom live a thousand years! A long-standing ambition had been fulfilled for Hiraman. Many a time he'd seen dreams like this. He was returning with his bride. Children were clapping and singing in every village. Women were peeking out from all the courtyards. The men were asking where the cart was from and where it was going. The bride had pushed the curtain aside slightly and was watching. And so many other dreams . . .

Leaving the village, he glanced back into the cart out of the corner of his eye. Heerabai was thinking about something. Hiraman was lost in thought too. After a little while, he began humming—

> O tell the truth,
> For one must go to God.

Without an elephant, without a horse,
Without a cart—
One has to go on foot . . .

"Don't you have any songs in your own dialect, my friend?"
Heerabai inquired.

Hiraman could now look unhesitatingly into Heerabai's
eyes when speaking to her. Could a company woman be like
this? The circus company owner had been a married woman. But
this Heerabai! Wanting to hear a song in the village dialect! He
smiled broadly—"Would you understand the language of the
village?"

Heerabai nodded her head, her earrings swaying.

For some time Hiraman drove the bullocks in silence. "You
really want to hear a song? Iss! Such eagerness to hear a song
from the village! But we'll have to go off this road. How can one
sing those songs on a public road?" He reined in the left bullock
and turned the right bullock off the furrow in the road. "We
won't go by way of Haripur then."

Seeing Hiraman's cart moving off the track, the driver behind called out, "What are you doing? Where will you go if you
turn off the road?"

Waving his whip in the air, Hiraman answered, "What do
you mean off the road? That road doesn't go to Nananpur!" Then
he muttered to himself—"People around here have this terrible
habit of cross-examining everyone on the road. . . . Country fools,
all of them!"

When his cart reached the road to Nananpur, Hiraman
slackened the reins. The bullocks slowed from a trot to a walk.

Heerabai saw that the Nananpur road was indeed desolate.
Hiraman understood the question in her eyes. "There's nothing
to worry about. This road goes to Farbisganj too, and the people
along the way are very friendly. We'll reach there by nightfall."

Heerabai was in no hurry to reach Farbisganj. She had developed such confidence in Hiraman that there was no question

of fear arising in her mind. Hiraman gave a contented smile.
What song should he sing? Heerabai liked both songs and stories.
Iss! The song of Mahua the rivergirl? "All right," he declared,
"if you're so interested, then listen to the song of Mahua the
rivergirl. It's both a song and a story."

After all this time, the Goddess was fulfilling this ambition
of his also. Praise be to the Goddess! Today Hiraman would pour
out his heart.

"Listen! Even today on the Paraman river there are several
ancient landings associated with Mahua the rivergirl. She belonged to that region. True, she was a rivergirl, but even among
saintly women she was one in a million. Her father stayed falling-
down drunk day and night. And her stepmother was a living
hellcat! A great sneak! She was acquainted with those who secretly sell ganja and liquor and opium at night, and with all kinds
of other people like that. She had some dealings with everyone.
Mahua was just a young girl, but that witch worked her to the
bone. She came of age, but nothing was even said about arranging
her marriage. Listen to what happened one night."

Hiraman hummed softly and cleared his throat:

"Oh Mother! The river is overflowing with August rains,
The night is fearful, the lightning is crashing.
I'm a tiny little girl, my heart is pounding.
How can I go all alone to the riverbank,
Especially to oil the feet of some traveler from afar?
My stepmother has closed the door.

Clouds rumbled in the sky and rain came pouring down. Mahua
began to sob, remembering her dead mother. If she were still
alive, she'd be holding Mahua close to her heart on such dreadful
days. 'Oh Mother, was it for this, to show me such terrible
days, that you bore me in your womb?' Mahua became angry
at her mother. 'Why was it that you alone died?' she asked
reproachfully."

Hiraman noted that Heerabai had sunk her elbow into the

pillow and was staring at him, absorbed in the song and the nar-
ration. How innocent she looked, lost in something this way!
    Hiraman put a quiver in his voice:

> "Oh bad mother,
> Why did you not feed me salt and kill me at birth?
> Was it for this day, O foolish one,
> You nourished your daughter with milk and butter
>                                        and utagan?"

Catching his breath, Hiraman asked, "Can you understand this
dialect or are you just listening to the tune?"
    "I understand it all," she replied. "That last word means an
ointment massaged on the body."
    "Iss!" Hiraman exclaimed, and then continued his story.
"So what good was all that weeping? The merchant paid Mahua's
full price, but then, grabbing her hair, he pulled her into a boat
and ordered the helmsman to cast off and raise the sail. The sail-
boat flew off like a bird. All night Mahua kept weeping and strug-
gling. The merchant's servants scolded and threatened—'Shut up
or we'll pick you up and throw you overboard.' Then Mahua
thought of something. The morning star came from behind the
clouds for a moment and then was hidden again. Mahua suddenly jumped into the water. Seeing her, one of the merchant's
servants was bewitched. He too jumped in, right behind her.
Swimming against the current is no sport, especially in the
swollen August river, but Mahua was a true riverwoman's daughter. After all a fish doesn't tire in the water. She cut through the
current, gliding like a migrating fish. And behind her the merchant's servant kept calling out—'Wait a minute, Mahua. I'm
not trying to catch you. I'm your friend. We'll live together the
rest of our lives. But . . .' "
    This was Hiraman's favorite song. The swollen August river
seemed to rise before him as he sang of Mahua. It was a night of
the new moon, and lightning flashed in the dense clouds. In those
flashes, he could catch glimpses of the young girl Mahua strug-
gling with the waves. The pace of that fish became even swifter.

He felt as though he himself were the merchant's servant. Mahua
listened to nothing. She didn't believe him, not even turning
around to look. And as she swam and swam, he grew tired. . . .

Now it seemed to Hiraman that Mahua had let herself be
caught. She'd come within reach of her own accord. He had
touched her, had obtained her. His weariness was gone. After
swimming against the current, in a river swollen for fifteen or
twenty years, his heart had at last reached the shore. Tears of joy
could no longer be restrained. . . .

He tried to conceal his moist eyes from Heerabai, but she
had long since crept into his heart and was watching everything.
Bringing his trembling voice under control, Hiraman scolded the
bullocks. "I don't know what it is in this song that makes them
both slow down as soon as they hear it. One would think a half
ton had been added to the load."

Heerabai gave a deep sigh, and a thrill ran through Hiraman.
"You're my teacher, my ustad."

"Iss!"

The winter sun shines only briefly in the sky and then begins
to grow dim. They had to reach Nananpur before sundown.
Hiraman was cajoling the bullocks. "Step up your pace and keep
your hearts strong. Hey . . . chi, chi! Get a move on, brothers!
Le-le-le-ey-he-ya!"

He kept exhorting the bullocks all the way to Nananpur.
Before each new challenge, he reminded them of past experiences—"Don't you recall all those carts in the procession for the
Chaudhuri girl's marriage, and how you beat them all? Yes, break
out that kind of pace! Le, le, le! From Nananpur it's only six
miles to Farbisganj. Two hours more!"

The market in Nananpur had recently started selling tea.
Hiraman went and brought back a jugful. He knew the woman
from the company! Every day, all day, she went on sipping tea.
Was it tea, or life?

Heera was rocking with laughter—"Hey, who told you that
unmarried people shouldn't drink tea?"

Hiraman blushed. What could he say? But actually he had

enjoyed tea one time—from the hand of the circus company lady.
Such a warming effect!

"Drink up, guruji," Heera laughed.

"Iss!"

Lamps and lights at the Nananpur market had been lit.
Hiraman lighted his traveling lantern and hung it on the back
of the cart. Nowadays even villagers living ten miles from the
city had begun considering themselves citified. They'd seize a
cart with no light and press charges. Such a nuisance!

"Please don't call me guruji."

"But you are my teacher. It's written in the scriptures that
a person who teaches even a syllable is a guru, and one who
teaches a tune is an ustad."

"Iss! You even know the scriptures! What have I taught
you? Am I . . . ?"

Heera laughed and began to sing—"Oh Mother! The river
is overflowing with August rains . . . "

Hiraman was dumbfounded. Iss! What a brilliant mind!
Just like Mahua the rivergirl!

Creaking and clattering, the cart started down a dry fur-
rowed slope. Heerabai put one hand on Hiraman's shoulder, and
her fingers remained there for a long time. Hiraman tried several
times to shift his gaze and focus it on the shoulder. When the
cart reached the incline, her slack fingers tightened again.

Glittering ahead were the lights of Farbisganj—or rather the
lights of the fair some distance from Farbisganj. A shadow was
dancing in the light of the lantern which hung from the cart. To
eyes filled with tears, each particle of light looked like a sunflower.

Farbisganj was familiar territory for Hiraman. Any number
of times he'd brought loads there for the fair. Accompanied by a
woman? Yes, once, the year his sister-in-law had come as a bride
to her husband's home. Then, too, the cart had been turned into
a room by covering the sides with canvas.

Hiraman had reached the camping grounds, and he was
covering his cart with canvas. The first thing in the morning,

Heerabai would talk to the Rauta Nautanki manager and join the company. The fair was opening the following day. This time the fairgrounds were full. Just one night! This whole night she would remain in the cart.

"Where's this cart from? . . . Who? Hiraman? From what fair? What are you carrying?"

Cartmen of various village communities seek out each other, group their carts together, and then set up camp. Hiraman was taken aback to see a group from his own village—Lalmohar, Dhunniram, Palatdas, and some others. Palatdas peeked into the cart and nearly exploded, as though he'd seen a tiger. Hiraman gestured them to be silent. Then, with a nod toward the cart, he whispered, "Quiet! It's a woman from the company, the nautanki dance company."

"From the company—ee—ee?"

"?? . . . ?? . . . xx . . ."

Now there was not just one Hiraman, but four just like him. They looked at each other in amazement. What power there is in the word "company"! Hiraman noticed that the other three had fallen silent. Lalmohar had stepped a little to one side and was signaling that he wanted to say something. Hiraman looked toward the canopy of the cart and said, "None of the restaurants will be open. I can get something from the sweet seller."

"Hiraman, listen. I won't eat anything right now. Take this and have something to eat."

"What's this? Money? Iss!" Hiraman had never yet had to buy food in Farbisganj. What were all these cartmen of his village for, after all? "Please don't argue needlessly. Put away your money."

Lalmohar found an excuse to approach the cart. Making a salaam, he said, "The rice for four can easily serve two extra. It's being cooked at the camp. We people are all from the same village. With his own people around, would Hiraman eat at a restaurant or sweet shop?"

Hiraman touched Lalmohar's hand. "Don't talk nonsense."

After moving away from the cart a few yards, Dhunniram

released his pent-up feelings—"Iss! You're quite a man, Hiraman!
That year it was the company tiger, this time the company
woman."

"Look, brother," Hiraman whispered, "she's not like the
women in our village who say nothing even when they hear loose
talk. For one thing, she's a woman from the western districts,
and besides, she's with the company."

"But I've heard that company women are prostitutes,"
Dhunniram said skeptically.

"Shut up!" The others immediately jumped on him. "What
kind of man are you? A prostitute? And in the company at that!
Just look at his stupidity! . . . How do you know? Just because
you heard it?"

Dhunniram admitted his error. Then Palatdas thought of
something—"Brother Hiraman, how can the woman stay all
alone in the cart? No matter what, a woman's a woman after all.
She might need something."

They all agreed. "What you say is right," Hiraman conceded.
"Palat, you go back and stay near the cart. And look, take care
when you talk to her. I mean it!"

The fragrance of rose perfume exuded from Hiraman's body.
An ox of a man, that other time the stench of the tigress had not
left his body for months. Lalmohar sniffed Hiraman's shoulder
cloth. "Ay!"

Hiraman stopped in his tracks. "What am I to do, Lalmohar
brother? Tell me. She's very persistent, saying I must see the
nautanki show."

"For free? Won't it reach the ears of our village?"

"Yes," Hiraman said. "Why be criticized the rest of one's
life just to see a nautanki show one night? How can a country
chicken put on a city swagger?"

"Would your sister-in-law object even if you saw it free?"
Dhunniram asked.

Next to Lalmohar's campsite was the camp of men who
hauled loads of wood. Old Miyajan, their leader, puffed on his

water pipe and called out—"Say, brother, who brought the load from the Ladies Bazaar?"

Ladies Bazaar! That was what they called the red-light district. What was this old man implying? "Your body smells of perfume," Lalmohar whispered in Hiraman's ear. "I swear it!"

Lahsanwan, Lalmohar's cart-helper, was the youngest of them all. What if this was his first trip to a fair? Ever since childhood he'd worked for big people. He wrinkled his nose, periodically catching a whiff of something in the air. Hiraman saw that Lahsanwan's face was flushed. "Who's that coming pounding up? Who? Palatdas? What is it"

Palatdas approached and stood quietly. His face was also flushed. "What happened?" asked Hiraman. "Why don't you say something?"

What was Palatdas to say? Hiraman had warned him to use caution in speaking. He had gone quietly to the front of the cart and taken the driver's seat. "Are you a friend of Hiraman too?" Heerabai had asked. Palatdas nodded his head, and Heerabai lay down again. Seeing her face and hearing her voice, Palatdas's heart began to quiver for some reason. Yes! At the Ramlila performance, the young princess Sita had lain down exhausted this same way. Hail! Hail to Ramchandra, the husband of Sita. Songs of praise filled Palatdas's heart. He was a devotee of Vishnu and a singer of hymns. Expressing his desire to touch the feet of that tired Sita Maharani, he moved his fingers as though making them dance across the keys of a harmonium. Suddenly Heerabai sat up—"Hey, are you crazy or something? Get away. Beat it!" Sparks seemed to be flying from her eyes. Bang! Crash! He ran. . . .

What could he say? He was trying to think of a way to run away from the fair. "It's nothing," he said. "I met a merchant, and I have to go right away to pick up a load at the station. The rice isn't yet cooked. I'll be back by the time it's ready."

Dhunniram and Lahsanwan castigated Palatdas as they ate. "He's a petty man, a wretch. Thinks of nothing but money."

After dinner, Lalmohar's party broke up camp. Dhunni and

Lahsanwan yoked their cart and went over to Hiraman's site, following the cart tracks. Hiraman stopped and said to Lalmohar, "Just smell my shoulder. Smell it and see!"

Lalmohar sniffed the shoulder and closed his eyes. "Ay!"

"All that sweetness from just a touch of her hand," Hiraman said. "You realize that?"

Lalmohar caught hold of Hiraman's hand. "She touched your shoulder? Truly? Listen, Hiraman, you'll never get another chance like this to see a nautanki show. Really!"

"You'll go too?"

Lalmohar's teeth sparkled in the light at the crossroads.

Reaching the encampment, Hiraman saw someone standing near the cart conversing with Heerabai. Dhunni and Lahsanwan spoke up simultaneously. "Where have you been? The company has been searching for you for a long time."

Hiraman went over to the cart. Well, here was that same trunk-carrying servant who'd put Heerabai in the cart at the Champanagar fair and then disappeared into the darkness.

"You've arrived, Hiraman? Very good, come here. Take your fare—and this is your tip. Twenty-five and twenty-five, fifty."

Hiraman felt as though someone had pushed him out of the sky onto the ground. No, not someone—it was this trunk-carrying servant. Where had he come from? The words he was about to say died on his lips. "Iss! A tip!" He stood there silently.

"Here, take it," Heerabai said. "And listen, tomorrow morning come meet me at the Rauta Company. I'll have a pass issued. Why are you so silent?"

"The lady is giving you baksheesh," Lalmohar said. "Take it, Hiraman."

Hiraman looked at Lalmohar in embarrassment. This Lalmohar had no idea of how to talk decently.

Everyone including Heerabai heard Dhunniram mutter, "How can a cartman leave his cart and bullocks to go see a nautanki show?"

"What can I say?" Hiraman remarked, taking the money and trying to laugh. The company woman was again joining the company. What was that to him? The trunk-carrier indicated the road and started off—"This way."

Heerabai paused a moment and called out to Hiraman's bullocks—"All right, brothers, I'm leaving."

The bullocks twitched their ears at the word "brothers."

"Bro—th—ers! Tonight! On the stage of the Rauta Musical Nautanki Company . . . come and see Gulbadan, yes Gulbadan! You'll be happy to know that this time we have with our company that famous actress of the Mathura Mohan Company— Miss Heeradevi, who charms thousands of hearts with her every move. Don't forget! This very night! Miss Heeradevi, playing Gulbadan . . ." This proclamation was arousing excitement throughout the fairgrounds.

Heerabai? Miss Heeradevi? Laila, Gulbadan? She's better than any film actress. O Sweetheart, I'm charmed by your sweet gestures. How can I describe them? My only desire is that you stay in my sight and that I stay in your sight. . . .

"Kirr-rr-rr-r," rolled the drum. "Kar-d-d-d-d-rr-rr-dhan-dhan-dhan-dharaam!"

Every man's heart became a kettledrum.

Lalmohar ran up to the encampment, huffing and puffing. "Hey! Hey, Hiraman! Why are you sitting around here? Go see all the excitement. They're singing the praises of Heerabai with music and drums."

Hiraman scrambled to his feet. "Uncle Dhunni," said Lahsanwan, "you stay here at the camp. I'm going to take a look too."

No one waited for Dhunni's reply. The three men fell in behind the publicity band of the nautanki company. At every corner it paused, the music stopped, and the proclamation was made. Hiraman shivered with ecstasy at every word of the announcement. Hearing the name of Heerabai and the praise of her charms, he slapped Lalmohar on the back. "Isn't it marvelous?"

"Now tell me," said Lalmohar, "are you still not going to see the show?"

Ever since morning, Dhunniram and Lalmohar had been

trying to convince him, and had finally given up—"Go to the
dance company and see her. She invited you when she was leaving." But Hiraman had stuck to the same old tune—"Dhatt!
What's the point of going there? The company woman has gone
back to the company. What am I to her any more? She wouldn't
even recognize me."

Hiraman had been sulking, but stirred by the public announcement he declared—"We really must see it. All right,
Lalmohar?"

After conferring briefly, they headed for the Rauta Company. Nearing the tent, Hiraman gestured to Lalmohar that the
burden of inquiry would be on his head. Lalmohar knew how to
make polite talk using the language of the city. "Babu Sahab," he
addressed a man in a black coat, "may I speak to you for a
moment?"

"What is it?" the man said, raising his nose and eyebrows.
"Why are you here?"

Seeing the man's annoyance, Lalmohar's fine speech fell
apart, and he stammered, "Gulgul . . . no, that's not it . . . Bulbul
. . . no . . . "

Hiraman immediately took over. "Can you tell us where
Heeradevi is staying?"

The man's eyes blazed. "Why did you let these people in
here?" he shouted to a Nepali policeman standing nearby.

"Hiraman!" It was that same bubbling voice. Where had it
come from? Heerabai pulled back the curtain of the tent and
called, "Come here, come inside. Look, Bahadur. Familiarize
yourself with this man. This is my Hiraman. Understand?"

The Nepali guard looked over at Hiraman, smiled a little,
and walked away. "It's Heerabai's man," he told the person in
the black coat. "She said not to stop him."

Lalmohar offered some betelnut to the Nepali guard. "Here,
have some of this."

Iss! Not just one but five passes, and all for the eight-anna
section! "Every night you're here at the fair," she had said, "you're
to come see the show." And she had remembered everyone—

"You have some friends. Take passes for all of them." Company women were marvelous. Right?

Lalmohar touched the pieces of red paper and examined them. "Passes? Good for you, brother Hiraman! But what will we do with five passes? Palatdas hasn't reappeared yet."

"Forget about him," Hiraman replied. "It's not written in the poor fellow's fate. But yes, first everyone will have to swear to God that not a whisper of this reaches our village."

"Who'd be so rotten as to go tell the village?" Lalmohar exclaimed. "If Palat causes trouble, I won't bring him along next time."

That day Hiraman placed his money bag in Heerabai's safe-keeping. One could never be sure at these fairs. All sorts of pick-pockets showed up, and one could hardly even trust his own companions. Heerabai consented, locking his black cloth bag inside her leather trunk. It not only had a cover of cloth, but also an inner lining of shiny silk. Now his mind was at ease.

Lahsanwan wore a hangdog expression. He had wandered all over listening to the proclamations and returned after dark. "You good-for-nothing loafer!" Lalmohar scolded him in a proprietary tone of voice.

Dhunniram was putting rice and dal on the fire to cook. "First let's decide who's to stay with the carts," he said.

"What do you mean? Lahsanwan isn't going anywhere."

"Ay!" Lahsanwan cried out, "I beg you, sir. One glimpse. Just one glimpse!"

"All right, all right," Hiraman said generously. "Why just one glimpse? Go watch for an hour. I'll come back so you can leave."

The drumming begins a full two hours before the start of a nautanki show. And as soon as the drumming begins, people start gathering like moths. Hiraman saw the crowd at the ticket office and laughed. "Look there, Lalmohar, at the way people are pushing and shoving."

"Hiraman brother!"

"Who? Palatdas! Where did you carry that load to?" Lalmohar inquired as though addressing a stranger.

Wringing his hands, Palatdas begged forgiveness. "I admit
I'm guilty. I'll take any punishment you give. But honestly, that
Princess Sita . . . "

The lotus of Hiraman's heart had bloomed with the beat
of the drum. "Look, Palat," he said, don't think she's like one
of our village women. You see, she has given a pass even for you.
Take it and watch the show."

"But you can only have it on one condition," Lalmohar
spoke up. "Every now and then Lahsanwan too . . . "

There was no need to explain anything to Palatdas, who had
just come from talking to Lahsanwan. Lalmohar then presented
the second stipulation—"If our village somehow finds out about
this . . . "

"Good god no!" Palatdas exclaimed, biting his tongue between his teeth. A moment later he announced, "The eight-anna
gate is over here."

The guard at the gate took the passes and scrutinized their
faces one by one. "These are passes," he said. "Where did you
get them?"

Now someone would hear Lalmohar's fine city language!
Seeing the scowl on his face, the guard became nervous. "Where
do you think we got them? Ask your own company—go ahead!
And there aren't just four. Look, here's one more." Lalmohar
took the fifth pass from his pocket and displayed it .

The Nepali guard was standing at the one-rupee gate. "Hey
there, brother," Hiraman called to him. "You were introduced
to me just this morning. Have you forgotten already?"

"They're all Heerabai's people," the Nepali said. "Let them
in. They have passes, so why are you stopping them?"

The eight-anna section!

This was the first time the three of them had seen the inside
of a "cloth-house." In front was the section with seats and
benches. On the curtain was a painting of Rama's journey to the
forest. Palatdas recognized the deity immediately. He folded his

hands reverently before the figures of Rama, Sita, and Lakshmana on the curtain. "Glory be to God!" His eyes filled with tears.

"Lalmohar," Hiraman asked, "are those pictures moving or are they still?"

Lalmohar had already become acquainted with the spectators seated next to him. "The play is behind the curtain. This is just an introduction, to attract people."

Palatdas, who knew how to play the drum, was shaking his head to its beat and keeping time with a matchstick. Hiraman also became friendly with one or two people by offering them a smoke. One of Lalmohar's acquaintances wrapped himself in a shawl and said, "The dance is late in starting. There's time for a nap meanwhile."

The eight-anna section was the very best section—all the way in the back and in the highest place! And with warm straw on the ground to sit on! Hey hey! The spectators sitting on benches and chairs in this chilly weather would soon be heading out to drink tea.

"Wake me up when the show starts," a man said to his companion. "No, not when it starts. Wake me up when Heeriya comes on stage."

A small spark flared in Hiraman's heart. Calling her Heeriya! Obviously a no-good man! With his eyes he signaled Lalmohar that there was no need to associate further with that person.

Dhan—dhan—dhan—dharaam! The curtain rose. The tent was completely packed. Hiraman's mouth gaped in astonishment. Why was Lalmohar laughing that way? He was laughing pointlessly over Heerabai's every move.

Gulbadan was seated amidst her court. She was announcing that any man who would make a splendid throne for her would be rewarded with anything he desired. "If there's any such artisan, then let him construct and bring that splendid throne . . . " Kirr—kirr—kirri! How she danced! And what a voice! "You know, this man claims Heerabai never touches betel or biris or cigarettes or anything like that." "He's right. She's a very righteous whore!"

"Who says she's a whore? She doesn't even paint her mouth! She must brush her teeth with powder." "Never!" "Who's talking such nonsense, calling a company woman a prostitute?" "Why are you so upset?" "Where's that whore's pimp? Beat up the bastard! Beat him! You . . . "

Hiraman's voice was ringing out through the uproar in the tent—"Come ahead! I'll break all your necks one by one."

Lalmohar was whirling his whip and whacking people in front. Palatdas was sitting on a man's chest—"Bastard! Calling Princess Sita foul names! And you a Mohammedan at that!"

Dhunniram had not been heard from since the beginning. As soon as the fighting started, he'd slipped out of the tent and fled.

The black-coated nautanki manager came running with the Nepali policeman, and the police inspector lashed out with his club. Feeling the club, Lalmohar bristled and began declaiming in his fine city language—"You want to chastise us, Inspector Sahab? Then go ahead and strike. But take a look at this pass. And there's another in my pocket, sir. Not a ticket, a pass! So how can we tolerate someone in front of us saying terrible things about the company woman?"

The company manager suddenly analyzed the whole situation. "I know what's happening, sir," he told the inspector. "The troublemakers are all connected with the Mathura Mohan Company. They want to start a fight and give this company a bad name. Let these people go, sir. They're Heerabai's men. The poor woman's life is in danger."

Hearing the name Heerabai, the inspector released the three, but their whips were confiscated. The manager then seated them in chairs in the one-rupee section. "You all please sit here. I'm sending betelnut for you." The tent calmed down and Heerabai returned to the stage.

The drum began to roll again.

Soon after, all three remembered Dhunniram. Hey, where had he gone?

"Master! Oh master!" Lahsanwan was yelling outside the tent. "Lalmohar, sir!"

"Over here, over here!" Lalmohar shouted. "Through the one-rupee gate."

All the spectators turned to look at Lalmohar. The Nepali policeman brought Lahsanwan over, and Lalmohar took the pass from his pocket and displayed it.

"Master," Lahsanwan said, "who was making remarks? Just tell me. Point out his face. Just give me one look at him."

The people noted Lahsanwan's broad and smooth chest. Bare-chested even in winter! These people must belong to some gang.

Lalmohar persuaded Lahsanwan to calm down.

Perhaps one should not question that bunch as to what they saw in the nautanki show. How could any of them remember the story? It seemed to Hiraman that Heerabai had fixed her eyes on him from the very beginning and was singing to him, was dancing for him. Lalmohar felt that she was looking at him. She must have realized that he was even more powerful than Hiraman! Palatdas had figured out the story. It was all the Ramayana. What other story was there? There was that same Rama, that Sita, that Lakshmana, and that Ravana. Ravana came in all sorts of disguises so as to snatch Princess Sita from Rama. Rama and Sita also changed their appearances. Here Rama was the gardener's son, the builder of the splendid throne. Gulbadan was the Princess Sita. The friend of the gardener's son was Lakshmana and the sultan was Ravana. . . . Dhunniram had developed a high fever! Lahsanwan liked best the part of the clown, especially when he sang, "Oh little bird! I won't take you with me to the Narhat bazaar." He wanted to make friends with that clown— "Won't you be my friend, Joker Sahab?"

Hiraman caught half a line in one song—"I am slain, O Gulfaam." Who was this Gulfaam? Heerabai was weeping as she sang—"Oh yes, Gulfaam, I am slain!" . . . Poor Gulfaam!

Returning their whips to the three men, the policeman remarked, "You come with whips and sticks to watch a dance?"

The next day a rumor spread through the fair that Heerabai had run away from the Mathura Mohan Company and therefore that company had not come this time. Its hoodlums had showed up instead. But Heerabai was a match for them. She had very cleverly found a dozen villagers armed with sticks. No one even dared call "Wah, sweetheart!" No one had the guts!

Ten days . . . days and nights!

All day Hiraman carried loads on hire. At dusk when the nautanki kettledrum began to roll, Heerabai's words would ring in his ears—"My brother . . . my friend . . . Hiraman . . . ustad . . . guruji!" All day long, some musical instrument kept playing in a corner of his heart. Sometimes it was a harmonium, sometimes a kettledrum, sometimes a hand drum—and sometimes Heerabai's ankle bells. Hiraman stood and sat, walked and turned to the rhythm of those instruments. Everyone recognized him, from the nautanki company manager to the curtain-puller. He was Heerabai's man!

At the start of the show every night, Palatdas would fold his hands reverently toward the stage. One day Lalmohar went to let Heerabai hear his elegant city speech, but she didn't even recognize him. He'd been crushed ever since. His servant Lahsanwan had stopped working for him and joined the nautanki company, having made friends with the clown. All day he carried buckets of water and washed clothes, saying "What's there in the village for me to want to go back?" Lalmohar remained sullen. Dhunniram had gone home ill.

That day Hiraman had hauled three loads to the station since morning. For some reason he found himself thinking of his sister-in-law. Had Dhunniram mentioned anything in the course of his fever? He'd been talking gibberish while he was here— about Gulbadan and the splendid throne. . . . Lahsanwan was having a fine time. He must be able to see Heerabai all day. Just yesterday he was saying, "Thanks to you, Master Hiraman, things are marvelous. After Heerabai's sari is washed, the water in the tub turns to rose perfume. I leave my shoulder-cloth in it to soak. You want to smell it?" . . . And every night he heard from some mouth or other—"Heerabai's a whore." There were so many people to fight! How could they say such things when they didn't know anything about her? But then, even a king gets cursed behind his back. . . . Today he would go tell Heerabai, "People are giving you a bad name for being in a nautanki company. Why don't you go work in a circus?" Hiraman's heart burned with jealousy when she danced in front of everyone. In a circus company she could make a tiger dance. No one would have the nerve to go near a tiger. Heerabai would be safe there. . . . But where was this cart coming from?

"Hiraman! Hey, brother Hiraman!"

Hearing Lalmohar's voice, Hiraman turned to look. "What have you been hauling, Lalmohar?"

"Heerabai's looking for you—at the station. She's leaving," he announced in a single breath. Lalmohar himself had taken her in his cart.

"She's leaving? For where? She's going by train?" Hiraman unhitched his cart. "Brother," he said to a watchman at the storehouse, "please keep an eye on the cart and the bullocks. I'll be right back."

"Ustad!" Heerabai stood near the gate of the ladies' waiting-room, her head and arms covered by a veil. "Here, take it," she said, holding out the money bag. "Oh, God, you've come! I had given up hope. I won't be seeing you again. I'm leaving, guruji."

Today the trunk-carrying man had been transformed into a gentleman in coat and trousers, and was ordering the coolies around as though he were a master. "Put the things in the ladies' compartment! You understand?"

Hiraman took the money bag and stood there in silence. She had extracted the bag from beneath her blouse and handed it to him. The bag was warm, like the body of a small bird.

"The train is coming." The trunk-carrying man scowled as he looked at Heerabai. The message on his face was clear: "Why that bag of money?"

Heerabai became agitated. "Come inside here, Hiraman. I'm going back to the Mathura Mohan Company. It's a company from my own region. You'll come to the Banaili fair, won't you?"

Heerabai placed her hand on Hiraman's shoulder, this time on his right shoulder. Then she took some money from her handbag and said, "Buy yourself a warm shawl."

At last Hiraman broke his silence—"Iss! All the time money! Keep your money. What would I do with a shawl?"

Heerabai's outstretched hand stopped. She gazed at Hiraman's face and then said, "Your heart has become very small. Why is that, my friend? After all, guruji, think of Mahua the rivergirl . . . " Her voice choked with tears.

"The train is here," called the trunk-carrying man from outside. Hiraman left the waiting-room. "Get off the station platform," said the trunk-carrying man, grimacing like the nautanki clown. "If you're caught without a ticket, it'll be three months behind bars."

Hiraman went and stood quietly outside the gate. At the station, the railway company was king. Otherwise he'd have fixed the face of that trunk-carrying man!

Heerabai entered a train compartment directly in front of Hiraman. Iss! What devotion! Even seated in the train, she kept her eyes fixed on him. He looked over at Lalmohar and his heart blazed. Always following him, always considering himself a partner . . .

The train whistle blew. Hiraman felt as though a sound originating in himself rose upward with the whistle—Koo-oo-oo! Iss . . . ! Chi-ee-ee-chakk! The train started moving. Hiraman scratched his left heel with the big toe of his right foot. Heerabai was wiping her eyes with a purple handkerchief. She was waving the handkerchief and motioning him to leave. The last compartment of the train passed by. The platform was empty—everything was empty . . . hollow . . . with only some freight cars parked on a siding. The world itself seemed to have become empty. Hiraman returned to his cart.

"When are you going back to the village?" Hiraman asked Lalmohar.

"What's there to do in the village these days? This is the best time of year to earn money hauling loads. Heerabai has left. Now the fair will break up."

"Very well. You want me to deliver any message for you at home?"

Lalmohar tried to reason with him, but Hiraman turned his cart toward the road leading to their village. What was left at the fair? A desolate fair . . .

The dusty bullock-cart road ran alongside the railway line for a long way. Hiraman had never been on a train. An old longing flickered in his heart—a longing to ride on a train, singing, and to go to the temple of Jagannath.

He lacked the courage to look back at the empty cart behind him. His spine was still tingling, and the champa flower was still blooming in his cart. Over and over the beat of a kettledrum sounded out the fragment of a song. . . .

He turned and looked—not even gunnysacks, not even bamboo, not even a tiger . . . angel . . . goddess . . . friend . . . Heeradevi . . . Mahua the rivergirl. . . . No one at all. Silent voices of departed moments were trying again to be heard. Hiraman's lips were moving. He was probably making a third vow—about carrying a company woman . . .

Suddenly Hiraman flicked his whip at the two bullocks. "Why do you keep turning and looking toward the railway tracks?" The bullocks picked up speed and broke into a trot. Hiraman began to sing softly—"Oh yes, Gulfaam, I am slain!"

KRISHNA BALDEV VAID

# My Enemy

Right now he's lying unconscious in the next room. Today I mixed something in his liquor, since ordinarily he gulps straight whiskey like lemonade with no particular effect. Reddish lines streak his eyes, the creases on his forehead glisten with perspiration, his lips become even more poisonous, but that's all—he remains in his senses as usual.

I'm surprised that this scheme didn't occur to me earlier. Perhaps it did and I then suppressed it after some reflection. I'm always pondering things and then suppressing them. Even today I was afraid that he'd recognize the taste in the very first sip and catch me redhanded. But as the glass emptied his eyes began to blur and my courage grew. I felt like wringing his neck, but then, imagining the consequences, my nerve faltered. I suppose every coward has a vivid imagination which comes to the rescue and saves him from danger. I did summon up the courage though to look directly at him for a moment. That in itself was no mean accomplishment, since my timid eyes ordinarily flutter all around when he's present. Even in ordinary circumstances my condition in his presence is very extraordinary.

His eyes closed and his head was drooping. Before he top-
pled over, his arms slowly rose up toward me like two weighted
branches. Seeing him helpless that way, I had the illusion that
he was breathing his last.

But I knew that the tyrant could still jump to his feet at any
moment. On regaining consciousness he would say nothing. Even
in those earlier days he used to talk very little, and recently one
might have thought he'd been struck totally dumb. Just imagining his silent disdain fills me with dread. I mentioned, didn't I,
that I'm a coward?

Somehow or other I'd figured that the long period of separation had freed me from any fear of him. It was probably that
happy misapprehension which led me to bring him home with
me that day. Somewhere in my heart there may also have been a
vain hope of dominating him, of abasing him. Perhaps I thought
that when he saw my live beautiful wife, my energetic healthy
children, and my handsomely-furnished magnificent home, he
would just give up and run away, liberating me from him forever.
Probably I also wanted to demonstrate convincingly to him the
marvelous extent to which I had ordered my life after leaving
him behind.

But these are all lame excuses. The truth is that I probably
didn't bring him with me that day; he came with me on his own.
Probably it wasn't I who wanted to abase him, but he who wanted
to humiliate me. This fine distinction must not have entered my
head at the time. I'm never able to think straight at the proper
time. That's one of my difficulties.

With Mala that day I had tried to present some such feeble
justification, but with no effect. As soon as she saw him, she flared
up. I then became aware for the first time of the whole situation
and of my own stupidity. Somehow or other I should have finished with the wretch right there, away from the house, by the
side of the road. If, breaking my cowed silence, I had placed before him all my constraints, drawn a quick sketch of Mala, and
told him clearly—"Look, guru, have mercy and stop following
me"—then we might have reached some understanding right

there. At least he'd have granted me a temporary reprieve. With
that much release, I'd have been spared the problem of settling
things simultaneously on two fronts. No matter what, I ought not
to have brought him home. But all this wisdom came too late.

Mala and he started glaring at each other like long-standing
mortal enemies. For a moment I was relieved at the thought that
Mala would handle the whole situation herself; but the next
moment I cowered, imagining her accusations and deprecations.
Trying to treat the situation lightly, I spoke in a gentle voice
which I preserve for such sensitive occasions. "Darling, we've just
come from a long walk, so please step aside a moment. Just let us
relax a bit and then you can dole out any punishment you wish."

She did step aside, but there was no lessening of her tension
and she didn't let me sit down. Furthermore, that cadaver looked
at me as though to say—"So, you've actually become a slave to
this woman." As for me, I was trying to eye them both, hoping
to evade the glance of one and hatch a conspiracy with the other.

As soon as Mala found a chance to take me aside, she began
berating me. "Now tell me, who's this no-good derelict you
picked up and brought with you? Some old friend of yours, right?
After all these years of marriage, you've not changed a bit. What
will my children say when they see him? What will the neighbors
think? Would you mind giving me some answers?"

I couldn't figure out what to say. In Mala's presence I speak
very little, spending most of the time weighing the situation,
which puts her in a worse temper. Of course her anger was justified. Her anger is always justified. The foundation of our successful marriage rests on this very thing: she's always right, whereas
I quickly and immediately admit all my errors. Moreover, whatever she may say, she has absolute faith in my compliance. Periodically she does make a kind of complaint intended to make
me happy—"What sort of mysterious pleasure do you derive out
of taking a stand against me on every little thing? I grant you're
more intelligent than I, but it wouldn't hurt you to agree with me
once in a while. . . ." Et cetera, et cetera!

In a way I enjoy these phony complaints of hers, though I

can't really feel happy about them. Anyway, she thinks that they let me retain my illusions, whereas I know that the reins remain completely in her hands. And that's as it should be.

Mala was gnashing her teeth and demanding, "Don't you have anything to say? What are my children going to say when they come back from the park and see this cursed man sitting in the living room? Think of the effect on them. Oof, such a filthy person! The whole house is stinking. Now tell me, what am I to say to my children?"

It was obvious that I could tell Mala nothing. So I just stood there, head bowed, while she, face upraised, kept pouring out her anger. Actually I should point out that Mala had not brought those children with her when she first came to this house as a bride. They're just as much mine as hers, but at such times she always calls them "my children," separating them from me as though lifting jewels out of the mud. Sometimes this makes me very unhappy, but then I reflect more coolheadedly and feel that, whatever the physical truth, in spirit our children belong solely to Mala. My part in their life-style is very small. And that's just as well, because if they took after me there'd be no telling how long it would take them, like me, to become upright. I'm pleased that they have a radiant future. And my only hand in that radiance is that I'm their legal—and probably their physical—father, that I support them, and that I'm bound heart and soul in service to their mother, day and night.

Well anyway, after standing there for some time with my head bowed, I finally spoke very meekly. "Look, dear, I didn't even recognize the wretch. There's no question of any friendship with him. But if one meets a person on the road, then . . ."

No telling how my sentence would have ended. Maybe it would have had no end. But Mala interrupted with a stamp of her foot. "Lies! Absolute lies!"

She then went inside and I, after standing there a little longer with head lowered, went back into the living room, where he was seated smoking a biri and smiling as though he knew everything I'd been through.

What happened earlier that evening was that I'd asked
Mala's permission to go for a little walk by myself and had left
the house just like that, with nothing in mind. Ordinarily she
doesn't give that kind of permission easily nor do I find the courage to ask for it. She hates walks that have no purpose. If she's to
go somewhere or meet someone or do something or not do something, she first of all determines the purpose clearly and accu-
rately. And it's right that she do so. I give credit to her wisdom.
Actually I usually can't go far from home alone, even for a purpose, being so accustomed to Mala's company that everything
seems sort of empty and desolate without her. When she's along,
no irrelevant thought can enter my mind. Everything appears
firm and purposeful. My inner state is like some room decorated
by Mala's hands, with everything in its place and no allowance
for disorderliness. But when she's not along, then the kind of
thing happens which occurred that evening; or perhaps I should
just say that some mishap occurs, since nothing quite like that
had ever happened before.

I don't know what got into me that evening when I drifted
a long way from home. Even far from home I usually think only
about things there. Not that there's trouble of any kind at home.
The cart of life was not only running; it was running beautifully.
With a woman like Mala in the driver's seat, what could a cart
do except keep going? No, there was no trouble at home—a good
salary, good wife, good children, good influential friends, their
wives also very robust and good, a good house provided by the
government, a good good-looking lawn, the neighborhood also
good, good regular meals despite the high prices, a good bed and
a good bed life. What else could a good man want, I ask you?

Alone, though, I frequently turn over the domestic situation
in my mind, finding the sort of satisfaction a healthy man must
get on gazing at himself in a mirror. What I mean is that time
passes easily, without feeling bored. This is also due to Mala's
good influence, as there was once a time when I constantly fell
prey to boredom.

For a while that evening my mind may have strayed to those bygone days. In any case, I had wandered far from home when suddenly he came up and stood confronting me.

It was as though some sinister stranger lying in ambush had spotted me alone and wanted to block my path. I stopped abruptly. My glance slid over his sunken eyes and fixed on his smile, where I caught a shimmering glimpse of that whole dusty era spent in his company. I felt as though, after years in hiding, I had finally been caught and ushered into someone's presence. Burdened by the prospect of this confrontation, my head drooped.

For some time, perhaps considerable time, we stood facing each other in the naked and profligate darkness of the street. Anyone watching might have thought we were praying over some corpse or muttering an incantation before attacking each other.

Matter of fact, Mala came to mind as soon as I recognized him, because I always invoke her name at any time of crisis. I wanted to turn tail and run for my life, but there was also an odd inclination to take up with the scoundrel instead of returning home. Wherever he led me, I'd go. I was startled at the idea, and I'm still astonished at it because after all it was precisely to leave him behind that I had sought shelter in Mala's arms. If I'd not rebelled against him years ago . . . but then I realized I'd be deluding myself to call that running away a rebellion, and my face flushed with shame. My face often burns with that fire.

The bastard must have sensed my distress. None of my weaknesses are hidden from him, which was one of the main reasons I'd sought refuge with Mala. In his laugh I heard the frightening rattle of dry leaves, a rattling together of countless memories from the time spent in his company. With great difficulty I raised my eyes and looked at him. His hand was extended toward me. Flinching, I stepped back, and his laugh became shriller. Teeth clinched, I looked him straight in the eye. Putting my hand in his coarse one and enduring the smelly warmth of his breath on my face, I felt as though, after all this time of freedom, I had now yielded myself again into his custody. Strangely enough, the realization did not disturb me as much as it should have. Perhaps every fugitive secretly hopes that someone will capture him.

Nothing was said all the way home. We walked slowly, each wrapped in his own silence, as though carrying a corpse on our shoulders.

When I straightened up and returned to the living room after Mala's tongue-lashing, that reprobate was sitting there happily smoking a biri. For a moment the room seemed to belong to him, not to me. Then I steadied myself somewhat. Avoiding his eyes, I opened all the windows in the room, speeded up the fan, kicked his shoes under the sofa, and was about to turn on the radio when there was a crackling laugh. Helpless, I backed away and sat down quietly.

I felt like facing him with folded hands and presenting him with the full truth—"Look, friend, take pity on me and leave quietly before Mala comes back. Otherwise the consequences will be terrible."

But I said nothing. Even if I had, he'd only have responded to my appeal with another venomous laugh. He's completely relentless, determined to get to the bottom of everything. And he abhors sentimentality.

Seeing him surveying the room, I began eyeing him furtively. Seated on the sofa with his legs curled beneath him, he looked like some sort of animal. His health looked very frail, but his appearance still resembled mine considerably. The thought troubled me and yet gave me a kind of strange satisfaction. There'd been a time when he was my one and only ideal, when we repeatedly resigned from our jobs together. . . . From one or two were fired together, when we considered ourselves superior to all the people moving along in the same old worn ruts, wasting their lives building unattractive conventional little playhouses, their minds imprisoned forever within the four walls of those houses, their hearts stirred only at the gurgling of their children, whose

stupid wives had them dancing in triple-time, and who were concerned with nothing but a show of respectability.

For some time I was lost in the memory of those days. It was
as though he'd brought a message back from that world, as though
he wanted to lure me again into the romantic wildernesses from
which I had fled and created a bed of roses for myself, a bed on
which Mala almost nightly demanded proof of my submission,
and where I was very happy.

He was smiling, as though having read my mind. Seeing him
gaining possession of me so easily, I tried to start a conversation.
"How long will you be staying here?"

His laughter again shook the neat and ordered atmosphere
of the house, and I was afraid Mala would come in and attack
him. But that fear was only proof that, despite all the years of
slavery, I still couldn't understand her. A few moments later she
walked in, smiling and enchanting, dressed in a gorgeous sari. She
greeted him charmingly and said, "You look very tired. I've had
hot water set out. If you'd like to wash up and then have a drink,
you'll feel better. There's plenty of time before dinner."

I was delighted. Mala had taken the matter into her own
hands and I had been worrying needlessly. I wanted to get up and
kiss her. I glanced at that bastard out of the corner of my eye and
he actually seemed slightly intimidated. I told myself that if he
didn't run away I'd lose all faith in the power of Mala's wisdom
and beauty. What fun if the wretch, instead of just giving up the
fight, were to get trapped by Mala's move. "Tell me, you bastard,"
I'd ask him then, "do you finally get the picture now?" Closing
my eyes, I imagined him dancing around her, enthralled by her,
lying down with her. This gave me a strange satisfaction.

When I opened my eyes, he'd gone into the bathroom and
Mala was bent over straightening out the sofa. I looked her in the
eye and tried to smile, but then, disturbed by her strained appearance, dropped my glance. Clearly she'd not yet forgiven me.

When he emerged from his bath, he was wearing clothes of
mine. Mala poured him some beer and asked, "Do you prefer

lots of spice in your food or just a little?" I could hardly suppress
a laugh, thinking that the bastard must barely get food at all. I
was pleased at Mala's strategy.

We sat there drinking for some time. Mala kept talking
cordially to him, asking all kinds of trivial questions—"How do
you like this city? Is the beer cold enough? Where have you left
your luggage?" Our children arrived and greeted their "uncle,"
took turns sitting on his lap and telling him their names and so
forth, sang a song or two, and then said good-night and went off
to their room. Mala's cordial behavior made it seem as though
some intimate friend from our own community had come to stay
for a while with his big car parked out in front of the house.

When Mala went to prepare dinner, I looked fearlessly toward the rogue for the first time that evening. He'd polished off
three or four glasses of beer and his face had lost some of its
pallor. But there was still poison and challenge in the smile he
gave as soon as Mala left, as though to say—"I like your wife, but
look man! You should warn her I'm not as soft as she thinks."

My spirits were dampened again. Apparently things were
not going to be solved so easily. I recalled that even in the old
days he'd been enamored of beautiful and spirited women but
that their charms didn't hold him for long. Nevertheless, I
thought, the matter has passed out of my hands now and all I
can do is wait.

Dinner that evening was delicious, and later Mala herself
escorted him to his room. But she wouldn't speak to me after
that. I tried to joke a little, saying, "He looked pretty good after
he got cleaned up, didn't he?" I coaxed and teased, making a
number of attempts to reach a truce, but she wouldn't let me
near her. I got no sleep that night, though inwardly I was still
convinced that she'd manage somehow to get rid of him the
next day.

My assumption proved wrong. Granted Mala was very clever,
very wise, very captivating, but she was no match for the audacity
of that bastard. For three days she entertained him graciously.
Wearing my clothes he began to resemble me completely, mak-

ing it look as though Mala had two husbands. I would take the car and leave for the office every morning. No telling what went on between those two after I was gone. But at every opportunity she'd take me aside and start scolding. "Look, isn't that slob ever going to leave? As long as he's in the house, we can't invite anyone over or go to anyone's place. My children say he doesn't even know how to talk decently. Just what is it he wants?"

What could I tell her about his wants? Sometimes I'd say, "Be patient just a little longer. He must be thinking about leaving." Sometimes I'd say, "What can I tell you? I'm ashamed too." And at times I would say, "It's you who has led him on. If you'd been stern with him, then . . ."

Mala did not alter her behavior, but on the fourth day she took the children and moved to her brother's place. I did everything to stop her but she wouldn't listen. That day the wretch laughed a lot, loudly and repeatedly.

Five days have passed since Mala left. I stopped going to the office. He reappeared in his true colors. Taking off my clothes, he put on that dirty outfit of his again. He didn't say anything, but I knew what he wanted. He was thinking that this chance would never come again, that she'd left and I'd be wise to run away before she returned. I shouldn't worry about her—she could take care of herself.

And today I've finally succeeded in knocking him unconscious for a little while. Two paths are open to me now. One is to kill him before he regains consciousness. The second is to pack a few essentials and get ready so that, as soon as he revives, we two could set out on the road from which, years ago, I ran away and took shelter in Mala's arms. If Mala were here, she'd come up with some third alternative. But she's not here, and I don't know what to do.

RAJENDRA YADAV

# A Reminder

IN bed that night, only one unpleasant shadow hovered briefly and then, melting into a torrent of files and telephone rings, disappeared. Nath could hardly remember the uneasiness that had made him grope in the dark and light a cigarette. In his mind he started reviewing the events of the day.

Although it had been unnecessary to lean over so far to set down the telephone receiver, that was the way Nath had done it. Somehow he felt very light. All at once the black telephone, files, paperweight, pincushion, and visiting cards—all sprang up clearly before him. He adjusted the collar of his shirt, glanced at his watch, and then pulled himself together. "Worthless wretch!" he repeated to himself. "Jackass!" Seeing a shadow on the other side of the dingy curtain over the doorway, he had dropped his squeezed-rubber smile and restrained himself again.

Kedar had been speaking on the other end of the phone: "Worthless wretch! Jackass! I hear you've become a real big shot along with your Minister Sahab. Phone a dozen times and your secretary says the Sahab's doing this or doing that. If I'd not

reached you this time, I wouldn't have spoken to you the rest of
my life, you bastard."

The two creases on Nath's forehead had deepened into
troughs. "Yes . . . yes . . . " he stammered, "I didn't recognize
you."

"Of course, of course, you grandson of a governor, why
would you recognize even your own father now?" came the
response.

The voice was very familiar but he couldn't quite place it.
The operator must be listening. Suppressing his irritation, he
said, "Look, I'm hanging up the phone, you . . . "

Lest the connection actually be cut off, the speaker on the
other end identified himself. "Hey, what are you doing? Don't
you recognize the venerable Kedarji?"

"Oh, it's you, Kedarji! Well, when did you arrive?" How he
produced that sentence, only he knew. Internally he had been
rocked by an explosion that made him want to wave the receiver
and start dancing—Hey, you bastard Kedarey! Where are you,
old pal? When did you get in? Come over right away. . . .

"I've been here since my arrival the day before yesterday
and have been trying to reach you by phone ever since. Please
stay where you are right now. I'll come there immediately. Just
explain, please, where the place is in relation to the Ashoka Hotel.
The problem is that the map of Delhi . . . "

"I'm delighted you're here, my friend. You must of course
dine with us this evening. . . . " His mind had translated Kedar's
remarks to mean that the audacious scoundrel was sitting there
trying to impress him with talk of the Ashoka! Why hadn't he
just come right over?

"It's this way, Mr. Nath. I'll first have to look at my appointment diary. Then something can be arranged." There was a burst
of laughter. "Wah! I understand, old boy! You've become terribly
proper. Of course we'll have dinner, but first I'm coming over to
shake up your grandness."

"Right now? Not just now, friend. I'm in the middle of a
lot of work. Tomorrow the Minister Sahab has to present some

extremely important papers in Parliament. I won't be able to visit with you. What are you doing this evening?"

"What am I doing indeed! Very well, hold on just a minute —uh, uh, oh yes, this evening there's a dinner with the trade representative. But I'm free from five until seven."

"All right, that's fine. Please meet me at the Volga at five-thirty."

"Hey, what's happened to you? 'Please meet me. . . . Please meet me. . . .' "

There was no response on Nath's end of the phone.

As soon as he heard "All right, five-thirty," he pressed the button, phone still in hand, and cut off the connection. His face hardened. That bastard was still a boor. I was giving so many hints, but there was only that same crudeness from him. Matter of fact, I'd heard that he was with some private company. Could he be coming to me seeking a license or something? Not inviting him here was a good idea. It would have created a problem. Kedar's position might be quite distinguished, but he lacked good judgment as to how status is maintained.

For a long time he couldn't figure out what work needed to be done. Perhaps there was nothing. But in time, one after the other and then hundreds of duties came to mind.

That evening when he reached the Volga at exactly five-thirty, he was stiff and restrained. When he opened the door, a pleasant coolness surged toward him, and simultaneously someone seized his shoulders from behind and hugged him—"Say, buddy, you're arriving right on time like a proper big shot."

"Hello-o-o," he said with forced enthusiasm and put out his hand. Kedar brushed aside the hand, put an arm around his waist and headed toward the chairs.

In summer, clothes don't stay fresh very long, and someone clinging this way messes them up even more. But Kedar just casually swept Nath along and they both plopped down at a booth. "Apparently that Minister of yours is an absolute blockhead. His whole machine is run by you alone."

"That's how things are." Nath straightened up and tried to sit properly. Coming here had been pointless. And he could have stalled. He was filled with a strange boredom and disappointment. I wonder whether he might be trying to judge how much influence I have on the Minister. Suppressing a yawn, he said, "Now please tell me something about yourself."

"Look, Nath, if you're going to talk, then don't use all this formal jargon," Kedar declared with real irritation. "Look, in Paris and London, where all the politeness and formality in the world was expected, you couldn't say anything without throwing in some foul language about mothers and sisters. Yet as soon as you come here, you become a total sahab." Maybe he too felt that this meeting was pointless.

Suddenly, however, they were both reminiscing. At parties and restaurants the two of them, dressed very formally, had represented their country by being models of smartness and propriety. Putting on serious airs, they would use pure Mughal politeness and manners, bowing to each other as they presented things, offered suggestions, and expressed agreement or disagreement. One would talk in whispers, while the other would assume a grave expression and listen attentively.

For example, at a meal, one would urge the other on with full courtly gestures. He would speak very slowly in Hindi—"You bastard, if you have to do things your way, then glut yourself with this cattle fodder." With equal solemnity the other would reply, "Thank you, you son of a bitch. First give me something to drink, though, you sister- ———." There was great pleasure in having their own language, unintelligible to those around. Nevertheless the words were spoken in such a way that even someone knowing the language could not have understood.

Ever since childhood, there was almost no abusive term they had not tried on each other, repressing their laughter as they softened the cursing with English words such as "sorry . . . sure . . . thank you." Back in seventh class, the two once arrived in class dressed as Ram and Lakshman and carrying real bows and arrows. Ever since, they had kept practicing the art of keeping a

straight face during their deviltry. Recalling all this, they both
rocked with laughter.

Nath began feeling that he'd been unnecessarily formal. He
was suddenly rejuvenated, released from the tight vise which had
been gripping him.

For an hour or more the two kept at it, their talk about old
times punctuated with statements such as—"This damn job's
been a disaster. . . . " "My work has kept me ground down. . . . "
"I thought that the very first thing I'd do on reaching Delhi was
to somehow dig you up and get you out, so that we could settle
down for a couple of hours of swearing."

Looking at his watch, Kedar rose with a start. "Shall we go
now, my friend?"

In the corridor, Nath suddenly remembered that he was the
Personal Assistant to a Central Government Minister, and decided that he was feeling bored from sitting for an hour and a half
talking about old times. It was only the chance to relax which
had been refreshing. His muscles tightened and he released
Kedar's hand, but to avoid drawing attention to the action, he
reached in his pocket and took out the car key.

Kedar stopped and said softly. "Hey, look! Who's that
ahead?"

"Where?" He turned with a start, afraid it might be the
Minister.

In the distance an old man wearing a three-piece suit was
heading toward them, moving slowly with a cane. It didn't take
long to recognize Professor Lal.

"That old man will be a bore. Let's duck out of sight here."

They stepped behind a pillar and a bamboo screen. For years
Professor Lal had paid Kedar's fees from his own pocket, while
Nath had received a check for two thousand rupees from him for
assistance in going abroad. After the professor passed by, lost in
thought, they both sighed with relief. They'd have had to bow
politely and greet him with folded hands, even then feeling
guilty at not touching his feet.

Whatever had been received would be returned by check in

the mail some day, accompanied by a note of thanks. Both of them were thinking along these lines, as they had done many times previously. Their intentions were not at all malicious, and it pleased them that somehow they had managed to remain honest.

The two of them walked beside each other like strangers. Waving goodbye to each other, one headed toward his car and the other toward a taxi. Nath realized after starting the engine and shifting gears that he could have given Kedar a lift. At least he should have arranged another appointment. Oh well, forget it, he told himself, and started the car with a jerk. With two fingers, he again adjusted the collar on his shirt.

He felt as though he'd emerged from some dark suffocating room into a fresh open place. He intentionally avoided looking toward the circular corridors of Connaught Place, lest he be spotted by another old acquaintance.

## RAMKUMAR

# *Sailor*

LOOKING at his face in the mirror that day, he happened to notice the eyes, and it seemed as though something was missing from them. When it had been lost, he had no idea, because he couldn't recall when he had last looked at his eyes in a mirror. For some time he stood that way, mirror in hand, gazing into it with an expression of uncertainty and sadness on his face—staring, vacant eyes, as though two doors had swung open of their own accord, revealing a wilderness stretching far into the distance.

And that day, that Sunday morning in the Company Garden, an observer would have been left with an indelible impression of his eyes, an impression that would have clung like an invisible shadow.

But there was no one else in the Company Garden. Alone, he felt safe. Red gravel crunched under his feet on the path between two sections of grass. Slanting rays of sunlight were glistening on the tops of the tall eucalyptus trees. And there were flowers—red, green, yellow. Except for three or four, he didn't know the names of the flowers, nor had he ever felt it necessary to know them. The breeze that morning was cold.

He recalled that he'd noticed that morning in the mirror that something had fallen from his eyes, or that something had lost itself in them. But he was not concerned.

Then he forgot everything in the freshness of the morning air. His hair began to fly in the breeze like loose ends of string. The first time he'd seen some grey hairs amongst the black, he had clutched the mirror in the same way, caught up in a dense gloom. Now he was used to them. He'd get used to his eyes also.

It had been about a month—he didn't remember exactly— since he'd been called to his father-in-law's room where the man, after a brief introduction, said that the hundred rupees a month he was paying for his own and his son's expenses was not enough in these days of rising prices. To substantiate the statement, he had quoted the prices of flour, dal, ghee, rice, and so forth. And then there was electricity, water, the servant girl, and his room. Noticing that his eyes were lowered, the man also mentioned quietly that since the son was getting bigger, his rations kept increasing too. Seeing him silent, the father-in-law added in a confidential tone, "If I were alone, it wouldn't matter. But your brothers-in-law are grown up now, their own children are growing, and they don't want to feed anyone else out of their earnings. And nowadays people don't even care about their own blood relations. So, son . . . " He paused a moment. "If you were living in a separate house, could you manage on a hundred rupees? Besides there are all kinds of comforts here—everything's just like in your own home. Your mother-in-law is fonder of your son than of any of her own sons' children, and that's a sore point with my daughters-in-law. But then, all this is no secret to you."

He had gone on listening to all this as though it referred to someone else. Then he went back to his room.

If it weren't for Munnu, he'd have rented a room somewhere else for himself. With the boy, though, how could he manage alone? This was the main reason for not moving out. Then too, living separately he'd be surrounded with other worries such as food and taking care of a household. He didn't believe his father-in-law's arguments. They all just wanted to get together and rob

him, taking advantage of him since they figured he was simple
and naive. No, he would not pay more than a hundred rupees.

Suddenly he was surprised to see a boy reading on a bench
in front of him. He felt like a thief caught red-handed. If he'd
spotted the boy from a distance, he would have quietly turned
around or slipped off the path to one side. For some time he kept
looking at the boy hunched over his reading, and gradually a
desire gripped him to sit down next to him on the bench. He
tiptoed up and sat down on the far corner. The boy glanced over
and then stared as though this were the first time he'd seen such
a person. Then he bent over his book again. He had smiled when
the boy looked over, but getting no response, he gazed straight
ahead at the historical ruins scattered there.

If his wife were alive, things would be different. As it was,
though, his living there was upsetting everyone. The shriveled,
toothless face of his father-in-law came to mind and he began
feeling worried. They'd be pressing him again and giving him
reminders. His older brother-in-law's wife periodically announced
in a harsh voice that she couldn't bake so many chapatis. And
when the mother-in-law whispered that the downstairs son-in-law
would overhear her, the girl's voice became even more shrill—
"I'm not afraid of anyone. I'm a woman who doesn't hesitate to
speak the truth." And in his room below he heard everything,
the voices upstairs carrying through the screen above his room.

"Excuse me," the student sitting next to him said. "Do you
know why there are eclipses of the sun and the moon?"

Taken aback, he looked blankly for a few moments at the
student whose eyes were holding back laughter. Eclipse of the
sun, eclipse of the moon. . . . In his mind two zeroes began racing
as though chasing each other.

"You must have studied geography?" The boy glanced at
the man's face and then continued, "All right, tell me this—what
country is it where night lasts for six months and day for six
months?" Then, staring at him, a faint smile spread over the
boy's lips. The student was now convinced that he had not even
finished high school.

He sat there as silently as a job applicant unable to answer a question and staring at the examiners. A definite smile appeared on the student's face. In those eyes was a glitter like stars on a dark night—and when he'd looked at his own eyes in the mirror that morning . . .

"I'm taking my exams," the boy said, closing the book in his hand. "After the exams, I'm going to become a sailor, so I can travel the whole world. I love to travel, and as a sailor I can go around the world without paying anything. Say, have you ever been on a ship?" the boy asked eagerly. This was the first time he had found a person who would listen to him with interest and never even open his mouth.

Looking at the student, he suddenly felt as though it was Munnu's face there in front of him. He ought to get Munnu into some school, too. With the child around the house all the time, they kept noticing that he was idle and giving him all kinds of chores to do—bringing curds from the sweet shop, filling the father-in-law's pipe, quieting the younger sister-in-law's crying baby in his lap. Sitting in his room, he kept hearing Munnu being ordered around, but he was never able to protest.

Munnu was afraid of him. He couldn't remember when the boy had last set foot in his room. When he had to deliver a message from upstairs, the child would stand out in the hallway and say quickly, "Auntie wants you to go get the wheat ground," or "You're to bring ten seers of green mangoes for pickle from the market." Then he'd dash back upstairs.

Looking at his son made him feel as though the inner fog might lift of its own accord. Many a time he had wanted to call the boy in, but the thought never got past his lips.

Any time there was a fight among the children, it was always Munnu who was beaten. He could hear him crying, but the boy never came to him and complained. Once when he went upstairs to deliver the vegetables he'd bought, he was unhappy at finding that Munnu was not with the other children. But he lacked the courage to ask anyone about the boy. Thinking the child might be playing on the roof, he continued up the stairs. From a corner in the dark came the sound of Munnu sobbing. Seeing him, the boy stopped crying and hid his face between his knees.

"What happened, Munnu? Did someone hit you?" He said nothing more. Hesitatingly, he caressed Munnu's head lovingly, but the child crouched over farther, as though there was no need for this sympathy. Munnu's long, dry matted hair caught in his fingers. It obviously had not been cut for two or three months. His shirt was torn and his shorts were covered with a thick layer of dust and dirt. The rough skin on his legs felt like dry leather. They sat there that way for a long time in the dark of the night, while all kinds of dim shadows circled about them. He felt as though he were touching his son for the first time, as though the child had just been born. . . .

"In the jungles of Africa you can see fights between ferocious lions and rhinos—that's what I've read in a book of mine. Say, have you ever seen the ocean? I haven't seen it either. But when I become a sailor, I'll have to be on it day and night. That's why I don't mind not having seen the ocean yet."

He was surprised to see the student still sitting there at the end of the bench. The light morning sunshine had reached them. Beneath the long row of trees there were flowers—red, green, yellow—but he didn't know their names. The sight of them was sufficient.

"I don't enjoy studying," the boy was saying, "and what good will it do? My big brother passed his B.A., but he couldn't find a job anywhere, not even for a hundred rupees a month, and finally he ran away from home. Father doesn't want me to be a sailor. If he opposes me, I'll run away from home too. By selling my books I can get enough money for a ticket to Bombay. I've even discussed it with a second-hand book dealer, and he has agreed. Say, you must have been to Bombay. Hundreds of ships go in and out of the harbor there. I could get a job on one of them, couldn't I? Sure I could. . . . "

Ocean depths filled the student's eyes. Had there ever been such depths in his own eyes? He felt as though he were seated next to the boy on a ship, taking a journey, surrounded by high, blue ocean waves through which the ship was moving forward. . . .

His wife also used to say that they'd give Munnu a good education. Cutting expenses, they'd not let him suffer any kind of
privation. Then, looking at her husband with great expectation,
she would add, "And you'll make progress, too. You won't always
be making just a hundred a month." Laughing, he'd agree with
her. . . . If she were alive now, she'd see how her dreams were
taking shape. On his Sunday holiday, instead of relaxing at home,
he was roaming around this garden, sitting on a bench talking
to a student.

His mother-in-law really was fond of Munnu. Occasionally
she'd have a piece of clothing made for him out of her small sav-
ings. Sometimes she'd bring him a toy bought at a fair. But this
affection upset her daughters-in-law, and out of fear of them she
never openly expressed her love for the boy. One day in the house
there was a quarrel about Munnu, and both daughters-in-law
spoke cuttingly to her. She cried all that day, and when he returned home that evening, she came to his room and said, "Son,
the state of this house is no secret to you. These days even blood
relations become strangers. And then daughters-in-law move in
from alien homes, unwilling to respect the old ties of their in-laws.
You're still our daughter's husband." She wiped her eyes with a
corner of her sari, perhaps reminded of her deceased daughter.
"It's time for us to go drown ourselves when a son-in-law has to
pay for his own food and the daughters-in-law get upset over
just baking a couple of chapatis for you." Then she too whispered
the suggestion that it would be best for him to go look for a
separate place. As for Munnu, she'd keep him with her for a year
or two until he got bigger. Everyone in the house would feel the
loss of his hundred rupees once he moved away, she had said.

That night he had tossed on his cot until all hours. His wife's
face kept coming to mind. Were it not for her death, he wouldn't
be having to face this problem. He decided to look for a new
place the next day. As it was, all he had here was a tiny cell where
nothing could be seen even during the day without burning a
light. And if he ever left a light on after dinner at night, the

father-in-law would stand at the screen upstairs and, instead of speaking directly to him, would make a general announcement that all lights in the house were to be shut off at once or he'd cut the wires to any room with a light burning. Next to his room the drainpipe opened, pouring out all kinds of foul-smelling muck from upstairs. He'd grown accustomed to that stench. But after his wife's death, when he first was forced to vacate the room upstairs and move downstairs, the dampness of the room and the smell of the drain had seemed intolerable. He could get a room like this anywhere for ten or fifteen rupees a month. . . . But by morning his resolution had faded and within a few days he had completely forgotten his plans. Life began flowing along again in its usual way.

Not that he hadn't entertained the idea of marrying again—but he had no family of his own to help arrange it, and why would his in-laws give any thought to a second marriage? One day, though, he took the afternoon off from work because he wasn't feeling well. No one in the house suspected his presence there. He had heard the wives of his brothers-in-law talking to each other while they did the household chores. The elder one was saying that if "that son-in-law" were to get married again, he'd move to the home of his new in-laws and they'd be free of him. With that room empty, it could be used as a study for the youngsters. Both started laughing, but the younger pointed out that if the room were empty, it wouldn't go to the children. The father-in-law would rent it out and pocket the income himself. . . . Despite his headache, he had sat thinking about that for a long time.

His glance happened to fall on the student seated there, and he saw that the boy was hunched over his book reading. He watched the student intently for some time. The faint shadow of a mustache had begun growing above his upper lip, but there was no dark shadow anywhere on his face. All of life was spread out before the boy like a smooth plain, and the expectation of new experiences must stir in his heart. Asleep at night, the boy must see the whole world in his dreams—the fight between a

lion and a rhino . . . that country with a six-month night and a
six-month day . . . jungles, mountains, oceans. . . . For a moment
he felt that Munnu had grown up and was seated in front of him.
He too must see dreams like this. As for himself, he never saw
dreams in his sleep. He had tried, but without success.

As he rose from the bench, he gave the boy an intimate smile.
He had begun to feel that they were old acquaintances, and that
the boy had been confiding thoughts which could only be expressed to close friends—secrets which only the two of them
knew. But on hearing a voice, the student raised his eyes for a
moment and stared as though trying to place him. Then, unconcerned, the boy became absorbed in his book.

He walked along slowly, feeling that same emptiness returning to his eyes which he had seen in the mirror that morning.

Once more he looked at the row of eucalyptus trees, now
filled with sunshine. This was Sunday, he was wandering around
the Company Garden, and the flower beds had flowers in them—
red, green, yellow—which would always remain unknown to him,
like that student seated on the bench. He was surrounded by
silence.

At the house, things would be in an uproar. Both brothers-
in-law would be home today, and it would be no surprise if one
of them was squabbling with his father. The children would be
on holiday from school, too. They'd be fighting with each other,
and Munnu would get beaten again if he got caught in the middle. That was the way he had seen it happen before. But even if
he were in the house, he'd be unable to give a word of comfort
to his crying son. Were he not even to return to the house, no one
would know the difference. There was no waiting for him at
mealtime. The servant girl prepared his tray and brought it to
his room, but when he needed more chapatis or vegetables, he
couldn't ask for them.

And yet the father-in-law was saying that his expenses were
more than a hundred rupees and that Munnu ate more food as
he grew bigger. But that day when he'd seen Munnu on the roof,
the boy's arms and legs had looked like dry twigs and his head

had seemed disproportionately large. And he'd also heard the father-in-law, or maybe it was the older brother-in-law, saying that his room could easily bring forty rupees in rent.

His wife's jewelry was also being held by her father. After the marriage, when he'd come here to live, his wife had turned the jewelry over to her father for safekeeping, asking for something when she wanted to wear it. And after her death the things had stayed right there. Once in the course of conversation the father-in-law had announced that when Munnu got married, they'd be given to his bride. He had said nothing. But one day he saw the younger sister-in-law wearing the necklace his wife used to wear. Though furious, he kept quiet. When he took a separate house he'd ask the father-in-law for the jewelry, but he suspected that he wouldn't get it back now.

Wandering around, he felt as though one load after another was being piled on his head. Each one was larger than the last, and there was no way to lighten them.

He came to a ruined monument in a corner of the garden, probably someone's tomb. Up on the dome, the remaining pieces of blue tile were sparkling in the sunlight. For some time he stood at a distance gazing at the black walls of the ruin and at the openings in the walls.

All at once he remembered the face of the student on the bench and heard a sound of something throbbing within him. Not moving a muscle, holding his breath, he kept listening to what sounded like someone filling the great chasm within himself.

From now on he would teach Munnu himself. If he gave him lessons for two hours after getting home every day, in a couple of years or so he could be enrolled in the fourth or fifth class at some school. Children younger than he were going to school while he just sat at home.

At that, his feet set out for the house. On the way he stopped at a store and bought a primer, a slate and pencil, and a notebook. Then he asked the shopkeeper to wrap all the things well in a piece of newspaper, so no one could see them. Asleep, he had no dreams; but occasionally while awake, lying on his cot or lounging on the empty roof or seated in the office, he could see bright spots glittering like pearls, which he would watch until they gradually grew dim and faded from sight.

He sat quietly on the cot in his room, slowly stroking the primer as though having seen nothing so valuable in years. Even in the dimness of the unlit room, he could make out everything. Noise was coming from upstairs—of the children and of the wives—and there was a delicious smell of food from the kitchen. . . .

Then his heart skipped a beat as he saw his father-in-law approaching. He couldn't remember the man ever coming before. Immediately he hid the primer under the blanket. There was another person coming too, someone he felt he'd seen before. When the man came close, he recognized the resemblance to his own face as it had appeared that morning in the mirror. Those eyes, too, looked as though something was missing from them.

Seeing the two of them standing at the door, he rose from the cot and stood up. But the father-in-law gave him not a glance. Turning on the light, he was saying to the man, "This is the room. A whitewashing will clean it up. Any number of people have come to rent it, but how could I give it to some total stranger? There are women in the house. The lawyer sahab sent you, and since he's one of my old friends, I agreed to give it to you." Seeing the man silent, he went on—"It's impossible to find an empty room in this area. Besides, this place has every comfort. The courts, the post office, the markets—everything is close by. In ten or fifteen minutes you can reach any place on foot. You'll save on rickshaw fares."

It seemed to him that the man was looking not at the room but at him. He didn't raise his eyes, feeling that the man would strangle him if their eyes met. Fear drenched his body with perspiration.

The man agreed to take the room. A smile spread over the father-in-law's pinched face. The tenant could move here the coming Sunday and meanwhile, the father-in-law promised, the room would be whitewashed. Before leaving, the man again looked at him intently. But he kept his head bowed. Just breathing seemed an effort.

Even after they had gone, he remained standing. He lacked the courage to sit down on the cot, as though the father-in-law and that person would only reappear and make him get up.

That afternoon he had to vacate the room. Up on the roof was a sort of tin-covered storage place, where the household junk was kept. During the monsoon it was used as a shelter for the beds of those sleeping in the open air. The two brothers piled the scattered objects neatly in one corner, and, after the servant girl had swept, his cot was put down in the empty space. His trunk and other belongings were placed to the side. He said nothing, not even a whisper.

When they had all gone downstairs, he lay down on the cot, from where only sky could be seen, stretching far, far away. There was nothing between him and the sky. It seemed strange, but after a while he felt only pleasure. Eagerly he took the primer, slate, and notebook from his trunk and gazed at them for a long time. Then he sat there, scratching wavy lines on the slate.

"All right, Munnu, what are you going to be when you grow up?" he asked, swimming in the large, wide-open eyes of the boy sitting beside him.

But Munnu's eyes remained blank—like a pond where the dropping of a pebble has made no ripple.

"When you're educated you'll become something, isn't that right? You won't just stay like this," he persisted, irritated. "Some people become doctors, some lawyers, some businessmen, some sailors. . . ." Thinking that Munnu might not know what a sailor was, he began giving a description. "A sailor sits on a ship and travels all round the world without paying anything. Any port where the ship stops, he can go ashore and roam around the city. New people, shops with new things, a place where lions and rhinos fight, places where it's night even during the daytime or where the sun shines even during the night. Tall, tall mountains covered with snow, thick jungles, and the ocean stretching for miles . . . a sailor sees all that. Are you going to be a sailor too, Munnu?"

The child was looking at him in astonishment. For a moment it appeared as though Munnu's mouth had dropped open in amazement and curiosity. It seemed to him that the boy's heart must be pounding and pearls must be shining in his eyes, as though he were imagining himself experiencing all these things. And his face should be wearing the expression seen a long time ago one Sunday morning on the face of a student sitting on a bench. But Munnu was as still and silent as though even the greatest things in the world would turn to ashes inside him. Why couldn't Munnu too, like that student, tell him excitedly what he was dreaming of becoming when he grew up?

"When you finish school, I'll send you to Bombay. I have enough money for a ticket. Hundreds of ships go in and out there every day. You'll surely get work on one of them. And when you become a great sailor, I'll come along on one trip. The two of us will travel the world together. I've never seen a night when the sun keeps shining, where it never gets dark." His voice filled with unconscious longings which rose like the soap bubbles that in childhood he used to send soaring in the air.

Seeing Munnu sitting silently in front of him, he was confounded. All this time he assumed that the boy had turned himself into a sailor and was sailing the seas. At the sight of the child staring at him in fright, he became angry. "Why don't you say something? Are you going to grow up and still be such a boob?"

At that tone of voice, Munnu's eyes filled with tears, his lips quivered, and he began to weep. He hid his head in fear between his knees.

"Is crying all you've ever learned?" His anger was mounting. Seizing the boy by one ear, he tried to lift his head, but Munnu kept his head down with all his strength and went on crying. Soon his tears were running down below his knees, leaving curled tracks on his dry and dusty legs.

Releasing Munnu's ear, he suddenly moved away. The sound

of the boy's weeping, finding no anchor on the roof, rose upward and then faded away, merging gradually with the murky haze of frightening silence.

With vacant eyes, he stared up at the mud-colored sky, as though searching for oceans, mountains, jungles. Munnu's crying gradually subsided and was lost in silence. Thin legs, with blue veins gleaming on them; and, resting on the legs, his large mis-proportioned head, its long, dry, tangled hair looking like weeds. For a long time they both sat there that way, quiet, far apart from each other.

Munnu was still supporting his head on his knees. All at once he saw the boy's eyes and sprang anxiously to the boy's side. Taking the young face in both hands, he raised it and looked very closely at those wide-open, unblinking eyes. He felt as though something was missing from Munnu's eyes also, just as he'd felt when he looked at his own eyes in the mirror that Sunday. Munnu's staring, vacant eyes—as if some locked door had swung open, through which he could see far into the distance. What was inside? Afraid to find out, he closed his eyes.

SHEKHAR JOSHI

# *Big Brother*

J AGDISH Babu saw him for the first time at the small cafe with the large signboard, on the left coming out of the marketplace. A fair complexion, sparkling eyes, golden-brown hair, and an unusual smooth liveliness in his movements—like a drop of water sliding along the leaf of a lotus. From the alertness in his eyes, one would guess his age at only nine or ten, and that's what it was.

When Jagdish Babu, puffing on a half-lit cigarette, entered the cafe, the boy was removing some plates from a table. But by the time Jagdish Babu had seated himself at a corner table, the boy was already standing in front of him, looking as though he'd been waiting hours for him—for a person to sit in that seat. The boy said nothing. He did bow slightly, to show respect, and then just smiled. Receiving the order for a cup of tea, he smiled again, went off, and then returned with the tea in the twinkling of an eye.

Feelings are strange. Even isolated in a solitary and deserted place, a man may feel no loneliness. Despite the isolation, everything is very intimate, very much his own. In contrast, though, there is sometimes a feeling of loneliness even in a bustling set-

ting among thousands of people. Everything there seems alien,
lacking in intimacy. But that feeling of solitude and isolation in-
evitably has roots in a history of separation or detachment.

Jagdish Babu had come from a distant region and was alone.
In the hustle and bustle of the marketplace, in the clamor of the
cafe, everything seemed unrelated to himself. Maybe after living
here for a while and growing accustomed to it, he'd start feeling
some intimacy in the surroundings. But today the place seemed
alien, beyond the boundary of belonging—far beyond. Then he
began remembering nostalgically the people of his village region,
the school and college boys there, the cafe in the nearby town.

"Tea, Sha'b!"

Jagdish Babu flicked the ash from his cigarette. In the boy's
pronunciation of "Sahab," he sensed something which he had
been missing. He proceeded to follow up the speculation—
"What's your name?"

"Madan."

"Very well, Madan! Where are you from?"

"I'm from the hills, Babuji."

"There are hundreds of hill places—Abu, Darjeeling, Mus-
soorie, Simla, Almora. Which hills is your village in?"

"Almora, Sha'b," he said with a smile, "Almora."

"Which village in Almora?" he persisted.

The boy hesitated. Perhaps embarrassed by the strange name
of the village, he answered evasively—"Oh it's far away, Sha'b. It
must be fifteen or twenty miles from Almora."

"But it still must have a name," Jagdish Babu insisted.

"Dotyalgaon," he responded shyly.

The strain of loneliness vanished from Jagdish Babu's face,
and when he smiled and told Madan that he was from a neigh-
boring village, the boy almost dropped his tray with delight. He
stood there speechless and dazed, as though trying to recall his
past.

The past: a village . . . high mountains . . . a stream . . .
mother . . . father . . . older sister . . . younger sister . . . big brother.

Whose shadow was it that Madan saw reflected in the form

of Jagdish Babu? Mother?—No. Father?—No. Elder or younger
sister?—No. Big brother?—Yes, Dajyu!

Within a few days, the gap of unfamiliarity between Madan
and Jagdish Babu had disappeared. As soon as the gentleman sat
down, Madan would call out—"Greetings, Dajyu!" "Dajyu, it's
very cold today." "Dajyu, will it snow here too?" "Dajyu, you
didn't eat much yesterday."

Then from some direction would come a cry—"Boy!" And
Madan would be there even before the echo of the call could be
heard. Leaving with the order, he would ask Jagdish Babu, "Anything for you, Dajyu?"

"Bring me some water."

"Right away, Dajyu," Madan would call out from the other
end of the room, repeating the word "Dajyu" with the eagerness
and affection of a mother embracing her son after a long
separation.

After some time, Jagdish Babu's loneliness disappeared.
Now not only the marketplace and the cafe but the city itself
seemed painted with a sense of belonging. Madan's constant cry
of "Dajyu" ringing out from all over the room, however, no
longer pleased him.

"Madan! Come here."

"Coming, Dajyu!"

This repetition of the word "Dajyu" aroused the bourgeois
temperament in Jagdish Babu. The thin thread of intimacy could
not survive the strong pull of ego.

"Shall I bring tea, Dajyu?"

"No tea. But what's this 'Dajyu, Dajyu' you keep shouting all
the time? Have you no respect for a person's prestige?"

Jagdish Babu, flushed with anger, had no control over his
words. Nor did he stop to wonder whether Madan could know
the meaning of "prestige." But Madan, even with no explanation,
had understood everything. Could one who had braved an understanding of the world at such a tender age fail to comprehend
one paltry word?

Having made the excuse of a headache to the manager,

Madan sat in his small room, head between his knees, and sobbed. In these circumstances far from home, his display of intimacy toward Jagdish Babu had been perfectly natural. But now, for the first time in a foreign place, he felt as though someone had pulled him from the lap of his mother, from the arms of his father, and from the protection of his sister.

Madan returned to his work as before.

The next day, heading for the cafe, Jagdish Babu suddenly met a childhood friend, Hemant. Reaching the cafe, Jagdish Babu beckoned to Madan, but he sensed that the boy was trying to remain at a distance. On the second call, Madan finally came over.

Today that smile was not on his face, nor did he say, "What can I bring, Dajyu?" Jagdish Babu himself had to speak up— "Two teas, two omelets."

Even then, instead of replying, "Right away, Dajyu," he said, "Right away, Sha'b," and then left, as though the man were a stranger.

"Perhaps a hill boy?" Hemant speculated.

"Yes," muttered Jagdish Babu and changed the subject.

Madan had brought the tea.

"What's your name?" Hemant asked, as though trying to be friendly.

For a few moments silence engulfed the table. Jagdish Babu's lowered eyes were centered on the cup of tea. Memories swam before Madan's eyes—Jagdish Babu asking his name like this one day . . . then, "Dajyu, you didn't eat much yesterday" . . . and one day, "You pay no attention to anyone's prestige. . . ."

Jagdish Babu raised his eyes and saw that Madan seemed about to erupt like a volcano.

"What's your name?" Hemant repeated insistently.

"Sha'b, they call me 'Boy,' " he said quickly and walked away.

"A real blockhead," Hemant remarked, taking a sip of tea. "He can't even remember his own name."

## MOHAN RAKESH

# Miss Pall

THAT figure in the distance could only have been Miss Pall. Nevertheless, before trusting my eyes, I adjusted my glasses. It was Miss Pall all right, no doubt about it. True, I knew she was now living somewhere in the Kulu region, but I didn't expect to run into her suddenly this way. Even seeing her in front of me, I couldn't believe that she would be living in this little village between Manali and Kulu, especially after all the speculations people had made about her when she quit her job in Delhi and moved away.

The bus pulled up and stopped beside the post office in Raysan. Miss Pall, a bag in hand, was standing outside talking to the postmaster. She thanked him for something and then turned towards the bus just as I stepped down in front of her. At first she was taken aback to find a man suddenly blocking her way, but as soon as she recognized me, her face lit up with delight.

"Why, it's you, Ranjit! What in the world brings you here?"

"I've come from Manali on this bus," I replied.

"Really? How long were you there?"

"Eight or nine days. I'm on my way back to Delhi now."

"You're leaving right away?" The enthusiasm dimmed on her face. "Look, this is terrible. You've been here over a week without even trying to get in touch with me. You must have known that I live in Kulu these days."

"I knew that, yes, but I didn't know where in Kulu. Even now, you just suddenly appeared. Otherwise how would I have known you had settled in this jungle?"

"Honestly, this is awful. You've been here all this time and now I meet you just as you're leaving."

The driver honked the horn. Miss Pall gave him an irritated look. "Please, sir, just a minute," she called, in a tone of both reproof and apology. "I'm going to Kulu on this bus too. Please let me have a seat for Kulu. Thank you. Thank you very much." Then, turning back to me, she asked, "How far are you going on this bus?"

"I'll go as far as Jogindarnagar today, spend the night there, and then catch another bus in the morning."

The driver began blowing the horn even more insistently. Glancing at him in angry submission, Miss Pall moved toward the door. "All right, we'll at least be together as far as Kulu and we can talk more on the way. I think you should stop over for three or four days here and then go on."

The bus had already been very crowded, and with the two or three passengers added at this stop, not even standing room remained. As Miss Pall stepped in the door, the conductor raised his hand and stopped her. I explained to him as clearly as possible that my seat was vacant, that the lady could sit there, and that I would find standing room somewhere, but the conductor insisted that no more passengers could be admitted. I was still arguing with him when the driver started the bus. Since my belongings were on board, I jumped on the moving vehicle. Once inside, I turned and looked back at Miss Pall. She was standing there looking as puzzled as though someone had just snatched the things from her hands and run off before she could do anything about it.

The bus rounded a few curves and headed for Kulu. I began

regretting that I hadn't unloaded my baggage there in Raysan, since Miss Pall had not found a place on the bus. My ticket was for Jogindarnagar, but that didn't mean I had to go all the way there. The encounter with Miss Pall had been so unexpected and brief, though, that the idea had not even occurred to me. With a little more time to think about it, I would certainly have stopped off for a while. In that hasty meeting I had not even been able to inquire whether she was getting along all right, and there were all kinds of other things which I was curious to find out.

People had been speculating endlessly about Miss Pall ever since she left Delhi. One person thought that she had married a retired English major in Kulu who had signed his apple orchard over to her. Another had heard that she was getting a government stipend and was just roaming around enjoying herself. There were even people who claimed she had gone off her head and that the government was sending her to the insane asylum at Amritsar for treatment. Because she had suddenly given up a five-hundred-a-month job and gone away, people were spreading all sorts of stories about her.

At the time Miss Pall handed in her resignation, I was not in Delhi, having left town on a long vacation. I knew quite a lot, however, as to why she had quit her job. We had both been working in the Information Department, and she lived just ten or twelve houses away, in the Rajendranagar section of town. Even in Delhi, her life had been rather lonely, since she was at odds with most of the office staff and didn't mix much with people outside either. The atmosphere in the office didn't seem to suit her, and she appeared to be just counting the days there. She kept complaining about almost all the other employees, saying that they were low-minded and that she couldn't associate with them.

"These people are so small and dishonest," she would say, "and their talk is so petty and mean, that I feel suffocated working amongst them. I don't know why people squabble with each other over such trivial matters, trying to make everyone else look bad for the sake of their own selfish little interests."

The main reason for her unhappiness there, however, was probably something quite apart from all this, something she would never openly admit. Other people knew what the problem was, though, and purposely said all kinds of things to provoke her.

Nearly every day, Bukhariya would make some comment about her looks. "Say now, Miss Pall! You're really looking radiant today!"

"And she's been getting slimmer too," Joravar Singh would chime in from the other side of the room.

Miss Pall would get very upset over these remarks, and on several such occasions got up and left the room. People kept commenting on her clothes, too. The poor girl, perhaps hoping to compensate for her corpulence, kept her hair cut short, wore sleeveless outfits, and spent a lot of time putting on makeup. As soon as she stepped into the office, though, someone or other would start making remarks—"Miss Pall, that's a very nice design on the new kameez you're wearing. You're looking stunning today."

Miss Pall took all these comments very much to heart and wore a very serious expression all the time in the office. When five o'clock struck, she would jump up from her desk as though released from hours of torture. Leaving the office, she would go straight home and remain there until returning to the office the next morning. Perhaps it was the heckling from the office staff that made her hesitate to expand her contacts with people outside.

Because I lived nearby, or more likely because I was the only one in the office who never gave her cause for complaint, she would occasionally come over to our place in the evening. I was living at my aunt's house, and Miss Pall became quite friendly with her and with my nieces. She often helped out with the household chores. At times we'd go to her place too. She spent her time at home practicing music and art. Arriving there, we'd hear the sound of a sitar from her room or find her, brush and palette in hand, engrossed in painting some picture. But when not doing either of those things, she just lay between the two pillows on the soft mattress of her wooden cot and stared at the ceiling.

For some reason, whenever I saw the thin silk cover over her bed, I felt very uncomfortable and wanted to snatch it off and throw it out the window. Her room was so littered with sitars, tablas, paints, canvases, pictures, clothes, bathing equipment, and cooking utensils that rescuing a chair to sit on was quite a problem. When I was forced to sit on that silk-covered bed, I'd become very disturbed and try to get away as soon as possible.

After searching the room, Miss Pall would unearth a teapot and three or four cracked cups from somewhere and start preparing "first-class Bohemian coffee." Sometimes she'd show us the pictures she had painted, and then the three of us—my two nieces and I—would praise them in order to conceal our ignorance about art. Several times, though, she had been too unhappy even to make decent conversation. Then my nieces would get annoyed and say they were never going back to her place, but I would feel even more sympathy for her.

The last time I visited her place, I found her extremely unhappy. I had just spent several days in the hospital for an appendicitis operation, and Miss Pall had come almost every day to inquire about me. My aunt had stayed with me at the hospital, but it was very difficult for her to collect everything needed for my meals. Each morning Miss Pall would bring over milk, vegetables, and other things. I had been released from the hospital just the day before I went to see her that time, so I was still rather weak, but I wanted to thank her for all the trouble she had gone to on my behalf.

She had taken the day off from work, and, with the door closed, was stretched out on the bed. I suspected that she had not even bathed that morning.

"What's the matter, Miss Pall? Aren't you well?"

"I'm perfectly all right," she said, "but I'm thinking of quitting my job."

"Why is that? Has anything special happened?"

"No, nothing special ever happens! It's just that I can't work with those people. I'm thinking of going somewhere far away, to some beautiful place in the mountains where I can live and practice my music and painting properly. I feel I'm just wasting my life here. I don't see any point in leading this kind of existence. I get up in the morning and go to the office. After ruining seven or eight hours there, I come home, eat dinner and go to sleep. The whole routine seems absolutely meaningless. I've been realizing how few things I really need. If I were to go somewhere and take a small room or shack of some kind, buying only a few essentials, I could get by on just fifty or sixty or perhaps a hundred rupees. I make five hundred here, but I spend every bit of it. Where it all goes is more than I can figure. If life is only going to continue this way, then why keep up the useless burden of going to the office? Living somewhere else, I'll at least have my freedom. I have some money saved up, and I can get some from my Provident Fund when I resign. With that, I could live quite a while in some small place. I want to go live somewhere away from all this filth, where people's behavior is not so petty. For a human being to live decently, he should at least be able to feel that the atmosphere around him is bright and clean, rather than having to wallow in dirty water like a frog."

"But how can you be sure that everything will be just as you want it in the place where you go? It seems to me that no matter where a person goes, he'll find both good and bad in his surroundings. If you leave because you're upset by the atmosphere here, how do you know you won't feel the same way about the atmosphere there? That's why I think you're wrong to consider giving up your job. Stay here and continue your music and painting. Let people go on saying whatever they please."

Miss Pall was not convinced. "No, you don't understand, Ranjit. I'll lose my mind completely, if I have to keep living with these people. You don't know all the things they've been saying, even about my taking milk and vegetables to you these last few mornings. How can anyone live around people who pervert one's best intentions? I've put up with all this for a long time. I can't stand it any longer. I'm thinking of moving away as soon as possible. The only thing I've not been able to decide is where to go. Being alone, I'm a little afraid to go live in some unknown place. You must know that I . . . "

She stopped in the middle of the sentence and suddenly stood up. "Well now, I must fix you some tea. You've just come out of the hospital and here I am, talking only about myself. You ought to stay home and rest for a few days. It's not good for you to start running around this way so soon."

"No, I won't have any tea," I said. "I can't seem to convince you, but I still think you're attaching too much importance to what people say. And I also believe they're not really as bad as you think. If you'd look at it from that point of view . . . "

"Please, that's enough," she interrupted. "I despise those people with all my heart. You consider them human beings? I prefer my Pinky to them. He's a lot more cultured than they are."

Pinky was Miss Pall's little dog. For some time she had been holding him on her lap and stroking him. Several other times I'd noticed her fondling the dog as though it were a child, and wiping its face with a towel after a feeding.

When I got up to leave, Miss Pall came as far as the outside door to see me off, the dog still in her arms. "Pinky, say 'bye-bye' to uncle," she urged, waving one of the dog's forepaws. "Bye-bye, bye-bye."

When I returned from my long vacation, Miss Pall had already turned in her resignation and left. She had told people only that she was moving to some village in Kulu. Their imaginations had filled in the rest.

The bus was rounding the curves along the Beas River and I was thinking of returning to Raysan. I had been bored after just ten days alone in Manali, whereas Miss Pall had been living here several months now! I wanted to know how she was managing alone and what she had accomplished since leaving her job. Besides, there's a certain pleasure just in meeting and talking with an old acquaintance in an unfamiliar place.

When the bus reached Kulu, I had my baggage unloaded and stored in the Himachal State Transport Office. Then I caught the next bus back to Raysan. In just fifteen or twenty minutes, it dropped me off in the Raysan bazaar. I asked a shopkeeper where Miss Pall was living.

He turned to a young man sitting next to him. "Who's Miss Pall, brother?"

"Isn't she that single lady with the short hair?"

"Yes, yes, that's the one."

Four or five other men were sitting in the shop. Their eyes all turned towards me, puzzling over what my relationship could be with that short-haired single woman.

"Come along, I'll show you where she lives," the young man said, stepping down from the shop. "Tell me, sir," he inquired once we were out on the road, "is this lady really all alone or is she . . . ?"

"Yes, she's all alone."

We walked along silently for some time.

"How are you related to her?"

I couldn't decide on an answer. After a moment's thought, I replied, "I'm not related to her. I just happen to know her."

Turning left, we climbed a little from the road and reached an open field surrounded by trees. In the middle were about half a dozen screened cottages looking like large chicken-houses. The boy told me that the first one was Miss Pall's, and then he turned back. I went up and knocked on the cottage door.

"Who is it?" her voice called from inside.

"It's a guest, Miss Pall. Open the door."

"The door's open. Come on in."

I pushed open the door and went inside. Miss Pall had spread her mattress and pillows on a rope cot and was stretched out just as she used to be on that wooden bed in Delhi. Near her lay an open book, face down—Bertrand Russell's *Conquest of*

*Happiness.* I couldn't tell whether she had been reading the book or just lying there staring at the ceiling. Seeing me, she sat up with a start.

"Oh, it's you?"

"Yes, it's me. You must have thought you'd seen the last of me."

"Honestly, what a strange one you are! If you were coming back, why didn't you get off the bus right then?"

"You should be thanking me for having gone seven miles and then returned. Instead, you . . . "

"I'd have thanked you if you'd left the bus then and let me have your seat."

I burst out laughing and began looking around for a place to sit. Everything was just as messy and chaotic as at her place in Delhi. Each object seemed to be serving a purpose for which something else was intended. One chair was piled high with dirty clothes, while the other chair was littered with paints. A plate was filled with nails.

"Sit down. I'll have some tea for you in just a minute." She started to get up.

"I've not even found a seat and you're already worried about making tea! Just tell me where I can sit, and forget about the tea. Right now I don't feel like drinking that Bohemian tea of yours, anyway."

"Then don't drink it! You think I enjoy the bother of making it? I'll clear a seat for you right now."

She emptied one chair by brushing the clothes and things off on the floor. On my left was a large table, but it was so piled with junk that there was no room to rest even an elbow. Sitting down, I tried to stretch my legs, only to discover that some of her sketches were under the pile of clothes. Miss Pall plopped back on the bed, leaning against the pillows. Spread over the mattress was that same thin silk bedcover that used to irritate me. I was again tempted to strip it off and tear it up, or throw it in a fire somewhere. Taking a matchbox from the table, I opened it, but then set it back down. There were no matches in the box, only a pinkish powder. I looked around for matches, but there were none in sight.

"The matches must be in the kitchen. I'll get them," she said, jumping up and going out of the room.

Meanwhile, I took a good look around. I was reminded again of that day at her place when I'd stayed late, talking with her. Remembering the way she had made Pinky say "bye-bye," I couldn't help laughing.

Just then Miss Pall returned with a box of matches. She must have thought it very strange that I was sitting in the room laughing to myself. All at once she grew serious. "Did someone give you a drink or something?" she asked, half joking, half accusing.

"No, no. I was just laughing at having come back here this way." Trying to sound convincing, I forced another laugh. "How could I have imagined that I'd suddenly meet you in this out-of-the-way place? And how could you have imagined that the man who left on the bus would be sitting talking to you in your own room just an hour later?" Convinced that I had justified my laughing, I then asked, "But where's Pinky? He hasn't put in an appearance yet."

Miss Pall became even more solemn. It struck me that her complexion had become rather coarse, and that there was a redness around her eyes as though she'd not slept well for several nights.

"One night after we arrived, Pinky caught a cold." She stifled a sigh. "I fed him all sorts of warm things, but in just two days he passed away."

I changed the subject and began reproaching her for having left without explaining the situation properly to everyone.

"I suppose people in the office are still laughing about Miss Pall?" she asked, as though inquiring about someone other than herself. Her eyes were so full of curiosity, though, that I didn't know what to answer.

"Why do you always attach such unnecessary importance to what others say, Miss Pall? People talk that way only because they have so little amusement in life. Once someone goes away, though, they forget in a few days that he ever existed."

I realized as I was speaking that this was the wrong thing to say. What she probably wanted to hear was that people were still talking and joking about her. She probably needed to believe that, in order to give some meaning to her present situation.

"Probably they don't talk in front of you," she said, "because they know that we—uh—uh—have been friends. You think those nasty people would ever stop gossiping? Never!"

I was glad Miss Pall didn't believe me. She probably thought I had lied so as to reassure her.

"Maybe they do still talk," I conceded, "but why should you care about that now? As far as you're concerned, those people no longer even exist."

"As far as I'm concerned, they never existed!" She pursed her lips contemptuously. "I don't consider any of them even equal to my little toe!" The look in her eyes suggested that she still wanted to get revenge on them.

I thought it best to change the subject. "Do you know that Ramesh has been transferred to Lucknow?"

"Is that so?"

Miss Pall showed no further interest in the matter. Nevertheless, I started giving an elaborate account of Ramesh's transfer. She nodded perfunctorily, but it was obvious that she was wrapped up in her own thoughts.

When I finished the story of Ramesh, we remained silent for a while. Eventually she spoke up: "Look, Ranjit, I'm telling you the truth—every moment with those people was becoming intolerable. I felt as though I was in hell. As you know, I didn't like even talking to anyone in the office."

Having left Manali that morning without breakfast, I was getting hungry, and thought it fitting to switch the conversation to the topic of food. I inquired about her arrangements for meals, whether she cooked for herself or had hired a servant.

"Oh goodness, you must be hungry!" At last she had dropped the subject of the office. "If you'd like something to eat, come with me to the kitchen. For now, you'll have to accept something already prepared. But this evening I'll fix you a proper meal. If I'd known you were coming, of course, I'd have more to offer. Hardly anything is available in the bazaar here, though. We consider ourselves specially blessed on days when there are good vegetables. Once in a long while we can buy a few eggs. This evening I'll cook trout for you. The trout here is excellent, though hard to obtain."

I was pleased at having successfully changed the subject. Miss Pall got off the bed and stood up. "Come on," I declared, rising from the chair, "I'll take a look at your kitchen. Right now I'm so famished that anything you have ready will taste better than trout to me. This evening I'll be in Jogindarnagar."

Miss Pall, who was just going through the door to the kitchen, stopped in her tracks. "Why did you turn around and come back if you have to reach Jogindarnagar this evening? Get this into your head—I won't let you leave today. Do you realize that you're my very first guest in three months? How can I let you go today? Do you have any luggage with you, or did you come just as you are?"

I explained that I'd left my things at the Himachal State Transport office in Kulu, telling them I'd be back in two hours.

"I'll have the postmaster phone them. Your things will be safe there until tomorrow. We'll go on the morning bus and bring them here. You're to stay at least a week, understand? If I'd known you were in Manali, I'd have gone and spent several days there myself. These days here I . . . oh well, first come along or you'll run away from here out of sheer hunger."

This new development took me by surprise. Deciding that the matter could be discussed later, I followed her to the kitchen. It was less chaotic than the other room, perhaps because it contained so little. There was a cloth-covered easy chair, practically empty except for the saltcellar on it. She probably sat on the chair while preparing her meals. Other utensils and ingredients lay on a dilapidated table. She quickly took the saltcellar from the chair and set it on the table, giving me a place to sit.

Then she lit the stove and put on a pan of vegetables. The ladle was dirty, so she took it outside to wash. Returning, she couldn't locate a dish towel, so she wiped the ladle on her kameez and then began stirring the vegetables.

"Is there enough for two, or will we both have to go hungry?" I inquired.

"There's plenty of food," she said, bending over and peering into the pan.

"What is there?"

She took the ladle and began probing at the contents of the pan. "Lots of things. There's potato, and eggplant, and probably —probably in the middle there are even a few teenda. I cooked these vegetables the day before yesterday."

"The day before yesterday!" I was startled as though my forehead had struck against something.

Miss Pall kept stirring. "I can't cook every day. If I did, I'd spend all my time preparing meals. And—uh—uh—being alone, I don't have any incentive for cooking every day. Sometimes I prepare everything a full week in advance. Then, with nothing to worry about, I gradually eat it up. But just say so and I'll make up something fresh for you."

I jumped to my feet. "Then are the chapatis two days old also?"

"Come here and see whether you can eat them or not."

I followed Miss Pall to a cane box in the corner. She lifted the lid. Inside were twenty-five or thirty dry chapatis, shriveled into all sorts of strange shapes. I walked away and sat down again.

"I'll make fresh chapatis for you," she said with a guilty smile.

"Forget it. I'll eat whatever's ready," I said, though inwardly disgusted at my own politeness.

Closing the lid of the box, she returned to the stove. "Vegetables don't last more than three days. After that I live on jam, onions, and salt. Plums are easy to get here so I make a lot of plum jam and keep it on hand. Taste it and see—it's good jam. Wait, I'll get you a plate."

She went out quickly and returned with the plate from which the nails had been removed. "The glass—ah—ah—has mustard oil in it. Will you take your water in a cup or . . . ?"

Trout! All through the meal and after it, Miss Pall was obsessed with the matter of the trout. She was determined to cook trout that evening. Because of her insistence, I'd agreed to stay over and leave the next morning. She had postponed further discussion of the subject until the next day.

There were other preparations to be made for the evening meal, since trout was not easy to prepare. The first thing needed was ghee, of which only a speck remained in the container. There were no onions or spices in the house, and some kerosene would be needed too.

After lunch we went for a walk and she took me first to the bazaar. The shopkeeper there had no ghee either, so Miss Pall asked the postmaster to send a pound from his place that afternoon, saying she'd buy some in Kulu the next day and return it. She also asked him to send over a few French beans and to get her two pounds of trout if a fish seller came by.

"Sorry to be so much trouble to you, Mr. Sabarwal," she apologized, having already thanked him seven or eight times. "But you see, this guest has arrived and there's nothing decent available here except trout. I'm going to check—if I can find Bali, I'll ask him to catch me a trout from the river. But Bali's very undependable, so please be sure to get some for me. I've also told Mrs. Atkinson. If she gets some too, I'll have fish both today and tomorrow. Don't forget, please. Lots of times the fish man doesn't call out, so I miss him. Thank you. Thank you very much."

She also arranged a phone call to Kulu regarding my baggage. Then, as we walked down the road, she started talking about breakfast the next morning.

"The trout will do for tonight, but what should I make for breakfast? We don't get bread here, or I could give you toast and honey. All right—well—we'll see."

The road was drenched with sunshine. A flock of sheep and

woolly goats was walking ahead of us. Patrolling alongside were two dogs, their tongues hanging out. An approaching jeep spread panic in the flock. The herdsman began driving the animals toward the hillside. One lamb slipped on the slope and, head raised, began bleating from down below. When none of the herders paid any attention, Miss Pall became distressed.

"Hey there, that lamb has fallen down. Hey, you with the goats, a lamb has fallen into the ditch. Go pick it up. Hey there!"

There'd been rain the previous day, so the level of the Beas was very high. The roaring water split and tore around the sharp rocks. Ahead, a rope spanned the river. A pulley was turning, gathering in the rope, and two men were clinging to the rope and crossing to the other side. All at once the two men clutching the rope began tittering, as though making fun of someone. Then one of them gave a loud sneeze. The rope reached the other side and the men got off, still tittering and sneezing. They let go of the rope, which hung in an arc from one side of the river to the other. Then from the opposite bank they let out another raucous laugh.

One of the men operating the pulley descended from the platform. Coming over, he began talking as though an unpleasant incident had just been averted. "Miss, that's the same Sudarshan who fed something to your dog. He's still not through with his mischief."

Miss Pall was more shaken by these words than by the earlier laughing and sneezing. Her face turned pale and her voice became brittle. "They're from that village over there, aren't they?" she asked.

"Yes, Miss."

"Please report this to the postmaster. He'll take care of the man."

"Miss, he tells me that you . . . "

"Now go do your work," she snapped. "Speak to the postmaster. He'll set them straight right away."

"But Miss . . . "

"Go on now. You can come discuss this some other time."

The man's head drooped and he walked quietly away.

We stood there for a while. Miss Pall, looking rather tired, sat down on a large rock at the side of the road. I gazed across the river at the long row of trees along the mountaintop. They seemed like a line drawn between the blue sky and the low-hanging white balloon clouds. Grey pillars, on which no bridge had yet been erected, stood on both sides of the river. Around the pillars, dirt was trickling into the river. I shifted my attention to Miss Pall. She was watching me, probably trying to find out what effect the cryptic conversation had made on me. Our eyes met.

"Shall we move on?" she asked.

"Yes, let's go."

She stood up, breathing heavily. As we started off, she began telling me how simpleminded the local people were. When Pinky was sick, they assumed someone had poisoned him. "They're uneducated people. I didn't even try to contradict them. These people can't give up their superstitions overnight. It'll take years."

As we walked, she kept glancing over to see whether I believed her or not. I had picked up a small stone from the road and was quietly flipping it in the air. We went along in silence for some time. When the silence began to seem unnatural, I suggested to Miss Pall that we head back to her house. "I'd like to see your new paintings. You must have done a lot of work in these three or four months."

"The first thing to do when we reach home is to have a cup of tea. Honestly, I'd give anything right now for a cup of hot tea. I intended to make some before we left the house, but then I realized that we needed to see the postmaster right away so as not to miss the fish man."

I was rather pleased that Miss Pall seemed to attach more importance to her first guest in three months than she did to her paintings.

As soon as we reached the cottage, she busied herself making tea. Though tired, breathing hard from climbing the slight grade, she didn't even stop for a brief rest. Her concern about the tea struck me as very unnatural, perhaps because I felt no need for it myself. She dashed around, searching for spoons and cups as though a dozen guests were waiting and she couldn't figure out how to prepare everything in time.

I strolled around looking at the pictures hanging in the room and on the veranda. They all seemed familiar. There were some large paintings Miss Pall had done of a festival in the Punjab. There were those same strange faces which we once ridiculed. Somehow she always chose to paint faces that were distorted in some way. I toured the whole room and the veranda. Except for a couple of unfinished works, I saw not a single new painting. Going to the kitchen, I asked Miss Pall where she kept her new pictures.

"Never mind that," she responded, rinsing the cups. "After tea we're going to walk up the hill. There's an ancient temple up there. The priest will tell you some stories that will amaze you. One time he was telling us about some temples here where people used to pray for rain. If the god didn't send it, they'd take his image to the Hidamba temple and hang it there from a rope. Interesting idea, isn't it? If a god doesn't do what you want, then string him up! I tell you, Ranjit, the people here are so superstitious—I can't tell you how superstitious they are! Even now they're still living in the days of the Kauravas and Pandavas, completely cut off from the modern world."

She glanced at me briefly and then busied herself with hunting for the sugar. "Now where has that sugar gone? I just had it in my hand and now I don't know where I set it. You see how absentminded I've become. There's only one cure—for someone to take a stick and set me right. Is this any way to live?"

"Haven't you done any landscapes here?" I asked.

"I've started a lot of paintings, but so far I haven't been able to complete them," Miss Pall said, as though trying to extricate herself from a difficult situation. "One of these days I'll apply

myself and finish them all. The turpentine is finished too, but
some day I'll go buy more. For several days I've been thinking of
going to the market and buying canvas and paints also, but somehow I'm just too lazy to go. There's some drawing paper that
needs binding too. One of these days I'll go and do everything
at once."

Miss Pall kept lowering her eyes while she spoke, as though
feeling guilty and trying to hide her feelings by talking continu-
ously. I watched her silently as she stirred the sugar into the tea,
finding myself filled with the kind of sadness that overwhelms
one on reaching a desolate seashore, or some lonely rocky ravine
surrounded by high mountains.

"First thing tomorrow I'll start straightening up the house
here," she declared, again starting a steady stream of talk. "First,
everything must be put in its proper place. Remember how en-
thusiastic I was about having those net curtains made for my
room in Delhi? They're still lying in the trunk here. I've not even
felt like hanging them up. Tomorrow I'll speak to the carpenter
and have him make rods. There should be food on hand in the
house, too—biscuits, butter, bread, and chutney are especially
necessary. I can at least stock up on whatever's available in Kulu.
And I can also buy turpentine there."

Even when she handed me a cup of tea, I was unable to say
a word, and began sipping it slowly and silently. My mind was
in a kind of stupor. To think of all the things I'd heard about
Miss Pall from people in Delhi—and then to find her in this
lonely mockery of a life . . .

Trout! Despite all her efforts, Miss Pall was unable to get
trout that day. The postmaster reported that the fish man had
not come; and despite all Miss Pall's cajolery, the landlord's
watchman Bali was unwilling to go catch a fish in the river. He
said he was polishing his stick and couldn't spare the time. Mrs.
Atkinson's son had caught a fish, but her husband had specifically
requested fish cutlets that day, so she couldn't give it to Miss

Pall. Yes, the postmaster did send French beans. Rice and dry French beans! Miss Pall lost all interest in making fresh chapatis. Her mind was not on cooking dinner, and as a result, the rice got slightly burned on the bottom. At dinner time, she kept offering apologies.

"I'm very unlucky, Ranjit, ill-fated in every way."

We had finished eating and were sitting outside on chairs carried from the house. Hands behind her head, she was gazing at the sky. The moon was nearly full, so the sky was suffused with light. The roar of the Beas echoed in the night. There was a rustling in the trees and a faint swishing sound from the grass in the field. The breeze was strong, and the clouds rising behind the hills in front of us were gliding slowly towards the moon.

"What is it, Miss Pall? Why are you so quiet? Just because some rice was spoiled is no reason to be so unhappy."

She kept staring ahead at the hazy line of mountains, as though searching for something. "I'm thinking, Ranjit, that my life is completely meaningless."

Then she began telling me the story of her early life, complaining bitterly that, from the very beginning, she had found no happiness even in her own home. There was no affection even from her parents. Her mother—even her own mother—didn't love her. That was the reason she'd left home fifteen years ago and taken a job.

"Just imagine, my mother didn't like my having my own home. And my father was opposed to my studying music. They used to say that my house should be a home, not a whorehouse. What affection I got from my brothers was snatched away when they got married. Only I know the difficulty I've had preserving my um . . . uh . . . purity. You can't imagine how hard it is for a girl all alone. I wanted to make a trip to Lahore, to paint some pictures there, but I didn't go because I realized that, confronted with the brute strength of men . . . uh . . . uh . . . what could I do alone? Even then, you know what terrible things those people in the department kept saying about me. That's why I say I detest

every one of them—your Bukhariya and Mirza and Jorawar Singh.
I even hated to sit down for a cup of tea with people like that.
You remember the time Jorawar Singh said to me . . . "

She began repeating little incidents that had occurred in the
office. When I saw that she was needlessly fanning her anger
again, I urged her once more to forget about the people in the
office and concentrate only on her music and art.

"Do some good paintings while you're here and then come
hold an exhibition in Delhi. When people see your work and
hear your name, they'll naturally start appreciating your worth."

"No, I don't want to get mixed up with exhibitions and
stuff!" She was still staring straight ahead. "Surely you realize
how much politics is involved in all that. I don't want to get into
those politics. I have three or four thousand rupees on which I
can manage for quite a while. When that's gone, then . . ." She
fell silent.

I was curious to hear more about her future plans, but after
some time she shrugged her shoulders and said, "Well, something or other will turn up. When the time comes, I'll think
about it."

The clouds were rising higher and the air was growing chilly.
The roaring breeze from the jungle made us shiver periodically.
Some Western music was coming from a radio in the next
cottage. In the house beyond that, people were laughing bois-
terously. Miss Pall, her eyes closed, began telling me about the
horoscope drawn up for her by an astrologer in Hoshiarpur. According to his findings, she was cursed in her present life to find
no happiness—neither in wealth nor in fame nor in love. The reason for this was also explained in the astrologer's book, the *Bhrigu
Samhita*. In her previous birth she'd been a beautiful girl, skilled
in the arts of dancing, music, and so forth. Her father was very
wealthy and she was his only child. The man she married was
extremely rich and handsome. "But I was so proud of my beauty
and my artistic talents that I didn't show the proper deference to
my husband. He lived in misery for some time and then passed

away. That's why I'm cursed to find no happiness in this life."

I kept watching her, saying nothing. Just that day she'd been making fun of the local people's credulity. All at once she stopped talking and fixed her eyes on my face. Something seemed to be trembling between her brightly painted lips. We sat quietly for some time. Clouds had covered the moon and intense darkness surrounded us. Then the light in the next cottage also went out, making the night seem even more dark and intense.

Miss Pall was still looking at me in the same way. The atmosphere was becoming oppressive. I pushed back my chair and stood up.

"It must be quite late. Let's go and get some sleep. We can talk more in the morning."

"Yes, of course," she replied, getting up. "I'll go get your bed ready. Tell me, shall I make it up on the veranda or ..."

"Fine. Put my bed on the veranda. It's probably too warm inside."

"Remember it'll get cold during the night."

"That's all right. I'll enjoy the breeze on the veranda."

Lying on the veranda, I stared out through the screen for a long time. Clouds had covered the whole sky, and the sound of the river seemed to have come very close. A spider web attached to the screen was swaying in the breeze. Nearby, a rat was gnawing on something. From the room inside came the sound of someone tossing and turning.

"Ranjit!" The voice made me shiver.

"Miss Pall!"

"Aren't you feeling cold?"

"No. There's a breeze, but that's why I like it here."

Then large drops of rain began splattering down. When the spray hit the bed, I shifted my position. I'd left a light burning on the veranda and could see things scattered helter-skelter. In making my bed, Miss Pall had been forced to turn the house almost upside down. Right next to the bed, a stool had been tipped over; and just beyond that, several picture-frames had fallen, blocking the passage. In the corner facing me, Miss Pall's brushes and clothes were jumbled together in a heap.

Inside, the bed creaked, followed by the sound of feet pattering across the wooden floor. Then I heard water being poured from a clay jug and sipped from a hand.

"Ranjit!"

"Miss Pall!"

"You aren't thirsty?"

"No."

"All right. Go to sleep."

It seemed for a while as though someone was breathing heavily nearby and as though that breathing was slowly and stealthily beginning to dominate the whole atmosphere, crushing everything with its pressure. When the rain eased a little, I turned and faced the screen and began looking out again. Just then something fell with a crash.

"What fell, Ranjit?" called the voice from inside.

"I don't know. Maybe a rat knocked something over."

"I've really been having a terrible time here with rats."

I kept silent. The bed inside creaked again.

"All right. Go to sleep."

The rain kept falling all night. It stopped early in the morning, but the sky was still overcast. From the time I got up until tea was ready, I didn't say much to Miss Pall. And even when we were drinking the tea, she spoke only in disconnected fragments. When I told her I'd be taking the first bus, she didn't once urge me to stay. Even in this casual conversation she was as formal as though addressing some total stranger. Her whole manner seemed very unnatural. She began busying herself with trivial matters, apparently to avoid conversation. A couple of times I tried joking mildly, to ease the tension and make it possible for me to leave in a friendly way. But not the slightest smile registered on her face.

"Well, Miss Pall, I guess we should discuss the matter of

leaving," I said at last. "You were saying yesterday that you'd come along as far as Kulu. It would be good for you to buy everything you need there today. Later on you might lose interest again."

"I won't lose interest. Someday I'll go and buy everything I need."

She picked up some clothes that were scattered around the veranda and set them down at random in other places. "It's raining today, so I won't go now. Perhaps tomorrow or the next day. There's so much to buy that I should first plan everything thoroughly. It's cloudy today, so today would not . . . "

"What if it is cloudy? Does that mean the shops close?" I kept talking, trying to persuade her. "Just tell me where you keep the ghee and turpentine containers. If there's a large bag of some kind, take that with you. The loose things can go in it. We'll go together in whatever bus goes from here. Then I'll catch the twelve o'clock bus in Kulu and go on. You can get a bus back almost any time during the day."

I was purposely talking as though it had been settled that she was coming along, though I knew she'd try her best to put off the trip. She was searching here and there for things to do, the expression on her face suggesting that my words were being completely wasted on her and that all she wanted was to be left alone as quickly as possible.

"Look," she protested, "sometimes you can't get even a single seat from here. To get two is extremely difficult. Why should you miss your twelve o'clock bus on my account? You go ahead. I'll buy what I need tomorrow or the next day."

As though remembering something that needed doing, she turned and walked into the other room. A little later she returned, carrying a petticoat partially eaten by locusts. Grimacing as though thinking only about that damage, she threw the petticoat in a corner and then blurted, "I've told you to go. You know it takes two seats just for me."

"Stop making all these excuses," I protested. "If there's no

room on the first bus, we'll find space on the next. Come here
and tell me where you've put those containers."

Miss Pall, perhaps tired of discussing the matter, stopped
objecting. "All right, sit down. I'll go look." Eyes averted, she
went to the kitchen.


It was true—we couldn't get seats on the first bus. The driver,
gesturing that there was no room, didn't even stop. There was no
room on the second bus either, but we somehow talked our way
into having space cleared for us. We were quite late in reaching
Kulu, though, as the road had been breached by the rain during
the night and was under repair. We reached there at almost the
same time as the twelve o'clock bus from Manali. It was then a
quarter to twelve. I went inside to check on my baggage and then
came back to where Miss Pall was waiting, the two empty containers in her hands. When I reached out to take them, she put
her hands behind her back.

"Come on," I said. "Let's first go to the bazaar and buy
your supplies."

"Never mind that now. Your bus is here. Go get on it. I can
buy my things any time. You won't find a seat on any of the later
buses. The two o'clock one is filled with passengers from Manali
when it reaches here. Another of your days would be wasted."

"What does wasting a day matter? First we'll go to the
bazaar and get your supplies. If I really can't get on a bus today,
I'll return with you and take one tomorrow. I'm not in that great
a hurry to get back."

"No, you go along," she insisted. "Why should I cause you
so much unnecessary trouble? I can make my purchases any
time."

"But I suspect you'd return today with those containers just
as empty as they are now."

"Oh no, I won't." Her eyes were brimming, and she looked
the other way while stopping the tears. "You think I don't take
care of myself. If that were true, would I be so fat? Come on,

give me the money and I'll buy your ticket. If you delay, there won't be room even on this bus."

"What makes you so insistent, Miss Pall? Honestly, there's no need for me to leave so soon."

"I told you—take out the money. I'll go buy your ticket. No, let it be. Your ticket yesterday was wasted on my account. So why am I begging you for money?"

Setting down the containers, she started for the ticket office.

"Miss Pall! Wait!" Embarrassed, I pulled the wallet from my pocket.

"You stay there. I'll be right back. Meanwhile, have your things brought out and loaded on top of the bus."

My mind hardly seemed to be functioning, but I had the baggage taken out and loaded on the bus. Miss Pall was still standing outside the ticket office. Since it was Saturday, when schools let out early, a number of children with satchels in hand had drifted down from the hills of Sultanpur to amuse themselves. Several of them had gathered around to stare at the bus passengers. Miss Pall was wearing an onion-colored salwar and kameez, with a black dupatta over her shoulders. The clothes made her look even broader than usual from the rear. The children began pushing ahead of each other to get near to the office. Miss Pall was leaning over at the ticket window.

"Fantastic!" one boy exclaimed softly. "A miracle, that's what it is!"

With that, the crowd of children standing around started laughing. I felt as though someone had piled another large rock on my heavy heart. All the children had now congregated around the ticket office, whispering among themselves. I couldn't say anything to them without attracting Miss Pall's attention. Turning away, I started watching the people who were approaching from the river. But I could still hear the children whispering. Two girls were murmuring to each other—

"It's a man."

"No, it's a woman."

"Look at the hair. Look at the body. It's a man."

"But look at the clothes. Look at everything else. It's a woman."

"Come here, children." I was startled to hear Miss Pall's voice. "Come closer and take a look." The ticket bought, she had moved away from the window.

"She's coming! She's coming!" the children shouted as they ran off. One boy dashed out on the street and yelled, "It's a miracle, brother, a miracle!"

"Come here, children. Come close to me," she kept saying. "I won't hurt you. In fact I'll give you some toffees. Come . . . "

Instead of coming closer, the children ran even farther away. Miss Pall stood there in the middle of the street for a while and then walked back to me, a strange expression on her face. Tears were about to overflow from her eyes and she was trying feebly to laugh, as though to deny they were there. Somehow she had managed to bite her lip in such a way that lipstick was smeared below her lower lip in several places. The stitching on her worn kameez was pulling loose near the shoulder.

"Lovely children, weren't they?" she said, blinking.

Nodding in agreement, my head felt like stone. After that I didn't really understand what Miss Pall was saying to me nor what I was saying to her. Thoughts no longer seemed to have any connection with words and eyes. All I remember is that I tried to pay for the ticket, but she stepped back and wouldn't accept the money despite all my urging. By some half-conscious process which I can't explain, we sustained a thread of conversation between us. My ears kept hearing her voice, and my own also, but they were like voices in the distance—stifled, indistinct, and meaningless. The one thing I heard clearly was this: "And when you reach there, Ranjit, please don't tell anyone in the office about me. Understand? You know how mean they are. In fact it would be best not even to tell anyone you met me here. I don't want anyone there to know or say anything about me. Understand?"

Then the bus started up. I peered out the window, watching Miss Pall. As the bus began moving, she started to wave. She was still holding the two empty containers. I waved back once, and until the bus turned the corner I could see the empty containers waving in the air.

SHRIKANT VARMA

# His Cross

A ROCK struck the windowpane, scattering broken glass over the floor. He scrambled to his feet. Meanwhile, a second rock! Hair disheveled and clothes in disarray, he ran down the stairs.

Reaching the bottom, he had just stepped into a long arcade of shops when a rotten tomato hit him in the face. Just as he raised his arm to wipe off the seeds and juice, a second tomato struck his forehead. Alarmed, he ran toward a cloth shop for shelter; but a rotten egg crashed and broke on his nose, and a yellow, stinking stream dripped down over his lips and chin. Then he was caught in a shower of rotten eggs and tomatoes. Covering his face with his hands, he dashed into the shop and hid behind a bale of cloth.

"What's the matter?" The shopkeeper and his assistant rushed over, sure that he must be in trouble.

They found him distraught and whimpering. He wanted to explain that those people had first broken his window and now were pelting him with rotten eggs and tomatoes. But despite his efforts, not a word emerged from his lips. Finally, with great difficulty, he stammered—"Eggs . . . tomatoes . . . "

They both stared at him in amazement. "But where?"

"Here," he said, pouting like a child and pointing to his face. But his face was perfectly all right, except that he needed a shave and his eyes were red and dull.

Reassured at seeing the two of them nearby, he had just raised his head from behind the bale of cloth when a tomato came flying and smacked his head. This time the tomato had been so big that his head felt squashed. Immediately he cowered and hid himself again, only to find masses of tomatoes and eggs raining down on him.

"There . . . " He pointed toward the street. "All those people . . ."

The two clerks looked with surprise toward the street. There was only the usual crowd passing by. "But there's nothing there at all," the shopkeeper protested in annoyance.

He stared wide-eyed at the two of them, unable to comprehend why they didn't see that all those people were pelting him with eggs and tomatoes. In despair he pulled open his shirt, to show them the way his body had been battered and bruised by all the blows. This time the two men exchanged glances and then went back to their seats.

"They're blind," he muttered angrily, and remained cowering behind the bale of cloth for some time. Meanwhile not a single tomato had fallen, so he rose and cautiously made his way out of the store. Once outside, he ducked behind a pillar and glanced all around, afraid that they were all hiding in the alleys, waiting to attack again as soon as he appeared on the street.

Reassured, he stepped out on the street and plunged into the crowd. He knew that no one could harm him once he was absorbed in that crowd. Tucking his hands in his pockets, he set off at a lively pace, his unusual height making him look like an ostrich in the crowd.

Having passed crossing after crossing through the crowds of pedestrians with no incident of any kind, he felt assured that nothing would happen now. Touching his shoulder, he realized that he'd been hurt and that his body was aching in a number of places from the blows.

But stronger than this pain was his anger toward those people. After all, what right had anyone to smash the window of a respectable man and then attack him? And such an attack too. Cowards! Sneaks!

Most of all, he was furious at that shopkeeper and his assistant. Bastards! Oh well, forget it. He was an honorable man, and ought not to curse others that way. Besides, what good would it do?

Having almost reached the outer limit of the city, he stopped, feeling tired and hungry. He searched his pockets, but found nothing. It would be necessary to return home at least once. But the thought of those people hiding in the vicinity made him tremble, and he hurried toward a neglected park nearby. He observed that it was deserted. Even the flower beds were desolate. A few dilapidated benches were scattered here and there. In front was a small pond filled with filthy water, its stench filling the air. Going to a bench, he lay down and tried to close his eyes. Though sure he'd be unable to sleep, perhaps he could at least relax a little. As his eyes closed, the sky seemed to whirl around and then disappear. The sight pleased him, and his mouth opened in a broad smile.

Suddenly he heard a whisper from a nearby bush and sat bolt upright, but he could see nothing. Then his eye lit on the limb of a tamarind tree in front of him, where he spotted two old vultures sitting and staring at him. At first taken back, he then told himself that there was nothing to fear. When he opened his eyes a second time, however, he found them still staring at him.

It's nothing, only my own silly fears, he reassured himself, and closed his eyes again. After some time his eyes opened once more, and he picked up a stone, took aim, and threw it at the vultures. There was a flapping on the branch and he lay down again, pleased.

He had just stretched out when he heard a noise in that

same bush. This time he saw four men advancing toward him with thick ropes in their hands. He got up, wanting to flee, but found his feet glued to the ground and his throat choked with terror.

The four men approached, tied him up with the ropes, stripped him naked, and then declared, "Now let the bastard have it!"

Having made him stand on the edge of the pond, where he could see his own reflection in the dirty, stinking water, they dampened some bamboo sticks and whacked him across the back. Leaping in pain, he pleaded, "Let me go! Don't beat me!"

But they continued wetting the sticks and beating him— whack! whack! He heard the sticks landing on his back, jerked with pain, and wailed, "What harm have I done you?" He couldn't figure out how he had hurt them, nor why he was being beaten this way.

During the beating, he glanced up once at the tree and noticed the two vultures jumping up and down on the branch. From pain or from pleasure? He couldn't decide.

After a thorough thrashing, they finally turned him loose. For several minutes he lay there by the pond, almost lifeless. Dying of thirst, he stooped over like an animal and drank from the pond, looking gratefully at the water. Then he began wondering whether they might still be hiding in that bush, waiting to spring on him again as soon as they noticed that he had regained consciousness a little.

Somehow he stood up and made his way, lurching, out of the park. Reaching the outside, he turned once to look back and then set off at full gallop. After some distance, he fell to the ground.

Opening his eyes, he discovered that some people had laid him at the side of the road, where they were fanning him and sprinkling his face with water. They all assumed that he'd not eaten for several days and had collapsed from hunger.

He tried to explain that this was not the situation, that actually he had been assaulted. But again he couldn't force a coherent sentence out of his mouth. Pointing toward the park, he declared, "Those people . . . they . . . " Then he tore open his shirt and began showing them what had happened, only to discover that they still could not comprehend. Finally he managed to pull himself together and told them that he had been showered with tomatoes and eggs that morning, and that just now he'd been tied up with ropes and beaten. Rolling up his sleeves, he showed how his wrists had been burned by the thick ropes and how his body had been lacerated.

He noticed the people looking at each other in astonishment. The crowd gradually dispersed. He was alone again.

Getting up from the ground and dusting off his trousers, he watched them leaving and clenched his fists. Selfish! Blind! He felt himself about to burst into tears. But no, nothing would be accomplished that way. His case must be heard. He was being attacked and no one knew about it or cared. He could lose his life this way.

There was only one alternative. Pleased, he started forward. Why hadn't he thought of this before?

Striding up to the police station, he went straight into the chief's office. The chief saw his agitation, but before he could formulate a question, the recital began.

He explained to the officer that he was a decent, respectable man, and that ever since morning he had been under attack but no one would even listen to him. First they had broken his window, then they had showered him with eggs and tomatoes; and just now when he had been resting, sore and suffering, in the park, they had tied him with ropes and beaten him.

The station officer eyed him intently and then, writing as he spoke, inquired, "Do you have a witness?"

A witness? He was taken aback, recalling that everyone had looked away during his beating, that people had gone about their business as though nothing had even happened. Selfish brutes, he fumed.

Seeing him silent, the officer spoke again. "Do you have any proof that you were beaten?"

Proof! He felt himself losing his temper. Here he had been so viciously beaten and this man was asking for proof.

"Why won't you try to understand?" he asked the officer, flushing. "They've beaten me all over, and nearly smashed my body to a pulp. I know they're still lying in wait somewhere, ready to attack me again the moment I'm alone."

This time the officer eyed him from head to foot. "All right," he said with a smile, "come along."

"But where?" He trembled with fear. Could the man be taking him back to them?

"A medical examination," the officer declared.

The words "medical examination" cheered him. In a few minutes the full truth would emerge. At the very least his humiliation and his suffering would be recorded in the official register.

On reaching the government hospital, he was taken into a doctor's office and stripped naked. He began touching place after place on his body, pointing out the injuries to the doctor as a child might do. "Here . . . and here!"

The doctor put a finger to his lips and said, "Quiet . . . quiet." He lapsed into total silence.

After a short time the doctor patted him on the shoulder. "Please stand up."

He stood up, glancing sarcastically at the police officer as though to say, "You see!"

Just then the doctor began washing his hands and said to the police officer, "There's no sign of any injury on his body."

"Liar! Fraud! You're blind!" he shouted, and left the hospital both whimpering and raging. By that time he had forgotten about his beating. All he could feel was his anger toward the doctor and the police officer, and then anguish at his own helplessness. He couldn't decide whether to cry or to laugh.

He was walking along absorbed in these thoughts when a tomato splattered on his head. He looked down in astonishment at the tomato on the ground. It seemed to be smiling at him sarcastically.

"So it has started again!" Overwhelmed with fear, he tried

to run. But meanwhile he was being pelted again with rotten eggs and tomatoes.

He couldn't decide which way to run. They had surrounded him and he was being attacked from all sides.

"Help!" he shouted. But then he realized that no one was listening to his cry. People were all going their own way, paying no attention to him.

Eggs and tomatoes were raining down on his back, his hips, his head, his arms. He felt that in minutes he would fall down dead.

Running forward, he plunged into the crowd. This time, however, they pursued him even in the crowd. Finding no escape, he fell down and clung like a child to the legs of a man passing by.

"What's the matter?" the man asked, raising him to his feet. He looked into the man's eyes, only to find them completely detached and expressionless.

"It's nothing," he mumbled in despair.

As soon as he moved away from the man, the pelting began again. Standing there, he writhed with pain.

In the course of the attack, he glanced up at the sky and muttered, "Have mercy!" But the heaviest shower of eggs and tomatoes seemed to be coming from the heavens. He started running again. Eyes closed, he ran wildly, his whole body reeling under the blows.

GYANRANJAN

# Our Side of the Fence and Theirs

Mukherji has been transferred and no longer lives in our neighborhood. The new people who moved in have no contact with us. They appear to be Punjabis, but maybe not. It's hard to know anything about them.

Ever since they arrived, I've been strangely anxious to find out about them. For some reason I can't stand staying detached. Even on journeys I have to get acquainted with the other travelers. Perhaps it's just my nature. But no one at our house is indifferent to those people. We're respectable, honorable people. Having young women in the home, we're forced to understand everything and to be constantly aware. We're full of curiosity, and keep forming impressions based on the activities of our new neighbors.

I'd like to invite the whole family over to our house and be able to come and go at their place. But probably they're completely unaware of my feelings. Their life is an unusual one. They spend a good part of the day sitting around on chairs set on the

firm ground near the veranda of their house. Those chairs remain
outside all the time, even at night. They're very careless, but the
chairs have never been stolen.

On one side of our house, there's a government office and a
high brick wall. Behind us is the back of a two-story apartment
building and, in front, the main street. As a result, we have no real
proximity with any other family. The new neighbors seem like
certain people found in big cities who establish no connection
with others and keep strictly to themselves. Both this city and
the neighborhood are quiet and peaceful. People come and go
at a leisurely pace and stroll around casually, since life has no
great urgency. That's why we find our neighbors strange.

I went outside. Those people were having morning tea, at
the late hour of nine. Besides the husband and wife, there's one
girl who must be their daughter. One always sees these same
three people, never a fourth. The daughter may not be pretty,
but she's a well-mannered young woman. If she used the right
make-up, she might even look pretty. I've noticed that she laughs
a lot—and frequently. Her mother and father laugh also. They
always look happy. What sorts of things do they talk about, and
why are they always laughing? Are their lives so full of delightful
circumstances which keep them laughing? Or are they insensitive
to the harsh, realistic circumstances of life? Amazed, I compare
my family with the neighbors.

They startle me by suddenly bursting into laughter. I'd been
concentrating on the rose beds, but now my trowel stopped.
Their laughter seemed unable to stop. The girl rose from the
chair and stood up, handing her teacup to her mother for fear of
spilling it. Instead of standing straight, she was doubled over.
Something funny in the conversation, perhaps a joke, must have
set off the explosion of laughter. The girl, helpless with laughter,
was unaware that her dupatta had slipped off one shoulder. The
movement of her bosom was visible—free and unrestrained. This
was too much! Her mother should have scolded her for that carelessness. What kind of person was she not to mind? But maybe,
unlike me, none of them had even looked in that direction.

Daily a kind of mild compulsion grips me, and my helpless fascination about the new neighbors grows. I'm not the only one. Puppi is very curious too, and keeps praising the material of that girl's kurtas. My brother's wife also glances periodically from the kitchen toward their house, and Granny even knows when the neighbors have bought water chestnuts or squash and when the stove has been lit. Nevertheless, those people don't show a scrap of interest in us.

The girl never looks in our direction, nor do her parents. It doesn't even seem intentional. So the thought of them conversing with us is remote and unimaginable. Perhaps they don't need us in their world. Maybe they consider us inferior. Or maybe they fear trouble because of our proximity. I don't know to what extent that could be true, however, since the sight of a young man in the vicinity doesn't seem to fill her parents with the fear which my father feels for Puppi at the sight of my friends.

We never hear a radio at their place, while ours blares constantly. There's bare ground in front of their house, with not even a blade of grass. Our house has a lawn, along with a vegetable garden and beds of strong-smelling flowers. Why doesn't that girl make friends with my sister and my sister-in-law? Why don't her parents mix with mine? Why don't they notice us drinking tea out of cups prettier than theirs? What they ought to do is add us to their list of acquaintances. They should be interested in everything of ours. Next to the fence, on our side, there's a big tall tamarind tree with fruit six inches long hanging from it. Girls are crazy about tamarind fruit, and yet this neighbor girl never even looks over longingly. She's never given me the satisfaction of breaking a piece of fruit off the tree.

I keep waiting. . . .

Our neighbors evidently have no problem that might make them want to seek our help. Perhaps the little internal problems that exist in our home and others don't exist in theirs, which is astonishing. None of the three ever appears worried. The girl's father must frown occasionally, and at times her mother must get upset, but nothing can be seen or heard from our place. Pos-

sibly the girl has some secret and private corner in her heart—
some complication or emotional conflict. Maybe so, maybe not.
Nothing definite can be known.

A light usually burns at night in their middle room, where
Mukherji and his whole family used to sleep. Apparently even
indoors they sit together and talk. They must have an endless
supply of stories and material for conversation. A sigh slips from
my lips. In our house the talk deals only with the weather, mosquitoes, the birth of children, the new wives of relatives, kitchen
matters, and ancient divine heroes who obliterate the present.

The fence between our houses is a barrier only in name.
It's only a foot high ridge of dirt with some berry bushes, a long
stretch of dry twisted wild cactus, and some unknown shrubs
with white ants clustered around the roots. In between, the
ridge is broken in several places. Paths have formed, used by the
fruit and vegetable sellers as well as the sweeper woman and the
newspaper vendor. The postman and milkman have been using
these paths for years. Despite the damage from dogs and cats
coming and going and from animals grazing on the plants, the
fence remains much the same as ever. Until a short time ago,
Mukherji's daughter Shaila used to take this route bringing books
over to me. It's such a convenient and simple fence that we can
easily ride bicycles through the gaps from one side to the other
without dismounting. And previously we used to pass through
that way, but no longer, because our neighbors interpret a fence
as something uncrossable.

They've been living here for three months. . . .

I often move my desk outdoors for study. At this time of
year the outside air is lovely, like ice water in an intense summer
thirst. But studying there is difficult. My eyes leap the fence and
my mind hovers around the neighbors' house. A young and unat-
tached girl. Cheerful and fearless parents. If only I'd been born
in that home! That's the way my mind wanders.

At times the neighbor girl sits outside all alone, doing some
work or doing nothing. Occasionally she strolls over to the wall
on the other side of her house. Elbows propped on the wall, she

watches the street. Then she returns. Loafers from other neighborhoods come into our area a lot. Not that there's any lack of them in our neighborhood too. But she always seems innocent and free, walking with small swaying steps.

At our place, in contrast, my sister-in-law takes Puppi along even when she goes outside to get flowers for worship. She's scared outside the house and in it too. She's kept scared. A sharp eye is kept on Puppi also. One time the neighbor girl's father put his hand on his wife's shoulder in the course of conversation, and Puppi was immediately called into the house on some pretext. That scene produced an uproar at our place. Such shamelessness! Gradually people in our house have begun considering the neighbors quite dangerous.

With the passing of time, the attraction toward the neighbors has changed into dislike, though they might as well be non-existent as far as we're concerned. In time, however, our family has made the neighbors a focal point for all the evils in the world. Our eyes cross the fence thousands of times in what has become a part of our daily routine. A new distress has crept into our minds, added to our other worries. I, too, waste a lot of time, but not a glance from there ever falls this way.

Somewhere nearby a diesel engine, finding no signal to proceed, stands shrieking. The novelty of the sound is startling. For a while all of us will talk about nothing but the diesel engine.

Yesterday those neighbors had not been home since noon. A few guests were staying at their place, but there was no hustle and bustle—just the usual carefree atmosphere. I rose and went inside. Sister-in-law was drying her hair. Then, I don't know why, she teased me slyly, connecting me with the neighbor girl. Smiling to myself, I went outdoors. Just then the girl and her mother returned, probably from the bazaar, carrying some packages. The father must have remained behind.

Both that evening and this morning people kept coming and going there. But it couldn't be considered a large number of people. Their house had the atmosphere of some ordinary festival celebration—just faintly. We were all astonished when the milkman reported that the daughter's marriage took place last night. It was some man from the other side of town. She'd had an Arya Samaj wedding. My sister-in-law threw me a teasing look of sympathy, and I started laughing. I laughed openly and freely, thinking what dreamers we all are.

Now and then three or four people would arrive at their house. They'd go inside, then come out a little later and go away. They were mostly serious and restrained people. At times children gathered, shouting and running around, but otherwise there was no commotion—as though everything were taking place easily and smoothly. There was no way to know just what was happening, nor how.

At our house this has been a day of great uneasiness. After several hours, the girl emerged. She was wearing a sari, maybe for the first time. She stepped out on the veranda straightening her sari and carrying a coconut. Her swaying walk was restricted considerably by the sari and she moved forward with an eye on each step. She hadn't veiled herself in any way, nor, even with her husband walking so close to her, did she show any of the embarrassment and coquettishness of a traditional bride. Her husband looked like some friend of mine. No one was weeping and wailing. Several times the girl's mother kissed her warmly on both cheeks. The father patted her head. The girl's eyes could no longer conceal a shimmer of tears reflecting her excitement over the new life ahead.

Squirrels were darting across the fence from one corner to the other. Mother expressed amazement to me over the girl's failure to cry. According to her, the girl had become hardened by her education and had no real love or attachment for her mother and father. "They're all like that these days . . . with not one tear for those who struggled and sacrificed to raise them."

I was not interested in listening to such things. I observed that Mother was enjoying the sun, shifting her position to stay in the patches of sunshine. Then Father made a pronouncement —"In the old days, girls would cry all the way to the edge of the village. Anyone who didn't was beaten and forced to cry. Otherwise her life at her husband's home could never be happy." Father feels very distressed that things are no longer like that. "The old days are passing and men's hearts have become machines, just machines!" At such times his voice grows sharp, and the wreckage of Kali Yug, this Age of Darkness, dances before his eyes.

A few small isolated fragments of cloud have appeared in the sky over our home and then passed on. The parents and relatives reached the gate and were waiting to give the girl a last farewell. The boy's party had brought a Herald car for the groom which looked like a colorful room. That colorful room glided slowly away and was gone.

Granny was the most astounded of all and kept muttering to herself. This marriage made no sense at all to her. "No fanfare, no uproar, no feasting. What's the point of such stinginess! And besides, not even asking the neighbors on such an occasion. What's happening to mankind? Good god!"

Having said goodbye to the girl, the people walked back to the house. Each carried out a chair and sat down outdoors. Ever since the girl's departure, her mother had been a little sad and subdued. A few people kept her company, probably trying to cheer her up. My friend Radhu swore that he could prove the girl was a woman of the world. I felt only the sadness of an intense loss. A sort of strange emptiness—an emptiness at being left behind and an emptiness produced by Radhu's loose talk about the girl. Absolutely unfounded! Maybe talking about a girl's misconduct provides a kind of depraved satisfaction. But perhaps in one corner of my mind I, too, like my family, can't tolerate the behavior of the neighbors.

Night is sloughing off the cover of evening. The people who were seated around a table across the fence have risen and dispersed. As usual, a light is burning in the middle room of the neighbor's house. Their night has become peaceful and quiet as usual, and there's no way to know how they're feeling about the absence of one member of the family. At our house, though, the bazaar of neighbor-criticism is doing a heated business.

# AWADH NARAIN SINGH

# Intimate

"If you have no objection," he asked me very casually, "then could I get your advice about something?"

The question struck me as very odd since the man appeared to be a total stranger. Nevertheless, to be polite I said, "Feel free to ask me anything you wish." I also inquired whether he was acquainted with me.

"What do you mean by 'acquainted'?" he asked very matter-of-factly.

Unable to produce any immediate definition, I remained silent. As though having received a satisfactory response, he then said appreciatively, "You seem quite trustworthy. Not that this means a great deal to me, but I know how to make use of it on occasion. Anyway, I gather there's no harm in seeking your advice on this matter. And even if there is, I don't care."

Forcing a tone of polite intimacy, I said that I'd be happy to be of assistance to him. My voice seemed tangled somewhere in my throat.

He read my feelings from the expression on my face. Leaning close, he said, "Borrowing words, my friend, is very dangerous. It strips off a person's mask and exposes it as artificial and worthless."

His talk was beginning to panic me. Previously I'd thought from his dress and behavior that he was worthless and stupid, whereas now he seemed extremely intelligent.

"As I was saying," he went on in a satisfied tone of voice, "I need some important advice from you. I think you're capable of it."

His personality was like a great rock crushing me. And he was piling still more weight on me.

As though realizing my state of mind, he assured me that it was not a dangerous question. "You can rest easy on that score. I'm not plotting to catch you in any trap. People do call me a double-dealer and a schemer but there's no truth to that. Actually you'll notice how much truth there is in what I say. I'm not trying to exonerate myself—because that's something I despise. I'm willing to reveal myself, holding back nothing."

Since some response appeared necessary, I remarked, "There's no doubt that you're a completely truthful and honest man."

"How would you know I'm a truthful and honest man when the fact is that you know nothing at all about me? That kind of pronouncement is false and worthless."

He seemed to be using a cover of intimacy to attack me deliberately. I tried to think of some counterattack but came up with nothing. "A person reveals himself by just his talk and his appearance," I said. "He doesn't have to wear a signboard."

Pressing my shoulder in a strange way he said, "You seem very naive, friend. I might very well be talking this way just to make you the victim of some trick."

Trying to appear casual and unconcerned, I replied that I had no fear of that. "I always keep myself ready for any such situation."

"How long have you been living in this city?" he asked, as though trying to size me up.

This question had little connection with his previous ones, and his talk kept drifting away from any point. I was trying to steer the discussion in some definite direction but he was frustrating all my efforts. Trying once more, I said, "I don't remember how long I've been living in this city. Nor do I feel that it has any particular importance."

As though twisting my neck he responded, "How much, after all, can one remember? Besides, these things aren't worth remembering. Oh yes, on that matter about which I was going to consult you, I wanted my wife's advice on it, too. But she's stupid and selfish, so I didn't discuss it with her. I've begun thinking it unwise to seek any advice from people who are very close, since they're usually prejudiced, and prejudiced people can't give impartial suggestions."

I was bored with his discourse and had begun to feel trapped. "What you say is right," I replied, hoping to put him off.

"What do you call 'right'?" he asked, as though seizing on my mistake. "What's the definition of 'right'? All I say is—don't consider whether it's right or not."

I was squirming with discomfort and irritation which finally burst forth, breaking the momentary silence. "All right then, it's wrong."

"You can't say that either," he interrupted, "because there's no formula for these things."

His rudeness was increasing. "I concede," I said, "that it's neither wrong nor right. It just is."

He looked at me intently. "Concessions accomplish nothing. By talking about conceding, we only expose our own helplessness."

When I kept silent, he pushed the matter further—"It's my conviction that things simply are, and hedging them with qualifications is an outrage against them. But you're getting bored. The point could be argued at length, but I don't want to elaborate any further since there's no advantage in wasting time. Of course I have so much time that to cut it short is a real problem for me. I'm amazed when people say they have no time."

His chin was quivering strangely. Aware of this, he said, "It's an old habit of mine. I don't consider habit a bad thing. In fact if I had my way I'd see that every man had some habit or other. Actually the trouble with our lives is that we have no habits. May I know what your habit is?"

I found it difficult to answer. "Unfortunately," I said, "I have no habit worth mentioning. But I'm trying and I feel compelled to find out why I have no such habit."

"That statement of yours doesn't pass," he declared. "There's no question of compulsion. You said you were trying, didn't you? In my opinion, trying has no meaning. I think we just use that word in self-defense, throwing it into all our conversations."

At this I exploded. "You're talking nonsense. I was wrong in considering you a keen intellect. You have no grasp of anything. You're a worthless person of the worst sort."

My anger seemed to please him. "All talk, after all, is nonsense, but only a few people have the courage to call it that. It delights me to know that you're one of those people. Yes, if by 'keen intellect' you mean 'wise,' then may you be blessed by it. I don't give a damn about intellect. As for knowledge, I'm no sycophant that I need knowledge as a crutch. People who depend on knowledge for support have nothing that's their own."

I was further convinced that he was the world's most useless and garrulous person, but I kept quiet, figuring that such a comment would only please him.

Guessing my thoughts, he looked over and said, "You're getting bored with my conversation. Boredom develops strength in people. You're not the only one. My wife gets bored with me, too, and my acquaintances call me foolish and talkative. But that doesn't hurt anything. Nothing anyone says or thinks can harm one, so I pay no attention to what they say. Isn't it true that the things which bore you provide a source of entertainment for me?"

"That may be so," I replied evasively.

"No maybe about it. It *is*," he insisted. "Now you've started talking about doubt."

"Are you in your right mind?" I asked. "You keep contradicting everything you say."

"Every wise man does that," he replied, "and if not being in one's right mind is madness, then everyone in the world is mad. If one weren't mad, he couldn't stay alive. Can you swear that you're not mad? With your permission, I'll prove to you right now just how mad you are."

I had a great urge to be rude to him. I imagined myself pounding him with blows and felt pleased. For a while he seemed helpless and pained. Then he said, "The expression that just appeared on your face shows your madness. Doesn't that prove my point?"

A wave of anger swept over me and a slap landed on his cheek. With double that force, he clenched his right fist and landed it on my nose. The blow knocked me to the ground. Before I could pull myself together, he sprang forward and lifted me up. Throwing his arms around me affectionately, he asked, "You weren't hurt badly, were you?"

I rubbed my nose. "It's nothing serious. The nose is just a little sore." When my eyes had cleared somewhat, I looked at his face. It showed no reaction.

Then he said sympathetically, "It's just this that is madness. That's the greatest truth in life." His face reflected unconcern. "There's nothing to worry about. It will be all right by tomorrow."

"What was it you wanted my advice about?" I asked.

"I don't remember."

"You forget very quickly."

"That's my fate," he said. "If I ever remember, we'll discuss it again. You come here often, don't you?"

"I have no regular schedule," I said. "I come here occasionally."

"Can you spend the night with me?"

"I have a wife," I told him. "I don't leave her alone at night."

"I have a wife too," he said, "but I don't show that much concern for her. Any time I don't feel like going home, I sleep somewhere else. If you don't mind, I'll stay with you tonight."

When I protested, he said, "That's all right. I'll go home. My wife doesn't mind my coming home. And it's no great problem to stay at home because she's very fond of me. Actually her excessive love sometimes creates difficulty."

Seeing me silent, he said, "I hit you very hard."

I apologized too. "It was my fault since I was the one who started it."

This talk of fault annoyed him. "You're talking in formulas again. A movement took place, nothing more. It can't be called anything else."

"Go home now," I said. "The night's growing late, and there's nothing to be gained by standing around here."

"I wasn't standing here in order to gain something," he responded. "If you want to go, then go."

He left even before I did, saying as he went, "Put a hot compress on the sore spot. It'll be all right by morning."

## DUDHNATH SINGH

# *Retaliation*

I**T** was as though they had been injected with morphine and as usual were sitting there sunk in a stupor. Not their looks but their actions made them all seem like drug addicts. Whenever someone pushed back the curtain and stepped inside, they would glance up for a moment through their spectacles and then bury their eyes in the files on their desks, as though those papers told of grisly murders or natural deaths which they were mourning.

As on previous days, he stopped momentarily at the door before going in, and smiled meekly at the attendant seated there. When in response the attendant shifted the wad of tobacco in his mouth and bared his teeth, he pushed aside the curtain and entered the room. As soon as he was inside, a feeling gripped him that they were all sitting there with pistols hidden in their pockets which they were about to fire at him. This fear had been developing because of the way they kept stalling him, until now, on his fourth visit, he had begun feeling apprehensive the moment he left home. But there was no alternative.

"I don't believe you even go there," his wife had charged. "Halfway there you turn around and come back." Time and again he had tried to exonerate himself, feeling as he did so that they were all listening and saying, "All right, boy . . . we'll see about it."

They are spread out on all sides. Even if they can't be seen, they know everything that is happening. They never fire bullets. They never even speak impolitely. They don't talk loudly. They remain silent, smiling. But their glances are piercing, their attack very sure. Murders take place. Somewhere or other there are any number of gutter pipes, of cellars, of dark tunnels where the corpses are quietly buried. However, these same people—or their skeletons—reappear walking on the streets. Thousands of men and women—all the way from Kalighat to Sham Bazaar, in the Bartalla fish market, on Elliot Street, in Tollygunge, in the dank alleys of Bhavanipur—everywhere! The sight of them is frightening. They are no longer human beings—only muffled shrieks in human form. This shriek spreads out over the whole country. . . .

He interrupted this train of thought, afraid. His legs were trembling for no reason. Several times after returning empty-handed, he had again set out from the house on the appointed date, only to have the fear seize him as soon as he stepped into the street. Then he would cover the long route on foot. This provided some relief, but the fear would begin hovering over him again as soon as he found himself standing at the base of that building.

The first time he went there, he sat down very casually on the chair in front. He had no previous experience in going to such places or dealing with such people. Blessed by good fortune, he had been living blissfully in his own limited world, believing that good, helpful, dedicated people were to be found everywhere. To some degree he still kept those hopes. This new situation had arisen only recently, and he assumed that everything would right itself very simply. So to a certain extent he'd been casual and unconcerned. No pallor of hopelessness had settled over his face. He was not in the habit of humbling himself in any situation.

Now, however, fingernails had slowly begun to dig into his back. Whenever he entered the door, a look of humility fastened itself to his face. That humble expression would automatically etch itself on his countenance. His mouth would open and he'd begin staring toward the street, or toward the rows of buildings beyond the roof, or toward the people walking on the street.

The man reminded him of a large rhinoceros. The first time he saw that stupefied rhinoceros, he had smiled and glanced around. They were all hunched over their desks, as though lying in wait. Then the rhinoceros gave a loud sneeze and began wiping his nose, after which he shoved a little snuff into his nose, raised his head, and sneezed repeatedly.

"Hm?" The man seemed to be returning to his senses.

"Yes," he responded with a smile.

"You're Mrs. Uma Malhotra's . . . "

"Her husband, Satyendra Malhotra."

"Let me see. The bills have all been approved. One or two are left. Why are they left? Let me see." He stood up and began rummaging through the files, very slowly and rhythmically as though doing a little dance. His grotesque neck was in motion and perspiration glistened on the man's smooth cheeks and bald skull. He kept staring at that skull, expecting the perspiration to drip onto the papers.

"Haa-oo," the man yawned and sat down, calling out, "Ramsaran—bring some water, tea, a biri to smoke." Then without even a glance at Satyendra, he closed his eyes and leaned back his head.

"There are biris in your drawer, sir," said the attendant.

"Uh, ye-es." He motioned the man to leave. His mouth had opened, exposing a reddish flap of skin. His face is going to split, thought Satyendra. There'll be a cracking sound. Everyone will gather around. "What happened? Who did it? The poor fellow's face split wide open. He was yawning . . . " A very simple man, Satyendra concluded, seeing the mouth close. The man opened his eyes.

"Find it?" Satyendra inquired.

"Eh?" the man said, as though startled. Then he stood up with only a single word, "Lunch," and a nod at his watch. He called to the others: "Let's go outside, Ghosh Babu. O Lord, I'm dead! Damn government . . . how many buffaloes does it need? There's not a single bull left. They all get crushed as soon as they come here." Looking over at a young clerk, he smiled—"Hey, your she-camel doesn't come around these days. Has she found a new rider or something?"

Satyendra followed the man out of the building. There was an office canteen in one corner of the grounds. The man headed that way with the other clerks. Satyendra also ordered a cup of tea, and seating himself at some distance from the others, began to observe them and to sip the tea.

"Hey, Chandul!" This was a Sikh speaking. He had swatted that man on the head.

"I find your pranks very annoying," the man responded hotly. The others burst out laughing and then became solemn, making fun of him. The man swallowed a samosa and then began sipping the tea he had poured into his saucer. They must behave this way all the time, Satyendra thought, but perhaps the presence of an outsider was making him act so irritated.

When lunch was over and they all went outside, Satyendra left too. Chandul went out the gate instead of returning to the office. Satyendra speeded up and trailed him at a distance. When the man stopped to have his shoes shined, Satyendra loitered nearby on the sidewalk. The man kept looking at his watch, glancing slyly at Satyendra and then gazing at the sky.

"Hey!" he barked into space. "Brush them some more. Only the government gives money for nothing. This is hard-earned cash." Ceasing his barking, he spat on the sidewalk, and then wiped the sweat from his forehead as though sprinkling sacred Ganges water.

Satyendra was waiting, and the man knew it and was becoming annoyed. They walked back, one behind the other. Entering the office, they sat down. Both were as before, he on the chair in front, Chandul on his office chair.

"Find it?" Satyendra repeated after a minute or two.

Chandul called an attendant and then was silent. When the man appeared, he handed over some files and began giving instructions. The attendant didn't understand, so he berated him. When the man had gone, he suddenly mellowed and began chatting with someone called Anandi Babu. They were talking about all sorts of things, none of which had any connection with their work. A number of words came up repeatedly—salary, cinema, tram and bus, rent, strike, jute mill, Marwari, B. C. Roy, Nimtola, Babu Ghat, massage. . . . Then a file of papers appeared and the two of them bent over it as though mourning. The attendant returned to say that he had delivered the papers. The man rose, drank some water, and then took off his glasses and began wiping them, staring straight ahead as though examining the clouds on the horizon.

"What do you do?" the man finally asked. He was speaking to him!

This expression of personal interest warmed his heart. He'd been taking offense unnecessarily. One name had been going around and around in his head—Chandul, "the blockhead." He began feeling apologetic. It wasn't right to judge people so quickly. He settled back comfortably in the chair, letting himself relax as though he'd been given permission to do so. He could speak the truth. That's what was necessary. The job would get done. "I've been ill for the last several months," he said. "At present I'm just taking it easy."

Suddenly he realized that the man's attention was elsewhere. Evidently he had forgotten his question and was not expecting an answer. He was centuries away. His head in the files, he was muttering—"Yes, in preparing the report for the auditors, that clown Anandi messed up all the papers. It must be right here. It ought to go through. Why would it be held up?"

Suddenly he removed his glasses and stared at Satyendra as

though having apprehended the real culprit. "There must be some problem. What problem? Go ask your wife. Come back with the full story. You're harassing us. There must be a reason. We don't have such delays here. I've taken care of all the bills." The man put on his glasses and rose from the chair. Was this a sign for him to leave? Satyendra also rose. All at once that same humble smile spread over his face.

"What's the problem?" the man asked before stepping away, as though saying, "Why don't you leave? Smiling won't accomplish anything now."

Suddenly he collapsed inwardly. Worthless! His conclusions had been worthless! He had been right the first time. Swallowing quickly, he spoke up—"What you say is right. There is a problem. There was a problem. My wife sent in the work late. She was sick. As a matter of fact, she . . . she was pregnant."

"Sent it late? Well! Then why are you making life difficult here? Go home. I'll look up the bill and send it to the boss. That will take time." He slid out between the chair and the filing cabinet, curving so as not to soil his white suit—as though doing a few fast steps of the Twist.

Now was the time. He couldn't slip away so quickly . . . as though strutting down some royal highway. Thinking quickly, Satyendra threw out one final comment—"But sir, I already told you why there was a delay. My wife was expecting a baby. And it's been three months since she sent in the records."

He didn't expect the man to stop. Having excused himself as busy, he was heading for the toilet so as to extricate himself, But he did stop—right there, in the midst of that unclean crowd, trapped in that confining place, silent—and began staring at Satyendra.

"She was expecting a baby!" he bellowed, looking with a smile toward his fellow workers. A middle-aged man, who was in charge and therefore always kept up a front of seriousness, suddenly took off his coat, hung it over the chair, and smiled. Seeing this, all the ghosts in that graveyard raised their heads and looked

at Satyendra. They were tired of mourning and were now enjoying themselves, having received the unspoken permission of the
man in charge. Chandul moved away and lit a biri. Now there
was no need to go to the toilet. The boredom had changed to
amusement.

He felt surrounded, with death inevitable—that death after
which he would reappear walking on the street, head bowed,
perspiration-soaked, mute, uncertain. They had surrounded him
and now could not let him go. They would certainly place him
among the shrieks in human form. They couldn't just leave his
black, curly hair and golden skin unmarked like this. . . . "Give
him some prescriptions for birth control, Dubeji," someone
fired from behind his desk. "You distribute them. Help him,
too. It will give him some peace of mind without affecting his
performance."

There was a round of laughter. He felt as though the window-
panes would shatter and everyone outside would see him being
finished off this way, in solitude. Did no one here feel sympathy
towards those being shot? Again that same smile of humility . . .

But they were quite genteel and were only amusing themselves. They were not accustomed to watching this kind of
bloodshed for long. Only grouped together did they find such
opportunities. Alone, they too feared death, even though they
had undergone thousands of experiences similar to this and so
were somewhat hardened.

Then Chandul liberated him. Putting an arm around Satyendra's shoulder, he escorted him outside. "Go home now. Come
back in three or four days. These are all my people. I'll take care
of everything." Halfway down the stairs, the man opened a door
and stepped through it. The door swung shut on a glimpse of
sparkling commodes and pairs of toilet footrests. There was no
point in waiting to say goodbye. He silently started down the
stairs.

"They're my own people—rubbish! My own people—bah!
They're all my own people indeed!" Uma lashed out as soon as

he returned. "I don't believe you even go there! You probably become very meek and mild. Nothing will get done that way. You're not begging for charity. I did the work for them. Laziness, robbery, dishonesty—that's all they do! You probably melt and fall right into their clutches." Each time he returned unsuccessful, she became upset and ended up close to tears—"Where am I to get money? Don't you realize? Even your medicine is finished. Don't you see the condition of the baby? You forget. You become a different person as soon as you step outside." Every day she repeated these accusations and then sat down, crushed.

Engulfed in one worry after another all the way home, he would prepare his defense—"It'll get done. I'm to return on such and such a day. They're our own people—all of them." Instead of criticizing them, he kept silent. Uma was used to thinking of happiness and sorrow only in simple terms. There was no remedy. . . .

Three or four days after his first visit, when he went there the second time, he was hopeful. As before, he went to the chair in front, sat down, and began smiling. But that man gave no sign of recognition, and he again began to despair.

"Yes?" The man peered from behind his glasses with the same unchanging expression. Where was he trained to do that, Satyendra wondered. Did they have some place where daily rehearsals were held so that they'd never make a mistake on stage?

"That bill of mine," he said at last.

"Oh yes, of course. Just a moment, I'll see." With that, the man started playing his role just as before, with no slipup. His shoes weren't dirty today though, so there was no shoeshine. Three hours passed. The man raised his eyes and stared as though Satyendra had just appeared. He began thumbing through the files and mumbling, "Must be here somewhere. Where could it be? All the bills have been taken care of. . . ." Then he lifted a paper in the air as though it were a rat he had caught while digging in the ground. "Here it is! Mrs. Uma Malhotra, 9 Shankar Mukerji Road, Calcutta 25," he read in a loud voice, as though announcing the location of some gambling den. "Right?"

Satyendra nodded. "Yes."

"I'll send it to the top boss today. It should be ready in four or five days."

"Yes sir." He joined his hands to say goodbye and stood up, afraid they would seize him if he remained seated or tried to apply pressure. Stepping outside was a relief. Walking home, he concluded that Uma would stop worrying once he told her that it would be only a matter of a few more days. They could manage somehow for four or five days. Uma was patient. She might be temperamental, but she was also understanding and could endure a lot. With that established, he felt more relaxed.

Four or five days later he returned again, feeling less fearful. This time he didn't smile or try to identify himself. The man saw him and immediately pulled out the file. The bill was still exactly where it had been the previous time. The man picked out the paper as though from a deck of cards and said again, "I'm having it sent this very day. It will be ready in four or five days. You may go now." Further discussion was cut off.

On the appointed day he returned again, feeling quite uneasy. As soon as he left home the sharp light, and the graveyard reflected in the window, began to dance around him. His body broke out in a cold sweat and he felt as though his hair were flying off and leaving him bald. They wouldn't crush his neck this time, nor would they trick him again. But their staring and their evasiveness—it was all so horrible. Inwardly he'd been defeated, and he just wanted to forget them.

Seeing no other solution, he had previously told Uma to come with him. Since women are highly respected in Indian society, there might be some change in their performance. Perhaps they would give a few lines to the two of them. Some alteration from the rehearsal might be allowed so that he and Uma could be included in the drama. Thinking of the phrase "respect for women," he couldn't help smiling, at which Uma became annoyed. Actually he merely wanted to be spared that cold feeling of fear and defeat. With Uma there, he figured that he could hide behind her while she settled the matter. Besides, it would be good for her to discover the secret weapons of those assassins. But he trembled at the thought that Uma too might become the target of their insults. What if they surrounded her also, killing her and burying her in those tunnels? Both of them would reappear on the street—heads bowed, sweat-drenched, mute, indifferent, defenseless, helpless. His decision to take her along had faltered. No, he'd go alone. He wanted to be inside the room there when he suffered this death of his. An open display of it would be even more frightening. He was not yet as shameless as all that. . . .

This time the man announced—"Come back after fifteen days. There's to be a meeting. A decision will be reached."

Now his courage had run out. He wouldn't go again. Leaving the building he set off on foot. Afraid to return home, he crossed Chowringhee Street to the large grassy park on the other side. The whole area was almost deserted that afternoon, and the Victoria Memorial was shimmering against a background of dark clouds. In the distance, large double-decker buses were moving slowly along the streets bordering the park. He felt imprisoned behind brown glass walls through which he was peering at the view outside. The bus horns sounded very faint. From that distance, the tramcars looked like toy trains that some child had wound up and released to chug along on their own. The passengers packed into them—or the people right now bowed in mourning over files in the big buildings of Chowringhee or Dalhousie or Barabazar—or these few individuals strolling like puppets on the grass of the park . . . all of them shared the same appearance, the same identity.

Shaking off that train of thought, he stepped off the path and stretched out on the damp grass, heedless of his clothes. A sharp wind was whistling from the direction of the river. Gradually a lethargy spread over him and he thought he might take a nap.

Only a few months ago they had moved into a different building. Their previous house had been nice and airy but they had to leave it. They moved into this place as quietly as though someone had given them a shove and then slammed the door. The walls had been colorwashed reddish-brown years ago, and peeling plaster fell off at the slightest touch. The ceiling was greasy and the floor moist. They placed most of their belongings in the damp closet, putting their books in a large trunk which they padlocked. The furniture was stacked in a corner. One wooden cot was set out, and a three-legged table and two chairs were placed on the narrow balcony.

The first night they slept unaware, but next morning they complained a lot about mosquitoes. The second night they put up a mosquito net but still kept tossing and turning. Unable to tolerate it, Uma decided to turn on the light and get rid of the mosquitoes which had slipped under the net, so that they could sleep in peace. That was when she discovered hundreds of big and little, brown and red, drunkenly scurrying bedbugs there on the white sheet.

"My God, where did these come from?" She woke Satyendra, and he got up rubbing his eyes. Look at them all! In the previous place there'd never been a single bedbug. When Uma lifted the baby, several large bugs scurried off. They raised the sheet. Locating the bugs on the purple mattress was difficult, but a few could be seen crawling around. The rest were hiding, as though lifeless, in the stitching of the mattress, or had crept into the legs and frame of the bed. They shook the sheet, spread it out, turned off the light and lay down.

"This is really bad," Uma said, her voice wide-awake.

"We'll see to it in the morning. We'll do something," Satyendra said, turning over.

"What do you mean morning! You think they'll let us sleep?" Uma sat up and took the baby in her arms. Standing, she turned on the light. "Look here! And you talk about tomorrow! Good heavens, they're so fat they'll drink all our blood!" She began squashing the bugs, not caring about the sheet. A strange rotten smell filled the room. "They've all run away. How could you sleep? Look! Move over! They're devouring you!" She began squashing the bugs hidden under his back. The baby woke up and began crying.

In the morning they questioned the landlord. "They're everywhere," he laughed. "You think they're not in my room? I've just become used to them, sahab. I crush them without even waking up, the bastards. I've tried everything. No telling where they come from. There's no sign of them during the day. Everyone who comes here makes the same complaint at first, but then people get accustomed. You'll have to get used to it too. Try whatever you like and just see. If you're going to live in Calcutta, sahab, then there's no escaping from trams and buses, mosquitoes and bedbugs."

That day they heated a bucket of water and washed the bed, table, and chairs with scalding water. But that night things were just the same. Uma was close to tears. "This is going to drive me crazy. All last night I couldn't sleep, and tonight it's the same. All that water, and not the slightest effect."

"So what am I to do?" Satyendra asked. All night they argued over all kinds of inconsequential matters, killing bedbugs every time they got up.

Two more days passed. They began sleeping during the day and staying awake at night. The downstairs tenant advised them to sprinkle kerosene around, saying that the fumes would kill the bugs. This would have to be repeated every week. Although they both despised the smell of kerosene, they had no choice but to pour it over the bed and the chairs. The stench was still terrible that night. Uma held her breath, inhaled quickly a few times, and then held it again. Satyendra lay facing the window, hoping that a breeze would keep the fumes from his nose. Now at least the bugs wouldn't come. With that in mind, they prepared to sleep. For a short while they dozed, but about midnight Satyendra's eyes opened. Uma was sitting on the floor, asleep. The baby was sleeping in her lap. The light was burning. As soon as he sat up, hundreds of bedbugs lurking under his head, limbs, and body began scurrying into the mattress. He looked at his watch. It was one-thirty. His flesh crawled. There would be no sleep again tonight. A strange feeling of helplessness seized him. What could be done? Finally he too sat on the bare floor and tried to sleep. The light was blazing through his eyelids. And sleep . . . if only I can get just a little, he thought.

They tried several other remedies. They spread out a rough blanket. Purchasing some poisonous spray, they filled the room with fumes, closed the doors and windows, and spent the whole day roaming outdoors. Returning in the evening, they opened the room which had become a regular gas chamber. But none of these efforts was very successful. The bugs were almost impossible to detect on the rough dark blanket. The poison proved ineffective. A smaller number showed up for a night or two, but the third night they filled the bed in greater numbers than ever, sucking their prey with relish. The predicament was strangely terrifying, and he could see no way to end it. Their faces had become simian from continuous nights of wakefulness. Their cheeks were hollow, the bones protruded at their temples, and their eyes, though sunken, bulged as though they'd been fasting for days. Only in the brightness of morning, when the bedbugs concealed themselves in the legs of the bed and other sheltered places, they slept deeply.

The tenants downstairs and the landlord all found this very curious. Did these people think they were living in some hamlet? No one in this metropolis would have the nerve to sleep so late in the day. Some people joked about it—"They must be newlyweds."

"What do you mean, newlyweds? It's the joy of unemployment!"

"That's all very well, but how do they fill their stomachs?"

On the ground floor, next to the alley, lived a goldsmith. Thump . . . thump . . . thump . . . thump, thump, thump. . . . Periodically he paused and listened to everything. Then he would hammer and shape the gold into strange forms. The whole neighborhood took delight in his performance. Grasping the single bow of his battered spectacles, he'd look upward and smile—"Oh what a world! How strange is your creation, O God!" And then once again thump, thump, thump.

They both were exhausted and looked ill. They were very worried about the baby, and spent the whole night taking care of him. Like his parents, he lay sleeping all day—or fussing. Meanwhile they were living in abject poverty. It was the rainy season. They survived mostly on mangoes and bread, but they lit a fire to give the appearance of cooking. Smoke would assure the neighbors that they were worthy to live in this house. Food was cooked in their home; they could pay the rent. They were not fugitives. . . .

Uma's milk was diminishing and the baby's stomach stayed empty most of the time. When he went to bed hungry and began crying in his sleep, she would lie down and put her breast in his mouth. The baby would pounce on the nipple and start chewing. Time and again she would feel his stomach and wait to get up. The baby would tire and scream with frustration.

"From now on, he's doomed to starvation," she declared reluctantly, as though this admission itself might change things somehow.

"They've promised," he would say.

"I'll believe it when it happens."

Then they would start making a list of necessary purchases, forgetting their problems briefly. But then Satyendra's glance would fall on Uma, lying on her side with hipbones protruding and buttocks shrunken. He found the sight incredible, and wanted to tell her to shift position and lie properly. He looked away. . . . Who would believe that they were starving? The whole matter seemed ridiculous when he thought about it, reflecting as though on some other person's situation.

There had been another delay, but on the eighteenth they were definitely giving the money, those people. During the days until then, the two of them seemed not to exist. On the eighteenth they would return and repossess their bodies. Meanwhile, he thought, let the days pass like seconds. Let only that day resume the form of a day!

On that date, the eighteenth, the man declared, "Come after fifteen days. There's to be a meeting. Your bill will be discussed." His courage ended, and for hours he roamed like an orphan around the big park near Chowringhee. He had considered taking a brief nap, but suddenly all these thoughts jolted him and sleep fled. He lay around that way until evening, as though he'd been shot and had fallen here. People were searching for him, to slaughter him before he could die. Otherwise it would be a waste. All their efforts would be wasted.

This was the fifth time.

He pulled off the expression of humility and discarded it. Now his face was blazing. As soon as he entered, that Chandul removed his glasses, set them aside, and began staring at him. He was taken aback by the look in Satyendra's eyes.

Satyendra was like a cobra who had raised his hood and then struck. "Where is my bill? Take it out right now!"

"Did you run all the way here?" the man wanted to ask. "Why's your face so red?" But he kept silent and waited—for that humility to plaster itself on Satyendra's face. Instead, though, there were two blazing eyes. This was a different man, a man presenting a challenge. This was not that person he could insult, put off, or sit dozing in front of. Somewhat intimidated, he looked for help toward his colleagues. Perhaps they were unaware of the misfortune. They were all engrossed in the pretext of being hard at work.

"You wish to say something?" he asked loudly, trying to attract the others' attention.

"What's there for me to say?" Satyendra fell silent.

The man had not expected this kind of answer. Dumbfounded, he stared at Satyendra with a contempt and hatred which his cowardice prevented him from discarding. Being skilled at attacking from the rear, he believed in waiting. . . .

"Please get me my money," Satyendra declared, making no mention of the bill.

"It has not yet been fifteen days!"

So the man was getting the message! "Today is the seventeenth day."

"You think everyone here is like you, with nothing to do but count the days?" he sputtered.

"Actually it's you who has nothing to do. All day you just stall here . . . " He left the sentence unfinished, knowing that the man would fry even if he spoke calmly.

This was just what happened. A frightening murmur sizzled from one corner of the room to the other. Then intense silence gripped the place and all eyes rose in his direction. He shouldn't have done that. Now they wouldn't allow anything to happen. If he had broken down completely, they'd have picked him up, tied up the pieces, and set him in running-order again. Now, however, they would just break him up and toss the remains in the wastebasket or out the window.

He sat there waiting for Uma. That morning they'd decided that both would go. She must be on her way. Respect for woman. . . . If she were to arrive now, he might be saved. He began feeling uneasy and saw that his humility was crawling around his feet, waiting. Should he pick it up and smear it on his face? That would probably satisfy them and they'd put their tiger-claw weapons back in their pockets. Or he could get up and depart with his triumph, leaving them dazed. But he found himself stuck to the chair, unable to stand up. Held as though by a rope, he was now beyond reach of help. . . . Just then Uma entered and saved him.

"What happened?" she asked Satyendra without sitting down or looking at anyone else. This was another challenge to them.

"Ask him." Satyendra motioned to the man.

Uma looked over expectantly. There was no response.

"Come on, we'll see the manager," Uma announced, and walked out. He followed her, feeling rescued and not daring to look back.

About an hour had passed. The manager had received them very politely and then had fallen silent. The two of them were sitting in front of him like fools while he dictated some important letters. Periodically papers were brought in for him to sign. Then he would put his hand to his head and start dictating again— "We don't take checks, so we are returning this one. Please send a bank draft." "The children are fine. Vilas has bought some shares in Manorma's name. He is giving up his job and will look after the business." "I regret to say that your payment has not yet been received. This kind of carelessness is very harmful in business. . . . You are well aware of the integrity of our firm, and of the efficiency and competence of our partners and other personnel. . . . "

Uma glanced at Satyendra. They both sat there, periodically looking out the window, at the color of the curtains, at the blazing sunshine outside, at the manager's concentration. Occasionally he would take a smile out of cold storage and hospitably offer it to them. Then the refrigerator door would close automatically. Several times he rang a bell. An attendant would enter and then, receiving no instructions, withdraw beyond the curtain at the door.

"You called?" The attendant stood there staring.

He barked an order and then, as soon as the man left, opened wide the refrigerator door. The stenographer quietly got up and slipped out. Will he put both of us in the refrigerator too, thought Satyendra, and save us from rotting?

Then that Chandul pushed back the curtain. File in hand, he stepped inside, looked cowed and disturbed. He had to face the manager but his fiery eyes also glanced once at the couple.

"Well, friend, what's the matter?"

"Sir, they've given me a lot of trouble. All the records had come. But they've kept after me. She went on making excuses.

This is the correspondence." He held out the whole file.

They were both speechless. So that was it! But he'd said nothing previously. And now? Now he would take a fixed position and give them more trouble, setting up a full blockade. Satyendra felt that the two of them had made a wrong decision. They ought not to have presented a challenge. Perhaps that humility would have done the job. But their patience had been exhausted and they had wanted to set up new defenses. He looked over at Uma. Now they both were repentant.

The manager glanced over the papers and then looked up at the two of them. The refrigerator door opened a little, then closed. He had not fully read any of the letters in the correspondence. "You may go," he ordered Chandul, and then, hands clenched together, looked at them as though to say "I knew there was no mistake on our part."

"Can't something be done?" Uma inquired.

Satyendra noted that she had picked up that humility and plastered it on her face. So it had happened just the way he had feared.

"Wait and see. I'll check." He rang the bell.

There were several minor actors in between the manager and that Chandul. He sent a note to the secretary and it came back with something written on it. He set the note to one side and began examining a file. Ten minutes later he finished reading it, again wrote something, and rang the bell. The attendant appeared as before. It was time for tea. The attendant set down the note and then picked up a small stove from the corner of the room and carried it outside.

"You may go. They've sent for you. Go see them right away. This can be handled without my help." He stood up and they also rose. Not bothering to acknowledge their gesture of farewell, he disappeared behind a curtain in the corner and could be heard settling into a sofa on the other side.

Coming outside, they asked the attendant for the secretary's room. He pointed the way and then turned his attention to the stove.

They were inside for a few minutes and then, wiping their perspiration, emerged again. They entered another room and then left it also. Now they were on the stage and the others were the spectators. Pouring hot water into the teapot, the attendant smiled. "What happened?"

Perhaps he too was a conspirator and could point out a secret passage through which to escape. "What is the sahab doing?" Satyendra asked.

"The sahab takes a little rest at noon. Then he'll have some tea."

"What now?" he asked Uma.

The official to whom the manager had sent them showed great politeness also. Satyendra and Uma were pleased when he sent for Chandul. But he had probably been lying in wait. This time his attack was even more dangerous. Placing a book of regulations before the official, he pointed with his finger. "Read this, sir." He appeared calm and assured.

"Read it to me." The officer sounded insulted. If these two outsiders had not been present, he probably would either have read it or have pushed it away saying he'd read it later.

" 'If the records are not submitted within the appointed time, then the company, according to its regulations, can reduce the remuneration at the rate of two rupees per day.' " Chandul drew himself up and completed the defense. "They sent it two and a half months late. They're bothering us unnecessarily. I told them that the boss would make a decision. It will be brought up at a meeting."

"How much was the bill?"

"Two hundred and fifteen rupees and thirty-six paisee."

He reflected for a moment and then said, "All right. You may go."

After that they were sent to the finance department. Maybe something could be done there. . . .

They went outdoors and began pacing up and down the lawn. They decided to meet the manager once more. Satyendra walked away and sat down. His wife went over and stood next to

him. Were they now going to attack each other? Then it was
lunch time. Hordes of employees headed for the canteen, including that Chandul and his associates. They looked over at the
couple, apparently made some dirty joke, and then laughed
loudly. Satyendra turned his face and looked out through the
bars of the fence at the street beyond. A tram was passing. He
could feel the rattling beneath his feet. . . . Would she be able to
attack from the rear? He couldn't stand it. "I'll go ask the attendant what time the manager returns from his rest," he said,
and started off with a glance at his wife. Perhaps she had not
heard, or perhaps she had understood. He ran up the stairs.

"Three o'clock," he announced when he returned. "What
about the baby?" He looked at Uma. They had left the child
with the landlord's wife.

She said nothing.

"I think there'd be no point in seeing the manager again.
The secretary and all those other people will get annoyed and
then it'll be even more difficult."

"Let them get annoyed. I'm not leaving here. Thieves!
Scoundrels! They're assassins, every one of them. I'm going to
leave with my money, and not before. I'll see to it!"

She was talking ridiculously. It was foolish to have such
simple expectations. But very well, maybe something would be
accomplished this way. Satyendra said nothing.

"What about the baby?" he repeated, thinking that he
might save his wife this way. She didn't realize what would happen. She couldn't endure it.

"Let it go to hell!" It was as though a hand grenade had
exploded. Satyendra was stunned. But a moment later Uma was
apologetic. How could she talk that way about the child?

They returned at three o'clock. The manager again sent a
note to the secretary, who wrote something on it and sent it back.
"Look, they're busy. They'll discuss it with me. You do this—
come next week Saturday. I'll have it settled and ready." He
folded his hands in farewell. He was being very patient and his
face showed no irritation. He was a man of vast experience.

Leaving without a word, they walked over and stood at the tram-stop. The tram started up and passed through the middle of the park. The cool air made both of them start to doze. At the Victoria Memorial stop, someone poked him and pointed to the sign saying the seat was reserved for ladies. Irritated, he got up. When a woman sat down next to Uma, she was awakened also. Her eyes were red. Looking out the window, she tried to discover how far it was to their stop, perhaps anxious to reach home where she could collapse in tears.

He'd be forced to go again! The thought was crushing him. Maybe this would be the last time. Would Uma go along? He lacked the courage to ask her. He began recalling all those people —that Chandul and his associates, the manager, the attendant, and the secretary—and that sparkling toilet beside the stairs, with the shining rows of paired footrests and the spring door which closed with a bang. He started falling asleep on his feet.

The thought of sleep and of night filled him with fear again. Sleep had become absolutely impossible there at night. To escape, they had begun spreading the bedding on the floor. For a night or two the deception worked, but one day they found them crawling all over the floor. And hordes of them were pouring out in lines from the chipped plaster on the walls. The next day they pulled off the peeling plaster and were confronted with a revelation. The whole wall was pocked, like the body of a terrible small-pox victim, and the thousands of tiny holes were full of them. After that they had abandoned hope of sleeping at night. They would sleep all day and keep watch all night. The bedding looked like a glaring desert in the bright light. Putting the baby to sleep between them, they sat on both sides. When it rained, drops formed on the ceiling as though it were perspiring. And below, in his dark crude room, the goldsmith pounded nails until late at night into the heart of the darkness. The whole room became permeated with the stench of rotten fish from the dirty pots and pans left lying in the courtyard by the downstairs tenants, and with the fumes of urine from the corner of the balcony. Occasionally his glance would fall on the mirror. He looked like a shriveled demon. Sometimes Uma and sometimes he would doze off. Perhaps they were growing accustomed to the situation.

But the bedbugs were no less clever. They began courting danger, coming out of the wall even during the day and taking up positions in the bedding. The dampness from the floor rose up through the mattress and sheet until a strange chilly odor crept into their bodies. At such times, emotionally vanquished, one word echoed in their minds—suicide. But it seemed to them only a word found in mystery stories. They'd heard and read of such a thing, but to do it seemed impossible. It was as though they were listening to some imaginary story, as though someone were looking at them and making fun of them.

This was the last day of the week, Saturday. It had not taken long—perhaps fifteen or twenty minutes in all. The matter had been settled. And he was back outside on the street—head bowed, speechless. The humility plastered to his face had dried up of its own accord. Only a thin film remained. When the film fluttered away in the breeze, a strange face appeared beneath it.

They had not delayed—"Yes sir, it's done. Take this. Where is the letter of authorization? Please sign here. A check has been issued for sixty rupees and thirty-six paisee. Yes, there was a meeting. The manager approved this. Tell me, how could we go against the rules? Your reason makes no difference. Our rules don't distinguish between reasons for delays. Whether your wife was pregnant . . . a delay is a delay."

As far as all of them were concerned, nothing special had happened. They were all calm and quiet. They'd reached a decision and had only to implement it. They had only to publish the news of their victory. He had not questioned the results. He had known. That was the reason he'd come by himself and had not brought Uma. For a moment he considered returning the check. Let it be given to charity in the name of the company! The next moment, however, he changed his mind. They would not permit their victory to be diminished that way. They could never allow him that satisfaction.

Leaving quickly, he was now walking down the street. A second fear had replaced the previous one. After one defeat, there was now the cold, sticky sensation of another defeat. They were everywhere, and they could not allow anyone to be different from themselves. They lay in wait to turn everyone into that shriek in bodily form. How was he any different from them?

Walking along, he wondered why he had never looked at things this way before. How easy it would have made everything! He noticed a strange similarity between his face and the faces of the crowd rushing by, the faces peering out of buses and trams. This similarity had probably not existed previously. It was a peculiar similarity—a strange acceptance of defeat, which left them bound to each other and unconcerned. At least he was not alone in his defeat. He looked over at a man standing in the line and suddenly broke into a smile, as though recognizing him. The man smiled back. Then they both faced forward and the line began moving ahead.

## RAMESH BAKSHI

# *Empty*

I HAD started cutting one minute from each task. Today shaving took only thirty seconds, I bathed in just two minutes, and it took one minute to dress. By saving time on each chore I hoped to leave early for the office, so as to finish the work there and use the free time to meet her. My mind is always scheming to find free time, to the point that even meals have become just a formality. Just as a miser is always multiplying and dividing, I'm always busy manipulating time. The result of all this is that I'm terribly busy—day and night.

After devoting my energy to stealing time for a rendezvous, it actually ends up being very brief. We barely manage to exchange five or six kisses before either her university bell rings or my boss's lunch is over. We end up rushing and racing.

Not only that, but if we go to the British Council Library then we have to dodge some girl friend of hers sitting there. Or we go to the zoo and some old-fashioned family sees our behavior and starts staring, at which point we try to do something to make them feel ashamed or, if they have a daughter, to make them resolve to keep an eye on her.

After buying a chocolate bar, we sit on a bench and take turns feeding each other. It's really a sight, and the passersby get very curious. We consider it crucial to disturb those people, and much more time is wasted in arguing over one thing or another than is spent in actual lovemaking.

One day we were feeding each other ice cream when a sweeper's moral sense was aroused. He came over and said, "A big sahab lives in the bungalow there in front. It might be good if you could sit somewhere else."

Scooping up a spoonful of ice cream, she responded, "We're not doing anything wrong. This boy doesn't know how to eat ice cream, so I'm teaching him."

The sweeper was about to say something when she stood up and held out the spoon. "Here, you taste it too."

The sweeper beat a hasty retreat and we both laughed for a long time.

Similarly I kissed her one day at Water Gate near the Hooghly River. A policeman in a white uniform came over and said, "I saw that."

Before I could say anything she had replied, "What's the rate for watching?"

A policeman is a policeman, but this question embarrassed him and he thought it best not to press the issue.

I told her that we should behave the same way with our parents. It would be a good way to stop them from taking issue with us. But at the mention of parents she always becomes serious and starts describing their tyranny.

Several times we got together and were suddenly in the mood to mesh when parents intervened. They're like a curse on us. As soon as we think of them, our bodies forget even their natural deviltry.

Suddenly the doorbell rang. I had just been thinking that I'd saved some time from the office, and was wondering what to do if she wasn't free. . . . Still buttoning my shirt, I opened the door and was taken by surprise—she was standing right in front of me. Eyeing her from head to toe, I couldn't figure out which aspect of my surprise to express first—her unexpected arrival or that outfit of hers.

"I just couldn't believe it was you!" I stammered. "What gave you the courage to come at this hour?"

She had seated herself casually on the sofa, after throwing her books on my table. Closing her eyes she said, "Well, what shall we do?"

Delighted, I leaned over her. "And what's this you're wearing today?"

"I was feeling terribly empty today. What's there to do?"

"Meaning what?"

"When my sister was around, I was always busy with something or other because of her. Last night she left by train for her in-laws' place. I went to the university, but it's a holiday there. I've had this emptiness since early morning. I had written nothing in my diary for two months, so this morning I got up and filled it in. Previously I used to elaborate on all kinds of little things in the diary, but now for any day I meet you I just write your name on the page and doodle around it. It makes me feel as though I'm writing my own destiny."

"But there are seven strokes, seven knots in writing my name. What are you going to do with a knotted destiny?"

"I'll have the knots stitched on my clothes!" She said this in response to my kiss, speaking only after I sat down contentedly next to her. She seemed to want to explain the emptiness which had somehow come over her. "The thing is that previously the thought of coming to your house would start a conflict in my mind as to how I could come—what if I did and someone saw me? Besides, I used to be afraid of you. Now there's no more conflict left. Meeting you is just a meeting. Mummy told me I've woven a cloak of public shame. You know what I answered?"

"What?" As was my habit, I was playing with her bare arm.

"I said—'Mummy dear, your cloak of public shame proved a bit too small. That's why mine's become so tight!'"

I laughed. "How did you get the nerve to say that to your mother? The mere sound of her voice used to scare you."

She rested both arms on my shoulder. "That's precisely my tragedy. That's why I'd get so upset when I was afraid, because then I'd feel that some incident had taken place and I'd been caught. . . . "

"You mean to say that no incident can take place now?"

"What could happen now? When one's not afraid of anything, then what can happen? All that's left now is to undergo the incident."

"What made you suddenly start thinking like this?" I asked pointedly.

"When I couldn't live without you. And once a person's determined to face whatever happens then what's the use of beating out his brains thinking about all those things, or of masturbating over a battle with those things?"

I liked what she said. The fact is that if we have the power to fight against a situation and yet are afraid to create a battle around it, then it's like the way we behave when we eat snacks. There's no battle involved when we enjoy asking for more hot pepper and yet exclaim as it burns our tongues.

"But if I'm forced to fight against Mummy and Daddy, then I'll fight. I'll suffer any consequences. I'll give any response that's called for. You keep describing our life as an armed siege, but it seems more like high jump to me. We each have to jump the right height for our own physical strength. If we fail, it's only because of weakness. As for me, I don't see a siege even when I look at this love of mine through a telescope."

I was watching her sparkling eyes. When she speaks with conviction, her whole body becomes still. Her eyebrows turn into a taut bow, and the collyrium pulling at her eyelashes lengthens. Her fingers intertwine and she forgets to keep adjusting her dupatta. She doesn't emphasize her words with gestures nor use long sentences for clarification. Her tears turn to acid, strong enough not only to start a fire but to destroy the frying-pan as well. Several times they've fallen on my dirty floor and cut right through the dirt there. Swallowed by this torrent of feeling, I pulled her very close.

"This morning Daddy got hold of a letter I'd written to a girl friend. I can't write emotional letters to people close to me. I only report what I've been doing. This was that kind of letter. Only one line in it might have suggested we were indecent friends, that we were having an improper relationship."

Mischievously I responded, "Meaning what? How could two girls have an improper relationship? Are you hinting at homosexuality?"

"Sure," she laughed, "I'm a homosexual. That's why I'm in love with someone girlish like you!"

At that I punched her waist and she doubled up with laughter. Her explosive answers to everything are the most pleasing bond in our relationship. We both seem most natural when we pretend to attack each other. It's become a habit with me not to feel right about something until she has reacted by striking out at me.

Repressing my delight, I said, "Well, what did your father say after reading it?"

"Oh my, he got absolutely furious about the letter. Said it was all vulgar." She began describing his anger as though telling a story—"I very quietly said just one thing—that there was nothing evil in what I'd written. Then, Daddy asked whether I thought any decent person used such language. I answered that it's the language of our new generation, at which he said that the people who used to be called hoodlums are now being hailed as the new generation."

She stopped to check my reaction, but there had been no reaction since I'd not been called a hoodlum. I just said—"Then why get upset? That's a perfectly correct evaluation of us." I assumed a loving expression and looked at her.

She gave me a slap and said, "Evaluation my eye! That puts us nowhere. Even Daddy has begun calling us hoodlums and loafers! And we used to be so good. . . . " She began weeping softly.

"Well come on," I said, "let's roam around Calcutta today."

"All right, let's go." She stood right up. "Honestly, I've been

feeling so empty ever since morning that I can't figure out what
to do or what not to. ... "

When she stretched as though ready to set off, I eyed her
closely—"You look very small in that blouse and skirt. Why did
you change to those clothes today?" This was the first time I'd
seen her in a skirt and blouse.

"What was there to do? I changed clothes hoping to break
the emptiness. When I was in high school, I'd get that deadly
feeling of emptiness on the last day of exams and put on a kurta-
salwar in order to feel composed."

"And now?"

"Now when I wear a skirt I feel naked!" Being risque seemed
an attempt to free herself from the emptiness which had engulfed her.

"And how do you feel in a sari?" I asked, closing the door
as we went out.

"A sari's a mosquito net! I think a sari is worn for protection
against mosquitoes."

I burst out laughing, but she didn't laugh. Walking down
the street, I tried to break through her emptiness by asking, "Say,
what ever happened to that Miss Goal? Did she go back to
America or is she still searching for her aims in India?"

A girl had come from America—Miss Mary. She had stayed
in the university guest house, wanting to meet the "new people"
of India, and we both had gone to visit her. Accepting us as repre-
sentatives of India's young generation, she had asked, "What's
the goal of the new generation? For instance, in America our aim
at first was the freedom movement. Then being anti-social became our goal. Now we're searching for some new god—but even
when we stand facing that god, we're responsible for our own
actions."

At that point we had started to laugh. I was still wondering
what to martyr in the name of a goal when she shot back—"We
don't have any goal."

Disturbed, the American girl declared, "How could the land

of Gandhi produce a generation which doesn't even have a goal?" She suggested that we make some one thing our goal. I asked what value that would be and she replied, "Those who have a goal are not empty." It was the recollection of that statement which prompted my question about the girl.

"She's still knocking about here in India," she answered and hailed a passing taxi. "Just four or five days ago she showed up at the Blue Fox. She was doing the Twist with a Beatle!"

"You're sure it wasn't her new god?" I said after the taxi started.

She shook her hair aside, wiped her face with a hankie and slid over near me. "Gods don't know how to do the Twist. Even my Daddy doesn't know how."

We both laughed, but only for a moment. I had a distinct feeling that she was forcing the laughter and that she couldn't have laughed spontaneously even over a joke. Her condition sobered me. "What's the matter?" I asked. "Are you unhappy today?"

"Of course not. I already told you I'm feeling terribly empty today. When I'm unhappy, I become calm. Look—where's the calmness in me today?"

I took her hands in mine, feeling uneasy as I do when she becomes sad. There are lots of ways I can remove her sadness. Several times, merely tickling her has broken the sadness. There've even been times when a stolen kiss or two eliminated her unhappiness. She herself admits that it melts away when I take her in my arms.

But what became of all that today? Seeing her in that skirt I'd become extremely aroused. I kissed the little mole glistening on her knee. With that, the tension usually gave way. I was convinced that she'd start sparkling again as usual and say in English, her body relaxed, "I'm the richest girl in Calcutta."

But today just the opposite happened. In response to my affection, she kissed me only once, and even that was fleeting. Just as I was feeling very contented, she'd said, "I just can't figure out what to do. I'm feeling so empty that ... that ... " It was then, to break that emptiness of hers, that I'd come up with the proposal of going somewhere.

Worried at my inability to ease her unhappiness, I asked, "Just what is it you're actually feeling?"

She looked at me and replied, "It's as though some great force were boiling deep inside of me."

"Any other day you'd have claimed that I'd fractured your limbs. Even after one of those experiences would you feel a force boiling inside you?"

"Yes." She put her hand on my shoulder, "That's the tragedy."

She began looking somewhere outside. There was no expression in her eyes, her face like a pressure cooker whose cover gave no indication of what was boiling inside. Earlier we used to spend all our time planning an attack on our problems. But now, though the problem is still there, it's no longer problematic. Maybe that was the reason she felt so empty.

I was about to say something when she spoke up—"Listen, Ramesh."

I looked over at her. She only calls me directly by name that way when she has something special to say.

"Dear, why did our country become free so quickly?" She looked me straight in the eye and I let her continue—"If the country were still enslaved then we could revolt, we could throw bombs, we could scatter English corpses around. Now there's nothing to be done. It seems as though there's a force inside which I'm battling against."

Her words were hitting straight home with me. It was as though she were carrying a sword and shield rather than wearing a skirt and blouse. My whole structure rested on the context of her dreams, so her emptiness was a problem for me. I pulled her close and put my trembling lips to hers. . . .

It sounded like something being ripped to pieces. The taxi braked so strongly that our kissing faces were knocked against each other. Locked together, we were thrown against the back of the driver. Passing cars had stopped and pedestrians rushed from the sidewalk to our taxi.

We pulled ourselves together, opened the door and jumped out of the taxi. An eight- or nine-year-old boy had been run down. The boy was crossing and the driver had lost control of the car.

It took me some time to comprehend the situation, but she immediately moved forward and pulled the boy from underneath. His right foot had been injured, and if the taxi had gone an inch farther he would have been mashed.

The boy was gasping, and blood flowed from his foot. The taxi driver began shouting. "People walk around blind and we'll be blamed when they get killed!"

This shouting irritated her. "What are you yelling about? Why don't you keep the taxi under control when you drive? What's the matter, don't you know how to use the brake?"

The driver couldn't very well remain silent. "Memsahab, I've been driving a taxi for ten years!"

"Show me your license," she demanded.

"I will not. Are you a traffic policeman or something?"

"Whoever I am, show me your license and then talk! You've smashed this boy's leg. You'll have to pay the damages."

"Yeah, yeah, yeah!"

"Watch your tongue when you speak!" She moved forward and seized the driver's hand. He freed it with a jerk that almost knocked her down.

Just then a Bihari stepped out from the crowd and repaid the driver with a hard slap. I stood watching as the whole crowd rained down on the driver. His turban landed some distance away. When he jumped in the taxi to escape, people smashed the front window. In no time a full-blown riot had developed on that Calcutta street. Three or four other taxi-drivers had pulled up, and it looked as though the two factions would start battling. A wailing siren approached and then stopped, while the excited crowd waited for the next scene.

A policeman asked, "Who hit the driver?" In response a rock came flying and struck against his helmet. Now there were three

factions. The crowd saw the policemen's sticks flailing and began
to run. The same Bihari who had first struck the driver came over
to us and said, "Your hand wasn't hurt, sister? That bastard gave
it a bad jerk. The hoodlum, raising a hand against a woman!
Rotten lecher!"

Neither of us replied and we set off in silence. Her eyes were
sparkling now and she was walking faster than I. She seemed to
have tightened her belt a notch. When she realized that she was
walking ahead, she stopped and took hold of my hand.

"Why are you going so slowly?" She pulled me with such
force that I was dragged alongside her.

"It's nothing. . . . I was wondering whether he might have
been watching us kissing through the rearview mirror and
whether that could have been the reason for the accident."

"Then the fault is his. Why was he watching what we were
doing?"

I wasn't surprised at this response. But I was still disturbed
at the sudden course of events. She interrupted my silence—"I
was getting furious at that driver. If I had the strength, I'd have
beaten him up myself."

I looked over and saw that she was brimming with emotion,
her eyes flashing and her hands shaking with excitement.

A minute later we were sailing along down Rajpath. Suddenly we were in front of Rajbhavan, the Presidential mansion.
"Say, why did you bring me here?" she asked.

"I didn't bring you. It was you who brought me here!" I
protested angrily.

Just then a police van passed by on our right, carrying away
the driver who had been arrested. Behind the van was our taxi,
driven by a policeman. I noticed that the meter was still running.

GIRIRAJ KISHORE

# Relationship

Mᴀɴᴋɪ opened the tin door of the garage, making quite a clatter. To her right was a cooking hearth, the coals dying out, surrounded by a small fading circle of light. Manki came inside and then fastened the bolt on the door.

'Hey!' she called, peering into the room. "Are you asleep?"

"Uh—no." The boy sat up.

"Have you baked the chapatis?"

The boy answered in a sleepy voice. "Yes, I've cooked them."

Manki stepped forward and her foot struck a cooking pot. "When are you going to get some sense?" she exclaimed. "Leaving the pot right in the middle of the floor!"

"Shall I light the lamp, mother?"

"Do you have to ask? Just light it." Manki plopped down and sat on the floor. The boy lit the lamp and the room grew larger. Manki looked over at her son—like a tall bamboo, standing there wearing a torn pair of shorts.

"Wretch!" she said with a smile. "Go cover up. You run around letting everything dangle like a bottle!"

He lifted a black dirty sari of his mother's from the floor and wrapped it around himself. "There!"

Manki laughed. "You're a full-grown man and yet your mother still has to tell you what to cover and what to uncover."

"Shall I serve the chapatis?" the boy asked softly.

"Is that something you have to ask about too? I'm so hungry my guts are cramped. Bring the food right away."

Placing the chapatis, wrapped in a dirty cloth, on a plate, he set them in front of her. He also righted the pot that had been kicked over and put it in front of her. She strained in the dim light to peer into the pot and then muttered, "Looks like you didn't add enough turmeric."

The boy sat there silently. Manki unwrapped two or three sweets from the end of her sari and placed them on the chapatis. Rolling up the chapatis, she gnawed at the sweets along with the bread. Periodically she also added some dal. The boy kept watching her face. "Mother," he said after a while, "you haven't eaten the dal. I took only a little so you'd have plenty."

Manki swallowed the chunk in her mouth and then responded. "How am I to eat it? There's not even any turmeric in it. I don't like plain grass and stuff! It was that lady-doctor's servant who gave me the two laddoos. With those I can manage." About to put the last sweet in her mouth, she hesitated a moment but then went ahead. After gulping some water from the jug, she declared with a chuckle, "The lady-doctor has gone away, so that rascal is entertaining in grand style."

Rising, she belched loudly and then squatted next to the closed door and washed her hands. Still squatting there, she urinated. The boy had lain down. Manki took off her sari and hung it on a peg. Removing the ragged loose blouse also, she draped it over the sari. For some time she massaged her bosom with both hands. Then, covering herself again, she lay down.

"Hey Girdhari! You haven't even put out the lamp. Go put it out."

Girdhari got up slowly and blew out the lamp. "You fool,"

Manki immediately scolded, "is that any way to put out an oil lamp, by blowing it? Better learn some sense or you'll end up just knocking around."

Girdhari went and lay down without a word. The coals in the hearth were dying out but some light filtered under the door from the electric light out front. The place where Manki had washed her hands and then urinated was still damp.

"Mother, what happened?" Girdhari asked suddenly.

"About what?"

"About that Ramtirth."

Manki chuckled. "What was there to happen with him? I'm the one who wasn't willing. He said he wouldn't take in such a big son along with me."

Girdhari said nothing. After some time Manki spoke again. "So I told him, 'In that case, go away. I've got plenty of others.' "

"Then you won't be going to live with him?" Girdhari's voice was full of eagerness.

"The bastard has nowhere else to go. He'll come back." Manki began to laugh loudly, the sound echoing in the semi-darkness.

Girdhari again spoke up softly—"You were mentioning a silver waist-chain yesterday, weren't you?"

"If he takes me in, he'll give one. The man earns a hundred and a quarter a month. If he were to die the next day, I'd already have his wealth in my hands. When your father died, I was left to go around scrubbing pots. He swallowed up everything we had." She smiled. "As for the silver chain, the old man's ready to give me one too. But Ramtirth is a young man."

"Which old man?"

Manki laughed again. "Oh, that lady-doctor's servant Baru. He has one foot dangling in the grave, but he's determined to make me a widow again, the bastard. From him I've demanded a gold chain."

"That would be nice if he'd give it," Girdhari said with little conviction.

"Suddenly he's going to become a big spender! Why, he'd have to hold an auction to afford even a two ounce chain, the old goat."

Girdhari kept still as Manki chattered on for a while. Then she fell silent also. After she turned over facing the other way, Girdhari asked, "Are you asleep, mother?"

"No."

Girdhari waited a moment and then raised the question about himself. "That Ramtirth doesn't want to take me in?"

Manki turned, trying in the darkness to see her son's face. He lay there quietly. "The scoundrel already has two children of his own," she tried to explain. "He says you're so big . . . that I can't keep supporting you forever. . . . And what would happen if I were to die?"

"Then you go ahead, mother," Girdhari murmured.

Manki lay in silence for some time and then called tenderly, "Girdhari, you must be feeling cold. Slide over next to me, son."

Girdhari crept over. Pulling him close, she stroked his back and said, "If we get you settled at his house, you'll be able to have a job at the cloth mill. Your marriage'll be arranged too. Who's there to care about you besides shameless old me!" She paused and then declared, "I'll settle it with him tomorrow afternoon. Baru has asked me over for lunch. Ramtirth will be there also. You come to the lady-doctor's house too and have your meal there."

"And the lady-doctor?" Girdhari asked fearfully.

"Oh, she's away on a four or five day trip."

Girdhari stammered, "The old man has invited Ramtirth too?"

"Oh, he's a friend of the old man. Baru says either I should live at his house or at Ramtirth's. The two of them are partners in crime!" Manki laughed.

Girdhari slid back to his own place. Manki turned over and before long she began snoring. Girdhari got up quietly and unlatched the door. The bolt clattered against the tin door. "What is it?" Manki asked from her sleep.

"Nothing—I was going outside to pee."

"Well, just squat there and do it. Why go outside?"

"All right." Girdhari was about to squat when he changed his mind and went outside. Standing there urinating, he stared up at the sky. Afterwards, he kept standing there for some time. Despite the jangling of the latch when he returned, Manki didn't wake up.

Girdhari arrived at the lady-doctor's house to find it all closed. After a full circle around the place, he sat down near the back door. A mixture of voices was coming from inside. Putting his ear to the door, he tried to listen.

The voice belonged to Manki. "Stop it. You're trying to steal all the fun free. First give me your promise."

Girdhari now put his eye instead of his ear to the crack. His mother was lying naked. Drawing back for a moment, he glanced around and then started peering inside again. His body trembled for some time. Squatting on the ground, he supported himself with one hand between his legs.

Ramtirth was clinging to Manki. The old man, standing, was watching the two of them intently. Suddenly Manki pushed Ramtirth aside. "Agree to my terms and then come ahead." Manki half rose from her prone position and said with a smile, "Both things have to happen, the boy and the chain. Give the chain alone if you can or . . . " She smiled at Baru. "Or else both of you do it together. Why sacrifice this poor old Baru? He can't do much anyway. Actually I'll be your woman alone."

In a flash Baru straightened up, leaped forward and stripped stark naked. "What's that you say? I'm not capable of anything? Take this and see!" He clamped himself to Manki, but was soon puffing heavily. Manki stroked his head and began to laugh.

Girdhari's lips were puffing a bit also. Now Ramtirth was standing. He tried to push Baru out of the way but the old man clung to Manki like a child. A strong shove and Baru lurched to one side, gasping as he fell to the floor.

Ramtirth was trying to fasten himself to Manki. She crossed

her legs and held them tightly together. Lying in that position she said, "First settle the matter. I have another man who'll give me a three pound chain. But it's you I love so I'm only asking a two pound one from you." She laughed. "My flesh has to be paid for in blood! If not from you, then from some friend of yours. I'm not a lady-doctor who can hire you and keep you under control."

Ramtirth was paying no attention to what she was saying. On his knees, he was trying to spread her legs apart, occasionally glancing up pleadingly at her. The tension was mounting steadily. Baru got to his feet, his nakedness very different from that of the other two.

Manki laughed at Ramtirth's great test of strength. "These are only two legs—there's no lock and no key. Tell me, are you ready to give in?"

Baru came over in all his nakedness and stood near them. Leaning over, he began looking at something. "Get out of here," Ramtirth snapped. "You weren't able to do anything."

"You miserable rotter," Baru retorted angrily, "carrying on this nonsense-wrestling. You're the one who's still young, and just what were you able to accomplish? Clear out of here or I'm opening the door." Each word was uttered with effort, but Baru went on babbling even while wrapping his dhoti around himself. "It's only me that's going to suffer. I'll lose my job. Hag! Bastard! Whore!" The old man's jaws clamped shut.

Manki looked over and barked, "Stop your jabbering." Then she turned to Ramtirth. "Answer me quickly. Girdhari must be on his way. I should get dressed."

Ramtirth's hand relaxed its grip on Manki's thigh. His eyes had begun to lose their sparkle and he was cooling down. Slowly he replied, "I'll take in Girdhari."

Girdhari turned and looked the other way.

"And the chain?" Manki asked immediately.

Almost in tears, Ramtirth replied, "Tyrant! Use your head! I have small children, and the debts aren't yet cleared from my woman who died." His body had begun to droop.

"Now you listen to me!" Manki propped herself up, hands

behind her back, and put her face close to Ramtirth's. He took
one look and then clasped her upper portion with both arms.
Manki brought her hands up and shoved him over backward,
saying, "You want to take away my honor completely free. Only
your children matter, not mine. Get away!"

Ramtirth tried to use force again but Manki warned, "Are
you going to move away or shall I start screaming? If my son's a
dumbbell, am I supposed to poison him? Shouldn't I look out
for him?"

Girdhari, face taut, was about to throw open the door when
he hesitated at the sound of a latch from the adjacent house.
Taking his eye from the crack, he glanced quickly around and
then huddled in a corner. A woman was coming out of the house.
Seeing Girdhari crouched in the corner, she came and stood right
over him. "Why are you sitting here?"

Girdhari stammered, "My mother's inside."

"Who's your mother?"

"She scrubs the pots and pans here."

"Manki?"

"Yes."

The woman flared up. "Then what are you doing here peeking and peering? Why don't you have the door opened?"

He continued to cower there.

"Look," the woman repeated, "what are you sitting around
for? Knock on the door. The doctor's away. If the house has been
robbed, who'll be held responsible? Where's that old man gone?"

"Inside," Girdhari murmured, his eyes glued to the ground.

"Are you crazy or something?" the woman said angrily.
"Either get the door opened or go back home. Why are you
crouching here like some thief?"

At that point a man emerged from the same house. "Come
on," he called to the woman and she went off with him. For some
time Girdhari kept looking around apprehensively, and then he
put his eye to the crack again.

The old man, bent over the other two, was thrusting his body
forward, rocking back and forth. All at once he cried, "Get out

of here. You've stirred up enough trouble. Shameless creature!"

There was no answer from Ramtirth or Manki. The old man leaned over and stared. "I'm opening the door," he shouted.

Girdhari stepped away from the door and looked the other way. His face had begun to droop from being in the sun so long. A couple of minutes later the door opened. Manki was adjusting her sari.

Seeing Girdhari at the door, Baru said, "You saw your mother's mischief?"

Manki became angry. "Are you completely shameless, old man? What mischief has his mother done? Bastard!" Turning to Girdhari she asked, "When did you get here anyway?"

"Just now." Girdhari looked crushed.

Ramtirth came outside and began staring intently at Girdhari. Girdhari avoided looking at any of the three.

"Go eat your food," Manki snapped. "Then help with the pots and pans. The morning has worn me out."

Baru interrupted immediately. "There's nothing to eat here for troublemakers. No shame and no modesty!"

"What are you jabbering about?" Ramtirth broke in. "What's there to blame anyone for? You certainly didn't forbid it."

This time Girdhari stared at each of the three in turn. His mother's face was distorted, and she was looking at Baru the way she'd been eyeing Girdhari a short time before. "Go inside," she told Girdhari. "What are you standing around gaping at here?"

After Girdhari had gone in, Ramtirth turned to Baru. "You killed it today and now you're fussing."

A faint smile appeared on Manki's face. "I haven't died!"

"As far as I'm concerned," Baru exploded, "I don't care who dies. But give back my forty rupees. When you grabbed the money you weren't concerned about my age!" Baru straightened up and leaped toward Manki. She burst out laughing.

Becoming still angrier, Baru roared, "What are you laughing about? I don't care what kind of bargain you've made. I won't let you leave without handing back the forty rupees. Talk to that lover of yours. He's going to give you a big silver chain when he can't produce even my forty rupees." Baru kept using his upper lip to control his sagging lower one.

"Nitwit!" Manki laughed. "Why're you making such an uproar? It's you who'll lose your job. That poor old lady-doctor hired you. . . . No one else would pay you even a cowrie."

Girdhari stood silently in the inner courtyard, staring at all of them. Baru began gasping again and moved inside, where he sat down in a corner trying to catch his breath. Manki came in from the kitchen with a metal platter of food. As she started to serve Girdhari, Baru shouted, "You're giving that wretched idiot his food on a tray? Dump it in his hand—in his hand."

Manki ignored him and went back to the kitchen. Girdhari glanced once at the old man and then started to eat. Manki brought out a bowl of the remaining rice pudding and handed it to the old man. He looked over at Ramtirth with a smile. For herself Manki brought the pot in which some rice was left. Pouring the remaining dal and vegetables into the pot, she started to eat.

Ramtirth laughed. "During your reign you'll give to everyone and only I'll be left out."

Manki smiled, "Why will you be left out?" Pointing to the pot between her outspread legs she said, "You come over here too."

"Go on, go ahead," the old man said. "That's right where you belong, Ramtirth."

Ramtirth laughed and said nothing. He too began eating out of the rice pot.

Girdhari had finished eating and was watching the three of them. As soon as Manki noticed him sitting there idly, she spoke up. "Hey, why are you just sitting there? Take care of the pots and pans."

He started gathering up the utensils.

"You saw that son of mine?" Manki smiled. "What a prince he is—a regular Raja Ram. And so innocent he doesn't even know how to wiggle his ears!" Ramtirth looked over at Girdhari. Eyes lowered, he was scrubbing the pans.

Baru came over and sat next to them. "Look," he pleaded, "you two have reached an agreement. Now give back my forty rupees."

Ramtirth turned to Manki. "Tell me, should I give you the chain, take in your son, or shall I pay the debt?"

Manki laughed. "Why should you get involved in this? And is it my fault that nothing happened with him?"

"So I'm to pay the money and others have all the fun?" Baru protested.

"Go away, you bastard!" Manki rebuked him. "As though I even have any money with me."

"Low-caste slut, get out of here!" Baru grabbed Manki's hand and sprang forward to give her a shove. Ramtirth reached out for Baru, but Manki had already knocked him aside.

"Now clear out! Your feet are dangling in the grave but still you run around foaming at the mouth chasing after women."

Girdhari stopped scrubbing the pans and looked over at them. Manki turned to him—"Go ahead, leave. Try to be nice to this rat and you get paid back with misery."

"Just let the memsahab come back! When this slut fell sick and was being eaten up by worms, I was the one who told the memsahab and had her treated. Now it's me who brings misery! Let her return, and just see if I don't have you dragged out of here by the hair."

"Do what you like. But you think I won't tell her why you gave the forty rupees? And with your mother . . . indeed!"

Manki took Ramtirth by the hand and started out. Beaming at the touch of her hand, Ramtirth followed along behind her. Manki returned once more to tell Girdhari, "Hey, come on, get out of here." Then she again walked out.

Girdhari continued washing and wiping the pans. After completing the job, he said a polite goodbye to Baru and went outside. Manki and Ramtirth had left.

When Girdhari had gone, the old man closed the door and quietly sat down, leaning his back against the wall.

When Manki returned, Girdhari was sitting cross-legged in front of the coals. She sat down affectionately beside him.

"Chapatis?" Girdhari asked without looking at her.

"Uh—no, I'm not hungry," Manki answered and then laughed. Girdhari sat in silence for some time, then rose and seated himself near the oil lamp.

"Hey, Girdhari," Manki said with a smile, "it's good we left today before the lady-doctor reached home. Otherwise she'd have eaten us alive. As it was, the old man couldn't do anything."

"Uh-huh," Girdhari murmured.

Manki looked over. "He complained to her about me, saying I owed him forty rupees. I asked right out, 'Rupees for what?' "

"Mother, where did you go this afternoon?"

Manki grew serious for a moment and then smiled, "He took me to the bazaar." With that she continued her report, "The matter was left hanging right there. I really turned the table on the old man—came right out with the whole story!"

"Mother, what's in that bag?"

"Oh, I forgot—your father bought some clothes for you. He was very angry at me, saying I've turned a nice boy into a regular madman who roams around in rage." She glanced at Girdhari. He was busy adjusting his torn shorts.

Manki opened the bag and held up a pair of shorts, an under shirt, and a shirt. "See what nice clothes your father bought f you."

Girdhari cast a quick glance at the clothes and rem seated in silence.

"What's wrong? Don't you like them?" Manki asked s

Just as mildly Girdhari replied, "They're fine."

"Then go and put them on. Let's see how you look

Girdhari stared at his mother and finally said, "P them up."

Manki was about to speak but said nothing. Rising without a word she walked over to the hearth, where she began removing the coals and extinguishing them. After putting out the coals she sat down to scrub the pots.

"I'll clean those in the morning," Girdhari said.

"No, I'll do them myself." She paused, "He's coming with a tonga tomorrow morning. There won't be time."

"I see." Girdhari didn't get up. After some time he asked, "Did he give you the chain?"

"He'll give it tomorrow." Manki laughed again. "I managed a good beating for that girl today. I was testing whether he'd listen to me or not. Just a bit of a thing, barely out of diapers, and yet she looks me in the eye and challenges me. I told him that if she gave me any trouble I'd skin her alive, and that he'd better not call me a wicked stepmother. The little bitch was asking why I had come to their house. As for the boy, he just sat there like an idiot-owl."

Girdhari lay down. The sound of pans being scrubbed con-
nued. Before long he rose, hitched up his shorts and went
·de. Manki saw but said nothing, standing on tiptoes to
̣s he walked over and sat down outside. He was seated
erect, the light from the lamppost shining on his body.
tood looking for some time and then called loudly,
what are you sitting there for? Come in the
ble she added, "The pig, sitting there naked
n bull of a man."

response and she called again. This time
g one way or the other and headed straight
e came and stood at the door.

?" asked Manki. "What made you get up

g him!" Manki muttered. "So grown up
ok after himself."

d lay down. Manki spoke again. "Now
pack and leave in the morning. Here I

have to do forced labor for the woman who owns the house. She doesn't charge rent but so what! She considers me just a servant. In our own home we'll live in comfort. I talked back to the lady-doctor too. Without knowing anything, she started scolding me—as though I'm her nurse or something."

Hearing no response from Girdhari, she inquired, "Are you asleep?"

"Well, no . . . "

"You lie there like a corpse, not saying a thing. If you act like that with your father . . . " She stopped and changed her approach. "Don't act that way with your father. With me it doesn't matter."

Girdhari now responded to her earlier statement very calmly. "That's fine," he said and turned over.

After finishing the chores, Manki lay down too. There was silence between them for a while. Manki thought that Girdhari had gone to sleep and she turned to face the other way.

Girdhari opened his eyes and looked over at his mother. Her back was completely naked. He reached out his hand, then pulled it back. Suddenly he blurted, "Mother . . . "

Manki turned over with a start. "Are you still awake? I thought you'd gone to sleep."

Girdhari said nothing.

"What is it? Why don't you speak up?"

He remained still.

"Come on, tell me," Manki repeated. What were you going to say?"

"The lady-doctor isn't married?"

"What does marriage mean to those people?" Manki said after a pause, chuckling in a vulgar manner. At this unexpected response Girdhari raised up, trying to see her. Loud laughter kept coming from her direction. He lay down again.

"What makes you ask, huh? Are you going to marry her?" She was laughing again. "She'll take you around in a motorcar. She swaggers around now, but we'll be well-off too then. I'll have her running around calling out 'Mother-in-law! Mother-in-law!' "

All this was accompanied by laughter, but then she paused to explain, "Those people don't believe in marriage and all that."

Girdhari said softly, "Mother, shall I lock the door?"

"I'll do it in a minute," she replied.

Girdhari adjusted his shorts, got up, and closed the door. "Now get some sleep," Manki said. "We have to get up early in the morning."

Girdhari lay there silently. After a while he sensed that she was still awake and asked in a low voice, "Are you asleep, Mother?"

"I'm going to sleep."

"Mother, what time is he coming?"

"Who?"

"He . . . " Girdhari paused and then said, "Ramtirth."

"You call him father from now on, understand?"

Girdhari gave no reply. "He'll be here by seven or eight o'clock," Manki said.

"Uh-huh," Girdhari muttered.

Hearing this acknowledgment, Manki felt relieved, and before long she was snoring. Girdhari slowly rose and walked to the door. He stood there quietly and then returned, but instead of going straight to his own place he leaned over his mother. The clothing had slipped off her breasts. He went on staring, then returned to his own spot and lay down. Manki's snores were growing louder.

Manki got up somewhat earlier than usual. Girdhari had already risen and gathered all his mother's possessions into one place. Sitting unperturbed, he was waiting for Manki to wake up. He had not yet put on the new clothes and was wearing the same old shorts, though a long undershirt somewhat covered his nakedness.

Manki rose and washed up in minutes. Girdhari kept sitting there like a statue. "Look son," Manki protested, "can't you do anything without being told? Go get cleaned up. Your father must be on his way."

Girdhari looked over. Manki was combing her hair, still wearing the petticoat in which she had slept. Transparent, it showed everything. Girdhari drew his eyes away and looked at her blouse. It was not as loose as usual, and the arms protruding from the sleeves pleased him. After doing up her hair Manki said, "Go on outside. I'm going to change clothes."

Girdhari went out. Manki took a sari and petticoat from the bag she'd brought the previous night and put them on. She marked a dot of color on her forehead and the red streak of a married woman down the part in her hair. Unwrapping a packet of powder, she applied it to her face. Then she put on a new pair of sandals. Everything done, she looked in the mirror and gave a little smile.

She was still smiling when Girdhari came in. He glanced at her out of the corner of his eye. "Tell me, Girdhari, how do I look?"

Girdhari gave a cursory glance and said softly, "Fine."

Manki laughed. Girdhari picked up his things and started off to bathe. Manki stopped him immediately—"Take your new clothes with you. Are you going to wear those same rags?"

Girdhari took one look at the clothes hanging there, then lifted them off the peg and took them with him.

He returned from his bath wearing the new clothes. Meanwhile Ramtirth had arrived with a tonga, and he and the driver had lifted almost all the luggage into the horse-carriage. Manki, speaking softly like a new bride, was telling them where to put the things.

As soon as he laid eyes on Girdhari, Ramtirth exclaimed, "Well! He's not ready even yet."

Girdhari stood there silently. Some luggage still lay on the ground. Manki called Ramtirth over and suggested, "Give Girdhari some money to take a rickshaw. He can bring the rest of the things."

"Look," Ramtirth protested, "he's just lucky to be coming at all. All the things can fit in the tonga. He's seen the house, he can come on foot."

Manki looked at Girdhari. Head bowed, he was standing there in silence.

"Let's go," Ramtirth told the tonga driver, and the carriage started off. Manki looked again toward Girdhari. His eyes were on the wheels of the tonga.

After the tonga had left, Girdhari made one round of the garage. Then he took off the new clothes, put on his old shorts, and lay down on the ground.

# Glossary

| | |
|---|---|
| Arjuna | A hero in the epic *Mahabharata* who is spurred on to battle by Krishna in the section known as the "Bhagavad Gita." |
| Arya Samaj | A reform sect of Hinduism stressing a return to the principles and practices found in the Vedic scriptures. |
| babu | A title, usually indicating respect. |
| biri | A small, cheap country cigarette made of tobacco rolled in a leaf. |
| chapati | A thin, flat unleavened bread, usually made of wheat flour and somewhat similar to a tortilla. |
| cowrie | A shell which at one time was the smallest unit of currency. |
| dal | Pulse or lentils, similar to split-peas and usually eaten as a kind of sauce with rice or chapatis. |
| dupatta | A long thin scarf worn over a woman's shoulders and sometimes also covering the head; usually worn with salwar-kameez. |

| | |
|---|---|
| ganja | A narcotic preparation from hemp which is smoked; similar to marijuana. |
| gazal | An Urdu lyric in the form of couplets. |
| ghee | Clarified butter, more expensive but usually preferred to other cooking oils. |
| guru | Title for an honored teacher, frequently used for a spiritual master. |
| Hanuman | The monkey who aided in the rescue of Sita in the epic *Ramayana*, and who is worshipped as a deity. |
| ji | An honorific suffix attached to Indian names or titles. |
| kameez | Shirt. A woman's kameez is usually about dress length and is worn with salwar pants. |
| Kauravas | Along with the Pandavas, the rival cousin-clans whose hostility is a major theme in the epic *Mahabharata*. |
| khir | A sweet pudding made from rice, milk, and sugar. |
| kurta | A long, loose shirt. |
| laddoo | A round sweet made from milk and sugar. |
| Laila | The heroine lover in a Persian story which has become a part of Indian literary and folk tradition. |
| Lakshmana | Brother of Rama in the epic *Ramayana*. |
| memsahab | Respectful term of address for a woman, especially a modernized or Westernized woman. |
| nautanki | A form of folk entertainment using song and dance and involving primarily themes of love and heroism. |
| paan | Betel. A rolled leaf containing lime, betelnut, |

spices, and sometimes tobacco, the chewing of which is a common habit in India.

papar           A very thin, crisp delicacy similar to a large potato chip.

Ram or Rama     The hero of the epic *Ramayana*, also known as Ramchandra, and considered an incarnation of the god Vishnu.

Ramayana        An ancient Hindu epic which tells of the exile of Prince Rama, his wanderings in the forest with his wife Sita and his brother Lakshmana, Sita's capture by the demon Ravana, and her eventual rescue with the assistance of Hanuman's armies.

Ramlila         Literally the "sport of Ram"; a dramatic folk performance of incidents from the *Ramayana* epic.

salwar          A woman's pyjama-type pant, usually tight at the ankles and worn with a long shirt (kameez or kurta).

samosa          A spicy fried pastry containing vegetables or meat.

Saraswati       Goddess of wisdom and learning.

sardar          Literally "chief"; respectful term for a Sikh man.

seer            Two pounds.

Sita            Wife of Rama, heroine in the epic *Ramayana*.

sitar           A string instrument, played in the manner of a guitar.

tabla           A drum played with the fingers.

tonga           A carriage, pulled by a single horse, in which the driver faces forward and the passengers face backward.

ustad           Master; teacher.

# Notes on the Authors

Amarkānt

Born in 1925 in Ballia District, U.P., he studied at Ewing Christian College, but left to participate in the Independence Movement, returning later to complete his B.A. at Allahabad University. Amarkānt worked in the editorial department of a daily paper in Agra and is now in the editorial department of a publishing company in Allahabad. He has published several novels and collections of short stories, and he came into literary prominence in the nineteen-fifties.

Ramesh Bakshī

Born in 1936 in Indore, he has completed an M.A. in Hindi literature. He has done editorial work with several journals, worked with All India Radio in Indore, and taught there at Hamidiya

College of Arts. Currently living in Delhi, Ramesh Bakshī edits the Hindi edition of *Shankar's Weekly* and is the convener and editor of Aavesh Forum, a group of young writers dedicated to the writing and publishing of avant-garde literature and opposed to "commercial" writing. His works include novels, short stories, essays, and drama.

Gyānranjan

Born in Allahabad in 1936, the son of a renowned Gandhian writer, he did his M.A. at Allahabad University. Gyānranjan began his literary career as a poet but now writes mostly stories, the first of them published in 1960. Collections of his stories were published in 1968 and 1971, the former having as its title story "Our Side of the Fence and Theirs." He and Dūdhnāth Singh won early acclaim as representing the new writing of the nineteen-sixties.

Shekhar Joshī

Born in 1934 in Almora, he studied in Ajmer and Dehra Dun and now lives in Allahabad, where he has for a number of years been a technical supervisor in a Defence Workshop. Shekhar Joshī became noted in the nineteen-fifties for short stories depicting urban industrial life. A collection of his stories was published in 1958 and a second collection is forthcoming.

Kamleshwar

Born in 1932 in Mainpuri, U.P., he did an M.A. in Hindi literature at Allahabad University and was first published in 1951. After some work with television, he was for two years the editor of the short story journal *Nayī Kahāniyān*. Kamleshwar currently edits *Sārikā*, a literary monthly published in Bombay and devoted especially to the short story. He was a leader in the writing and discussion of "nayī kahānī," the "new story" of the nineteen-fifties, and is also a writer of novels, drama, and literary criticism.

Girirāj Kishore

Born in 1936 in Muzaffarnagar, U.P., he lived in Allahabad for some time and now holds an administrative position at Kanpur University. He completed an M.A. in social work and served for five years as a social worker and probation officer. Author of several novels, children's books, a play, and collections of short stories, one of which has "Relationship" as its title story, Girirāj Kishore is considered a leading representative of the new writers of the nineteen-sixties who depict changing values in urban India.

Ramkumar

Born in Simla in 1924, Ramkumar's literary work includes novels, short stories, and a travelogue. A collection of his stories in English translation has been published by the Writers' Workshop in Calcutta. Also an award-winning artist, he lived for two years in Paris studying art, and has since exhibited extensively in India, Europe, and America. In 1970 he spent eight months in the United States on a Rockefeller Foundation grant.

Mohan Rākesh

Born in 1925 in Amritsar, he attended Hindu College there and then Oriental College in Lahore, completing the M.A. in Hindi and Sanskrit. Mohan Rākesh taught at Elphinstone College in Bombay, and was head of the Hindi Department at DAV College in Jullundur. After twelve years of teaching, he resigned so as to give his time to writing. He did editorial work in Jullundur and Delhi, edited *Sārikā* for a year in Bombay, and now lives in Delhi, devoting himself to writing. First published in 1947, he was a leading figure in the "nayī kahānī" movement and is known for his novels, plays, translations, and travel writing, as well as for his stories. A novel of his has been published in English translation with the title *Lingering Shadows,* by Hind Pocket Books in Delhi. In 1971–1972 he was given a Nehru Fellowship for research on "The Dramatic Word."

Phanīshwarnāth "Reṇu"    Born in 1921 in a village in Purniya District, Bihar, he left his studies at Banaras Hindu University in 1942 to join the Quit India Movement, involved especially with worker and peasant agitation. After a long illness in the early fifties, he turned from politics to literature, living primarily in Bihar. Although first published in 1946, "Reṇu's" major literary recognition began when his novel *Mailā Ānchal* was hailed in 1954 as originating a new trend of "regional fiction." Other novels and stories have followed. "The Third Vow" was made into an award-winning Hindi film.

Awadh Nārāin Singh    Born in 1933, he began publishing stories in 1966 and is one of the young Hindi writers in Calcutta associated with *Rūpāmbara,* a "little magazine" primarily publishing new writers. A collection of his Hindi stories has been published with the story "Intimate" as its title piece. The volume is dedicated "To my generation."

Dūdhnāth Singh

Born in 1936, he completed an M.A. in Hindi literature at Allahabad University, where he is currently a lecturer in the Department of Hindi. Prior to that appointment he lived in a variety of places, "for fifteen years drinking the sweet poison of freelance writing in the underworld of society." Two years were spent in a tuberculosis sanatorium. Known primarily as a story writer and critic, Dūdhnāth Singh has also written poetry, a novel, and personal essays. He began writing in 1960.

Krishna Baldev Vaid

Born in Dinga, Punjab, he did an M.A. in English at Punjab University and a Ph.D. in English at Harvard University. Krishna Baldev Vaid taught at Hans Raj College in Delhi, Punjab University in Chandigarh, and now teaches English at the State University College at Potsdam, New York. A writer of stories, novels, and literary criticism in both Hindi and English, he has translated many of his stories into English, and one of his novels, entitled *Steps in Dark-ness,* has been published in English translation by Orion Press, New York.

Shrīkānt Varmā

Born in 1931 in Bilaspur, M.P., he did an M.A. in Hindi literature at Nagpur University. He is renowned as a poet and as a writer of stories, novels, criticism, and translations into Hindi of such authors as Pasternak, Lorca, and Wallace Stevens. After several years of editorial work with Hindi literary periodicals, Shrīkānt Varmā took a senior position with *Dinamān,* a Hindi news weekly in Delhi, and now handles press relations for Mrs. Gandhi's Congress Party. He has visited a number of European countries and in 1970–1971 was poet-in-residence in the International Writing Program of the University of Iowa.

Nirmal Varmā

Born in Simla in 1929, the younger brother of Ramkumar, he spent most of his childhood in the hills and then did an M.A. in history at St. Stephen's College in Delhi. He taught for several years and was influenced by the terrorist movement at that time. After working for a leading English daily newspaper, Nirmal Varmā lived for a number of

years in Prague, where he studied and translated Czech literature. He has traveled extensively
in Europe. When in India he
lives in Delhi, primarily writing
fiction and travel reminiscences.

Rājendra Yādav                  Born in 1929 in Agra, he did his
M.A. at Agra University. After
living for several years in Calcutta, he moved to Delhi where he
helped to establish a publishing
company. A leader in the writing and discussion of "nayī kahānī," Rājendra Yādav has published extensively—short stories,
novels, literary criticism, an-
thologies, poetry, and translations into Hindi of such writers
as Turgenev, Chekhov, and Camus. His first work was published in 1947. Some of his
writing has been done in col-
laboration with his wife, Man-
noo Bhandari, a noted story
writer herself.